ANOTHER MAN'S SON

**Center Point
Large Print**

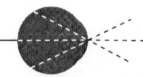

**This Large Print Book carries the
Seal of Approval of N.A.V.H.**

ANOTHER MAN'S SON

KATHERINE STONE

CENTER POINT PUBLISHING
THORNDIKE, MAINE

Library of Congress Cataloging-in-Publication Data

Stone, Katherine, 1949-
    Another man's son / Katherine Stone.--Center Point large print ed.
      p. cm.
    ISBN 1-58547-427-4 (lib. bdg. : alk. paper)
     1. Large type books. I. Title.

PS3569.T64134A85 2004
813'.54--dc22

                                                    2003024907

Prologue

Montlake High School
Seattle, Washington
Wednesday, September 12
Eighteen years ago

"There's something you should know, Mr. Collier, before we meet with Kathleen."

Ian Collier didn't like the high-school principal's tone—ominous—or her expression, which was sheepish. And he felt that the worrisome "something" should have been revealed to him long before now.

Kathleen Cahill had been selected as this year's Rain Mountain Scholar. The scholarship was Ian's idea and Ian's money. But he left it to a committee of educators to decide which high-school senior was most deserving of the all-expenses-paid opportunity to attend the college of his or her dreams.

All the applicants were deserving. Bright students from impoverished backgrounds. Ian would award the scholarship to every name on the list if he could.

But Rain Mountain Scholars were funded with personal not corporate money, and there was a limit to the number of college educations Ian could underwrite at one time—especially since the first three recipients were doing exactly what he'd hoped they'd be doing: getting the best education money could buy.

At present, thirty-six-year-old Ian Collier had a freshman at Harvard, a sophomore at Stanford and a

5

junior at Yale. It was an admirable investment in other people's children, Ian's accountant conceded. But the C.P.A. urged caution.

True, Rain Mountain—the company—had exceeded all expectations. The Pacific Northwest *had* needed another winter-sports outfitter. And Rain Mountain Enterprises was enjoying a national presence, too.

But consumers were fickle, and trends were unpredictable and one mustn't forget that perennial wild card: weather. This past December had been particularly instructive. Torrential rainfall between Christmas and New Year's had washed out the holiday ski season and made slush of January's ski-area revenues as well.

Rain Mountain had, of course, been fine. The slopes had been powdery perfection from Thanksgiving till Christmas Eve. Rain Mountain skis, boots, parkas and goggles had topped the Christmas wish lists of skiing enthusiasts, and the company's inaugural line of fluffy sweaters and mittens for the snow-bunny crowd had sold out by December fifteenth.

Had the rain come a few weeks earlier, however . . .

El Niño weather patterns or not, Ian's scholarship students would be fine. Their entire four years' tuition-and-living-expense money had been placed in trust. Rain Mountain employees—and their retirement funds—were similarly protected.

But there were no such guarantees for Rain Mountain Enterprises' CEO. Ian didn't care. He and poverty had been sparring partners for a very long time. He could think of no better use for his hard-won wealth than sponsoring exceptional students' dreams.

"Something I should know." Ian repeated Mrs. Petersen's words. "About Kathleen?"

"Yes. Well, about her feelings toward the scholarship. It's possible she won't want it."

"Even though she applied."

"Actually, we applied for her. Last spring, when we told her we were going to nominate her, she said she'd decided not to go to college after all. We couldn't believe it. College and medical school were what she'd been working toward *forever.* Needless to say, we went ahead with our plans, hoping that when she returned to school this fall she'd have reconsidered."

"But she hasn't."

"No."

"Any idea why?"

"None."

"I take it she doesn't know about today's meeting?"

"No. I just had my assistant pull her out of third-period study hall."

So Mrs. Petersen was planning a surprise for Kathleen Cahill. An ambush. Well-intentioned, of course. The unexpected gift of a dream.

But it was an ambush, nonetheless.

Ian hated being any part of it. His loathing was based on experience and pain. . . .

Ian Collier had been ambushed for the first time at age ten. Wanting to know what everyone else seemed to know about his parents—and the reason prospective adoptive couples never gave him a serious look—he'd managed a middle-of-the-night break-in at the administrative offices of the orphanage.

In his naiveté, the hopefulness of a lonely boy, he'd created a happy reason for being perennially overlooked. He wasn't truly a candidate for adoption. His own parents would be returning for him any day.

The real reason was far from happy. Gordon and Eileen Collier wouldn't be coming for him. Indeed, for all practical purposes, Ian had been orphaned before he was born.

Gordon Collier's assault on his pregnant wife had left Eileen near death. She'd been maintained on life support only until her unborn son could mature enough to survive outside the womb.

Gordon was dead, and long since buried in a pauper's grave, before Ian's birth. The gunshot to Gordon's head hadn't been self-inflicted, a final mortal act of conscience by the suddenly repentant murderer. The bullet had come instead from the high-powered rifle of a Seattle cop. And in the neatly typed recounting of the carnage that was Ian's legacy—and pedigree—there'd been nothing to suggest that Gordon Collier had felt the slightest tug of remorse.

So there it was. The truth that had been withheld, presumably for his own good, was hidden no more. Ian was a murderer's son.

The knowledge was freedom of sorts. Ian understood that it was his destiny to remain unclaimed. He used the knowledge as a defense against pain. Never again would he let his caretakers see, let anyone see, how it hurt to be unwanted.

And never again would anyone know more about

Ian than Ian knew himself.

No one did, either, until a twenty-four-year-old socialite surprised the eighteen-year-old murderer's son with a dream he'd never imagined he'd want.

"I'm pregnant," Vanessa Frances Worthing had informed him. "And guess what, Ian? The baby's *yours*."

At the time, Ian remembered Vanessa only vaguely. She and the sex they'd had were indistinguishable from all the other girls and all the other sex that was readily available to him.

Ian's sexual liaison with Vanessa had occurred during ski season at Crystal Mountain, the popular ski resort located seventy-six miles southeast of Seattle. Ian was on the ski patrol at Crystal, the culmination of a work history that had begun as a ski-lodge busboy five years before.

Although Ian didn't recall the specifics of sex with Vanessa, he was very certain about when it had taken place: after midnight and before dawn. He partied only when the lifts were closed and it was too dark to ski. It was as good a way as any to pass the hours until he could return to the slopes.

The weekend Vanessa and her friends spent at one of the resort's pricier chalets had been memorable. Crystal Mountain had played host on that weekend to what investors, sponsors, skiers and viewers had hoped would be the resort's first of many international skiing events. The eyes of the skiing world had been focused on Crystal's snowy slopes. What kind of downhill course could be fashioned from the terrain—how fast, how treacherous, how steep—and would there be enough mountain for world-class slalom and giant slalom as well?

The consensus had been yes, although there'd been the predictable dissenters, wedded to the excellence of their venues and no others. A virtual unanimous opinion had emerged, however, when it came to the skill—and future—of the local skier who'd been the forerunner for the downhill course. No one had clocked Ian's time. It hadn't occurred to them to do so. But those who watched most closely—ski team coaches from around the globe—suspected it was as fast as that of the eventual downhill winner, the reigning French superstar anyone had yet to beat.

Most likely Ian's run had been a fluke. But his straight-down-the-mountain descent appeared so effortless, and so fearless, that it was tempting to imagine what a little formal training might do. There was something else the experts noticed as Ian flew by them: an expression of joy.

By the end of the weekend, Ian had been given home phone numbers of coaches, agents and athletes alike. And he had the memory of what a U.S. ski team coach had said. "It's two years until the Olympics. You could be there, Ian. You could own the place."

By weekend's close, Ian Collier had also become a father.

Who could still become an Olympic champion, Vanessa insisted. Yes, it would mean lots of travel. But she'd go with him. Hadn't he discovered on that weekend at Crystal how well great sex with her made him ski? And as for the baby, it—he, she—could be left at the Worthing family mansion on Seattle's Queen Anne Hill. That was what money and nannies were for.

No, Ian replied, that was what fathers were for.

Vanessa wasn't accustomed to being denied. But her anger at Ian, at his plan to quit skiing and find a job in town, vanished when her parents confronted her with a more monumental no.

The Worthings had investigated Ian Collier, as she'd expected they would. She knew they'd discover he'd dropped out of school at thirteen, not seventeen, and had been lying about his age to employers, bartenders, lovers, ever since. He lied, he drank, he smoked, he was eighteen. He was, in short, wholly unsuitable for their daughter.

Vanessa hadn't decided exactly how provocative to be in her reply. But its essence was certain: If her wild and incorrigible teenage lover never did anything other than take her to bed, she'd be happy—and wasn't that what her loving parents wanted her to be? The issue of Vanessa's happiness, and the widely discrepant definitions offered by her parents and her, was a recurrent theme in the relationship that had become increasingly difficult with each passing year.

Vanessa thrived on attracting the wrong men. But she'd never been this wrong before—a murderer's son.

Vanessa hadn't known that little tidbit and was secretly jubilant when her parents told her. Ian could forsake his skiing career, cut his hair, swear off alcohol and cigarettes even before the baby was born, and bring home such meager paychecks from restocking grocery shelves that, in Vanessa's opinion, it was hardly worth a trip to the bank.

But nothing could purge him of his dangerous pedigree, or the way she felt when they made love.

Vanessa wasn't pleased, however, that Ian had such a vague memory of their weekend at Crystal. She was as unaccustomed to being forgotten as she was with being denied. It worried her, too, how much she wanted the murderer's son. In contrast to Ian, she'd thought of little else in the weeks following the passion they'd shared.

Vanessa expected adoration from Ian, as she expected and received it from every other lover she'd known. Of course, once the man's heart was hers, she became bored, eager to move on. That was what would happen—eventually—with Ian. And, Vanessa realized, she'd want it to. As much as she'd enjoy their time together, and as satisfying as it would be to flaunt this worst—and final—fling, she'd be somewhat relieved when her slumming days were through.

Vanessa Frances Worthing was more like her parents than she cared to admit—or than she was ready to let them know. But her place in society was important to her, her rightful place and with the right man. As it happened, Vanessa already knew the man she'd one day marry. The only man she'd marry.

Ian had proposed marriage to her—for the baby's sake, the baby's legitimacy, not because he wanted to make formal pledges of everlasting love to her . . . and not even because he wanted a nuptial claim on her millions.

In Vanessa's view of the world, a child born out of wedlock was vastly preferable to divorce. The child wouldn't suffer, not in the long run, not *her* child. He or she would be raised as Vanessa herself had been, with class, with manners, a worthy Worthing heir.

Besides, for this last and most outrageous dalliance the idea of living in sin—in the gardener's cottage on her parents' estate—was too delicious to resist.

It could be so delicious, she thought. So decadent. The perfect final indulgence before beginning her "proper" life.

Perfect . . . assuming Ian fell in love with her, became devoted—and disposable.

And what if Ian Collier didn't toe the line, and her own feelings for him didn't wane? The very thought scared her, and enraged her, then was confidently dismissed. Ian would fall in love with her, and her obsession with him would vanish, and she'd live happily ever after with the man she was born to wed.

Ian was unaware of Vanessa's agenda—beyond her wish, which he satisfied no matter how tired or disinterested he was, for sex. He was determined to keep her happy, and, until the day she left, he believed she was. She had sex with him on demand, enjoyed Sam in small doses, and spent the rest of her time shopping, dining and traveling with her friends.

Four years after Sam was born, Ian was ambushed anew. It was almost Christmas, and he and Sam had great plans. Returning from his night at work, Ian was smiling as he approached the cottage where Sam and Vanessa should have been sleeping.

But both were gone. So were Vanessa's parents. A note from Vanessa, an instruction really, informed him that there were documents for him to sign. Her attorney would explain.

The final ambush, the last surprise, was that Vanessa had always known the aching truth discovered by Ian the day Sam was born. He had no legal claim to the little boy who was his life. Vanessa could take Sam away from him whenever she wished and there wasn't a thing he could do about it but hurt, and rage, and vow never to inflict such pain on another living soul.

But now, on this splendid autumn day, Ian Collier had become an unwitting conspirator in the ambush of a sixteen-year-old girl.

Neither his voice nor his expression conveyed the fury he felt.

"Where's Kathleen now?"

"In the conference room."

"I'd like to meet with her alone."

"Oh, Mr. Collier, I'm not sure that's a good idea. Kathleen's brilliant. Well, you know that. You've read her file. But her social skills are . . . undeveloped. It's sometimes quite difficult to get her to talk."

Ian waited politely, impatiently, as Mrs. Petersen reiterated what he already knew. He'd read Kathleen's file. Of course. Carefully and more than once. And he'd been intrigued.

Kathleen Cahill was unlike Ian's future Harvard, Yale and Stanford grads. She was academically exceptional, like the previous three, but she lacked the outside interests and talents the others possessed. She was not, as one had been, student-body president and accomplished violinist. Or quarterback and debate team captain. Or year-book editor and Maria in her school's rendition of *Sound of Music.*

Kathleen's letters of recommendation differed, too, both in content and style, from those of the others. Such raves as "extraordinary maturity" and "remarkable poise" were absent, as were "lovely," "gracious," "articulate and charming." And there was no between-the-lines affection in the letters Kathleen's teachers wrote for her, no wish that she was their daughter, sister, grandchild, niece.

Kathleen Cahill had just that one claim to fame. Her brilliance. "A rare and stunning intelligence," her science teacher proclaimed. "She has no difficulty in grasping even complex abstractions."

Kathleen progressed through her schooling at an accelerated clip. She'd only recently turned sixteen. But it would have been a crime to hold her back, just as, the scholarship selection committee had decided, it would be a "miscarriage of their responsibilities as educators" not to afford her the chance to become what they all believed she could be—"the kind of scientific mind that could make significant, perhaps monumental, contributions to the world."

Nothing in the description of Kathleen Cahill was in any way reminiscent of Ian Collier at age sixteen. At any age. Nonetheless and with astonishing certainty, Ian felt sure that Kathleen disliked surprises as much as he.

"Mrs. Petersen."

"Yes?"

"Where's the conference room?"

The principal opened her mouth to object again but didn't. Ian had permitted just a flicker of his annoyance to show. And it was more than enough.

"The last door on the left."

The door was ajar. But Ian knocked lightly and waited to enter until he heard the tentative reply.

"Come in?"

"Thank you." Ian smiled despite what he beheld on the face of the girl seated at the immense wooden table. Fear. *Terror.* "Hello, Kathleen. I'm—"

"It's my mother, isn't it? She's—"

"No."

"No?"

"No." Ian's fury returned as he realized how Kathleen had interpreted the request that she leave study hall and come to the principal's office. She'd anticipated an ambush. But she'd been expecting it to be with a nightmare, not a dream.

Mrs. Petersen should have known. Hell, Ian should have known.

He'd read Kathleen's file. He'd even mused, as he'd read about her family, that she, too, had been orphaned before birth. Her father, like his, was truly dead before she was born. And his death, like Gordon's, had been violent. But Daniel Cahill had died honorably, in the service of his country in the jungles of Vietnam.

And when a pregnant Mary Alice Cahill received the news, she had died as well, an emotional death that was just as final. Oh, there were times—or so the school counselor noted—when Mary Alice seemed to function

16

fairly well, when she could hold down a job and wasn't irretrievably depressed.

But depression was the major theme of Mary Alice's life. Just as worrying about her mother was Kathleen's.

Kathleen was also her mother's keeper. She did their grocery shopping, cooked their meals, balanced their frugal budget and paid their bills on time. Kathleen wrote the checks herself, drawing from a bank account that was the sum of survivors' benefits from Daniel's death in combat and the money she and Mary Alice made.

Kathleen was the more reliable worker of the two, but the part-time jobs available to a teenage student weren't as well-paid as anything Mary Alice could get. In order to keep those better paying jobs—the school counselor also noted—Kathleen filled in whenever Mary Alice couldn't work, or accompanied her mother when it was clear Mary Alice needed help.

According to the file, Mary Alice's—and Kathleen's—most recent known place of employment was a hotel in the University district. She worked in housekeeping as an assistant to an "actual maid." Her task was to collect used towels and sheets from the rooms and cart them off to the laundry.

Nightmare scenarios regarding Mary Alice Cahill were easy to conjure. No brilliant mind required. And when the person imagining the worst was a girl, a daughter, the idea of a desperately depressed mother leaving her laundry cart by the stairwell, climbing to the rooftop and leaping to the sidewalk twenty floors below . . . No wonder he'd seen terror.

"I'm not here about your mother."

"You're not?"

"No, I'm not." Ian sat directly across from her, which was not to say close to her. An expanse of varnished pine stretched between them. "Really."

His reassurance was transforming. The body that had been rigid with fear softened with relief. It wasn't that Kathleen slumped. Her posture remained quite perfect. But she was breathing now. And she hadn't been. The hands that had been clasped to ghostly whiteness on the tabletop pinkened ever so slightly as she loosened them.

Kathleen didn't return Ian's smile. She'd retreated so deeply into her thoughts, her relief, she seemed to have forgotten him entirely.

Who he was or why he was there didn't matter—as long as he hadn't come with tragic news about her mother.

Ian waited without impatience for Kathleen to focus. And as she gazed unseeing at her faintly pink fingers, he gazed at Kathleen.

There'd been no photo with the application that had been submitted on her behalf. Ian had painted his own portrait, however, as he'd read the file. She'd be small, he'd supposed, compact and intense.

But once freed of her terror, Kathleen Cahill seemed . . . serene. And far from the tightly packaged dynamo he'd pictured, she was long and slender. Very long. She must tower over her classmates.

Still, the serene—and socially awkward?—girl didn't slouch. Unembarrassed by her height, perhaps, or merely oblivious to how different she was.

She wasn't completely inattentive to her appearance. Though clearly the worse for wear, probably second-hand, her burgundy jumper, faded blue turtleneck and navy-blue cardigan were clean and wrinkle free.

Clean, too, and spectacular was her sable hair. It fell long, straight, tidy—except for the bangs. They were short and ragged, as if cut with pinking shears, and Ian sensed emotion in the close-cropped fringe. Precisely what emotion was unclear. Sadness, perhaps, at having to cut them herself, her depressed mother unable to manage even that.

Or maybe the carelessly shorn bangs were further proof of Kathleen's serenity, a calm with who she was. How her bangs looked didn't matter. Her priority was to provide an unobstructed view for her intelligent eyes—which were what color? Ian realized he didn't know. In terror there'd been only blackness, pupils dilated in an adrenaline rush of fright.

And now that the terror had abated? Difficult to say, since she was still staring down at her hands.

On reflection, though, Ian found a fleeting memory of blue.

An accurate memory, he discovered, when she finally remembered him and looked up.

Kathleen Cahill's eyes were blue, but it was a startling shade, more ice than azure. Her eyes were haunting in their stillness—and without a flicker of recognition of him.

Ian Collier's photogenic face was invariably searched for by television reporters assigned to sporting events and charity galas. There was usually an on-camera interview, after which there'd be an allusion to his "extraordinary life story"—which was familiar to the overwhelming majority of the city's population.

It was a feel-good story and an inspirational one. Rags to riches. Shattered bones—a career-ending injury during a downhill race at Kitzbühel—to dazzling success. It was from what might have been his deathbed in the Austrian hospital that twenty-four-year-old Ian Collier had come up with the idea of Rain Mountain. And thanks to the steady stream of well-wishers, the movers and shakers of the skiing world, Ian had lined up the necessary seed money by the time he was well enough to travel home.

The media knew everything there was to know about Ian's murderer father—and not a single thing about Ian's life with Vanessa and Sam. Vanessa's parents had sold their estate and moved to southern California within three months of their daughter's middle-of-the-night vanishing act. And although the Worthings' coterie of elite friends knew about Vanessa's relationship with Ian, it wasn't the sort of unfortunate blemish on a family's otherwise untarnished reputation that anyone with any class would ever reveal.

And when Ian was asked about the missing years between his downhill run at Crystal and his emergence on the international ski-racing scene?

Ian lied, for Sam's sake, as he'd promised Vanessa he would. He'd been in training, he said. No one pushed for more or suspected more. If Ian hadn't tried to conceal Gordon Collier's crime, and he hadn't, there weren't likely to be other secrets of significance waiting to be revealed—not a clandestine romance with an heiress, much less a loved and lost little boy. And not even a hidden meaning to the name Rain Mountain. A private meaning . . .

Many Seattle teens, male or female, would recognize Ian on sight. Particularly those who skied. His short but memorable racing career had become the stuff of legends—he'd become a legend—among aspiring racers. Videotapes of his most notable runs were studied for both his fearlessness and his style, and he'd signed more autographs in recent years than at the height of his brief yet dramatic career.

But he'd signed no autographs for Kathleen Cahill—and he felt quite sure she didn't ski.

So she looked at him, and he looked at her, and the silence was oddly . . . serene.

Eventually curiosity prevailed.

"Who are you?"

"My name is Ian Collier."

Ambush! Kathleen might not recognize his face, but she certainly knew his name.

And understood at once why he was here.

"There's been a mistake."

"You're right, Kathleen. There has been. Neither of us was told the truth. You didn't know an application had been submitted on your behalf, and until a few moments ago I had no idea you weren't interested in being considered for the scholarship—much less being awarded it."

"Awarded it?" It was a whispered wish, faraway . . . and impossible. "But you can still give it to someone else."

"Yes, I can. And I will if you really don't want it."

"I . . . don't. But thank you."

Ian smiled. "You're welcome." His focus remained on Kathleen, but he was aware of the living tableau behind her. Trees dressed in their autumn finest fluttered crimson and gold in the morning sun. Ian loved this time of year. The autumnal fires, spectacular in their own right, but more wondrous to Ian in the promise they held. Winter. Snow. Escape. "As long as I'm here, would you mind telling me why you've changed your mind about becoming a doctor?"

"You know about that?"

"It was in your application."

"And that I'd spend my life doing research? That's what everyone thinks I should do."

Ian had to admit it was very easy to envision her in a research lab, her concentration broken only when an errant strand of hair fell into her pale blue eyes—a situation promptly remedied by a decisive and mirrorless snip.

Very easy to envision—but hard to wish for when it was so obviously not what she wanted.

"Not everyone," he said. "Not me. And not you."

As her hands knotted again, whitened, Ian noticed for the first time the fingernails chewed to the quick.

"What would you like to do, Kathleen?"

"Deliver babies."

She made the confession with apology. And defiance.

"I can see you doing that."

"You can?"

"Absolutely." In fact, it was even easier to envision—

her long, slender hands, the first cradle for the just-born life, providing careful passage from womb to world. "You'll be a terrific obstetrician, Kathleen. So terrific I'd love to pay your way through medical school as well as college. It would be an honor for me to do so."

"Oh, Mr. Collier. *Thank you.*"

"Is that a yes?" Ian asked, even as he saw her reply before she spoke it. The yes made a fleeting appearance, an evanescent temptation swiftly quashed.

"No."

"Because your mother needs you?"

"No. Not really."

"But?"

Kathleen gnawed on her lower lip as ferociously as she'd devoured her fingernails.

She gnawed. He waited.

At last she spoke. "No one can know."

"You have my word."

The girl of rare and stunning intelligence didn't question Ian's promise. She believed him, trusted him, at once. Or maybe it was simply time for the secret that gnawed so mercilessly within to be let out. It escaped in a rush. "I don't know where she is! She left one night and never came home."

Just like Sam. "When was that, Kathleen?"

"Two hundred and fifty-six days ago. On December thirtieth. I didn't want her to go! It was raining *so hard.*"

The Rain Mountain Enterprises CEO remembered the rain, the ski season that had been drowned. And Ian the man, the father, remembered a time when he'd counted in days—not weeks, not years—the nights since he'd lost Sam. "But she had to go to work?"

"No. I'd have gone with her." Kathleen's tormented thought was clear. If only it had been a work night, mother and daughter would have been together during the storm. But it hadn't been a work night, and . . . "She just needed to go out. To be with people her own age. To have fun."

"Had she done that before?"

"A few times."

"Do you know where she went?"

"Not specifically. It would've been a bar, or a cocktail lounge."

"Did she drive?"

"No. We don't have a car. But we live a block from North Forty-fifth."

North Forty-fifth Street, which changed to Northeast Forty-fifth at the junction with I-5, was a main arterial. If Mary Alice Cahill had caught a bus on Forty-fifth, she could have gone anywhere.

Ian knew without asking that Kathleen believed her mother would have returned if she could. He'd seen Kathleen's terror when she thought he'd come to tell her what, in some hated corner of her mind, she must know to be true: that her mother was no longer alive.

No one can know, Kathleen had said. And no one did know, Ian realized. Kathleen's friends hadn't wondered about her missing mother—because the girl, whose life was devoted to her studies and her mother, had no friends. And neither did Mary Alice. As for her co-workers at the hotel, Kathleen must have explained, as she'd explained so many times before, that Mary Alice was ill and she was filling in.

Ian's mind's eye saw what the past 256 days had been for Kathleen, living alone, waiting alone, desperately missing the woman no one else missed at all.

Ian knew about grieving, alone, for a missing loved one. He wanted the aloneness to end for Kathleen. And it had. He was here.

"You haven't told anyone."

"No. I called all the hospitals, though, in case she'd lost her ID and been admitted with amnesia."

Kathleen had made those hopeful calls. But no matter what truth she might suspect, she'd been unable to make the logical—and hope-shattering—calls to the police, to the morgue. Equally impossible had been a search of newspapers for the devastating words in black-and-white.

She would wait, Ian thought. And keep waiting. Her isolation would become greater over time, her loneliness unbearable. And, as she spent her lifetime shuttling carts of used sheets and towels to the hotel laundry, there'd be babies born who'd never know the safe passage afforded by her cradling hands.

"Would you like me to see what I can find out?"

"I . . ." Kathleen hesitated, obviously afraid, not wanting to know but realizing she must. The not knowing, the relentless fear, was ravaging her. "Okay."

"Okay."

Ian asked Kathleen to tell him about Mary Alice, and what he heard in reply was a daughter's unconditional love. Kathleen was proud of the mother who'd lost her beloved husband but had gone on despite her anguish, giving all she could, all she had, to make a life for her child.

Kathleen understood her mother's need to go out sometimes. She wanted Mary Alice to find whatever happiness she could however fleeting it might be. It couldn't be more than fleeting.

Still and always, Mary Alice wore her wedding band. Yes, even when she went out at night. Worn always, too, was a heart-shaped locket with her husband's photo, a snapshot of him in uniform as Daniel Cahill left for war.

"Does she look like you?" Ian asked—using, as Kathleen did, the present tense.

Kathleen shook her head. Vigorously. The long strands swayed. Her bangs didn't move. "No. She's *very* beautiful."

Three days later, Ian discovered that Kathleen's reply had been true, and not true.

The Jane Doe photograph taken in the King County morgue on the morning of December thirty-first revealed that even in death, even in murder, Mary Alice Cahill was very beautiful.

The postmortem portrait also revealed that Mary Alice looked exactly like Kathleen.

It was Ian who told Kathleen of her mother's death and guided her, so gently, through the aching farewell. No one else even tried to help. The friendless girl who'd always been a little different was now viewed by others as frankly strange. What kind of daughter would fail to report her mother's disappearance for all those months?

Ian gave Kathleen the answers she needed about the

murder, and asked the questions that had to be asked. Would she like her mother's wedding band? No, came the swift reply. Mary Alice had worn the ring in life. She'd choose, as Kathleen chose for her, to wear it in death . . . wear it forever.

Kathleen would have made the same choice about the locket—if during the rain-drenched night when her mother had been lost, Mary Alice's necklace hadn't been lost as well.

Ian was at Kathleen's side when she buried her mother, and he drove Rain Mountain Scholar Kathleen Cahill to the airport the following June. She'd been accepted into the accelerated program at Johns Hopkins; in six years she'd graduate with both her Bachelor of Science and her medical degree.

As a medical student, Kathleen wrote often to the man who'd made possible her dream—and who, even then, was her only friend.

"Dear Mr. Collier," her neatly written letters always began.

The letters were polite, grateful, formal, and as solemn as the motherless daughter who wrote them.

Ian worried about the solemnity of her letters; he knew she was grieving, knew it would take time. He doubted her classmates in Baltimore knew her mother had been brutally murdered. Kathleen wouldn't have wanted them to know. She'd have become a curiosity at best, an object of pity at worst.

As it was, the girl who'd always been isolated distanced herself even more. It was a defense, Ian knew, against her pain. He'd constructed a similar barrier between himself and the world.

"Dear Kathleen," he always replied, encouraging her to address him as Ian—and since it was obvious that studying alone was all she ever did, he also encouraged her to tell him what she was learning.

There was energy in her letters when she wrote about her schoolwork, a passion despite her grief. Science was an escape for her, as certain for her, and as comforting, as retreat to the mountains was for him.

But Ian found exhilaration in his snowy escapes, a quiet joy.

There was joy for Kathleen, too, at last, when she reached her clinical years of medical school. Caring for patients was what she was meant to do. She loved being able to help and wrote with great affection about her patients—as if they were friends—and with great respect for the doctors and nurses from whom she was learning so much.

Kathleen still had no life beyond the hospital walls. But she was happy with the life she had. The more time she spent in the hospital, the happier her letters were.

In the spring of her final year at Johns Hopkins, Kathleen was accepted into her first-choice residency—OB-Gyn at Brigham and Womens in Boston. Three months later she graduated at the top of her class.

"Dear Dr. Cahill," Ian wrote.

"Dear Ian," she replied.

Her letters became less formal during her residency, and quite a bit more rushed. Doctors weren't necessarily born with illegible handwriting, Ian decided. It was simply a consequence of writing on the fly. The tidy handwriting of Kathleen's med school letters gave way to writing that looked as if hand and paper were moving in opposite directions as the pen tried to anchor as many words as possible before all contact was lost.

But Kathleen loved what she was doing and wanted him to know it. Letters became postcards, however, the first of which was mailed ten days after it was written—because, as she jotted in the already crowded margins, it took her that long to "get organized enough to find a stamp!"

Ian responded by sending her a stack of hot-off-the-press Rain Mountain postcards. The company logo—Mount Rainier shimmering gold—was pictured on the front, along with the newly minted slogan Altitude with Attitude. Pre-addressed to Ian's Wind Chimes Towers condo, each postcard was already stamped.

Nine years and countless written communiqués after Ian had watched Kathleen board a plane for Baltimore, they finally spoke.

She called him at home at ten in the evening Seattle time, one in the morning in Boston.

"Ian?"

Calls from women—lovers—were frequent. But Ian didn't recognize this particular woman's voice. "Yes?"

"It's Kathleen."

"Kathleen. *Hello*."

"Is this a bad time to call?"

"Not at all. No time is bad. How are you?"

"Good. You?"

"I'm good, too. Kathleen? What's wrong?"

"Nothing really. It's just that every so often . . . do you

ever get angry with her, furious with her, for letting herself get killed?"

"Angry with your mother, you mean?" *You bet I do.*

"I actually meant your mother, Ian. I know I'm furious with mine. I'm just trying to decide how normal—or pathologic—my reaction is."

"My guess would be pretty normal. Don't you think?"

"I don't know. It feels awful. So selfish. She didn't want to meet a deadly stranger. She just wanted to have a few hours of fun."

"You wanted that for her, too."

"I did. But she must've known that meeting strangers in bars was dangerous. And she had a teenage daughter who needed her. She should have been more careful—should have cared more."

"I'm sure she cared, Kathleen."

"I am, too. That's why I feel so guilty about my anger. And disgusted, too, for making it about *me*. My loss. She's the one who died. The greatest loss is hers."

"But your loss was also great. You can't minimize the pain for the loved ones who survive."

"You survived."

"With plenty of anger. I spent the first eighteen years of my life at war with the world. I don't recall a specific fury directed toward my mother, but if I'd known she was aware of my father's violence and intentionally provoked him, I can assure you I would've had a lot of trouble forgiving her for putting herself in harm's way."

"Even though she was a victim."

"A victim, Kathleen, but not the only victim of her carelessness."

"Victims blaming victims."

"Maybe, but I'd bet our mothers would understand."

"I hope so. Thank you."

"You're welcome."

Silence fell, a few thoughtful beats during which they both felt so comfortable they didn't want the conversation—or even the silent connection—to end.

Both spoke at once.

"This is nice," Ian said as Kathleen asked, "At war with the world?"

And both replied at once.

"Sure," Ian acknowledged as Kathleen agreed, "It *is* nice."

Both smiled, then frowned, as her pager sounded.

"I'm not on call, but I asked the resident who is to let me know if one of my patients goes into labor. I promised her I'd be there when she delivered."

Ian thought about the patient to whom Kathleen had made the promise, one of so many patients who trusted her, confided in her, placed their dreams of having babies in her hands. Kathleen was like a best friend to the pregnant women in her care. But it was a one-sided friendship, professional and finite. Only the hopes—and stresses—of the patient were relevant, and once the baby was delivered, and the mother's routine post-partum visits were through, Kathleen might never see her again.

And as for the personal friendships Kathleen had? As far as Ian could tell, what Kathleen did in her free time was jot postcards to him. And tonight, in her free time, she'd called.

But now her time was no longer free.

"You'd better go."

"Yes. But . . ."

"I'd love it if you'd call again, Kathleen. Anytime."

"You can call me, too, Ian. With rare exceptions, if I'm here—my apartment—I'm not on call."

"But sleeping."

"That doesn't matter. I wake up quickly."

The prospect of talking to Kathleen again, the sheer possibility of it, sounded wonderful to Ian. Necessary, somehow. But there were other necessities, practical ones. "You need your sleep."

"Not—" *as much as I need to talk to you* "—really."

That need, for both of them, won out.

Kathleen wanted to hear about Ian's eighteen-year war with the world, and how and why it ended, and Ian wanted to tell her.

He'd never told anyone about Sam.

But he wanted, and needed, to tell her.

1

Sarah's Orchard, Oregon
Monday, December 30
Present day, 2 p.m.

"I do have the one puppy left," Marge Hathaway said. "She's yours if you want her."

"I do." Sam Collier's voice was soft. And husky. He hadn't spoken to anyone in the entire month since his previous conversation with Marge.

Sam had called her on that day. He'd done an Internet search—"cocker spaniel puppies" and "Oregon"—and discovered Marge's Web site, OceanCrestCockers.com. The site had been decorated for Christmas, a festive display of clip-art wreaths and candy canes adorning what was first and foremost a photo gallery.

Marge was pictured with Glenn, her husband of fifty years, with whom throughout that half century she'd provided a happy home for children, grandchildren, great-grandchildren—and dogs.

The newest Ocean Crest litter boasted eight pups. A photo of the proud mama and papa, the latter sporting a Santa's hat, provided colorful proof that the babies came by their honey-and-copper coloring honestly and should similarly inherit standard-for-breed bright eyes and shiny coats.

Marge did a little editorializing below the photos of the Yuletide newborns. Why not? It was her Web site. Her beloved puppies.

She didn't give a hoot what the books said. None of her pups ever left their Ocean Crest Ranch home until their fifty-second day of life, which in the case of the Christmas litter would be December 28. Not that she'd have let them go before Christmas even if they'd been old enough. Puppies bounding out of beribboned boxes on Christmas morning might seem cute. But as all dog lovers knew, a puppy's adjustment to its new home was confusing enough without the frenzy of Christmas Day. It was a dangerous time, too, for small mouths that chewed everything in sight.

Marge's Christmas puppies could be spoken for in

33

advance, however. Interested parties were welcome to call.

Marge didn't describe on her Web site her selection process of owners-to-be. But Sam hadn't been surprised to find himself subjected to an over-the-phone screening when he called.

Marge had wanted to know his age—thirty-six—and where he lived.

"Sarah's Orchard."

"Ah." The single syllable was warm with approval. Marge was obviously familiar with the small rural town, its quaint charm and friendly folks. "That's a wonderful place to live."

"Yes, it is."

"Have you lived there long?"

"Eight years. I have an apple orchard here."

"An apple orchard is perfect for a lively little dog. And what about your family, Sam? Your wife, your kids, your pets?"

"I haven't any."

"A significant other, then?"

"No. I live alone."

Silence had fallen at the revelation. Crashed. When the interview resumed, Marge's tone was firm. "Cockers are extremely social creatures. Our cockers especially. Once the babies are old enough to begin the socialization process, we put their playpen in the middle of the family room. They become accustomed to the constant parade of kids, other dogs, the occasional cat."

A happy place in the center of a family sounded wonderful to Sam. And entirely foreign. Oh, he knew about circles of love. But he had no experience of being *within* one.

"Of course," Marge offered in a softening tone, "I suppose there are plenty of interesting goings-on at your orchard. And I know Sarah's Orchard is dog-friendly—and filled with kids. At least ten of our cockers have found wonderful homes there."

For whatever reason—a leap of faith—Marge had taken a liking to him. As a result, she was trying to make more agreeable in her own mind the prospect of giving him an Ocean Crest puppy.

It was what Sam himself should have been doing, convincing Marge that solitary though he was, he'd give the puppy a happy home.

But as certain Sam was that he wanted a dog—and as confident that he'd give it the best life he possibly could—he was wondering if the social little creature might be happier elsewhere.

Sam's wish for a dog was certain and longstanding. Throughout the years of his boyhood—the years he was able to remember, from age six on—he'd wanted a puppy. The yearning had been year-round, but it crescendoed every Christmas, becoming so desperate, so aching, he found the courage to speak the longing aloud . . . even though he knew the reply—"No, you may not!" He'd retreat then, away from the circle of love from which he was excluded, and hide once again in the silence of his room.

And when, at age sixteen, Sam Collier left the Greenwich estate to become a restless, reckless wanderer, he'd found peace, during his tormented wanderings, in the company of dogs.

The dogs he'd encountered had been—unlike Sam himself—creatures with homes. Happy, wanted, safe.

Someday, he used to think, perhaps he'd have a home of his own. And once he'd found that home and knew it was where he was meant to be, meant to stay, he'd make a home for a dog.

Sarah's Orchard was that place, and it had felt so right, this Christmas, to welcome a puppy into his Sarah's Orchard home.

So right—until the nice woman on the other end of the phone made him wonder just how selfish a decision it was. Yes, virtually all the dog owners who'd seen Sam with their pets had commented that he had a remarkable way with dogs. A dog *whisperer,* in the opinions of some.

But Sam knew the truth: Dogs had a way with him. All dogs had ways with humans.

"Is there a reason you're particularly interested in a cocker?" Marge asked in the renewed silence.

Reason? No. Emotion . . . yes.

Sam had long since suppressed his unhappy boyhood memories. He'd discovered that it was a decision entirely within his control. The memories—and the emotions that accompanied them—were locked away. Sam alone had the key.

But there were other emotions he couldn't so easily control—and he didn't really want to lock them away. There was a hopefulness to the emotions that came from nowhere, untethered to any memories he could recall. Hopefulness . . . even when entwined with a longing he didn't understand and a hurt too deep to name.

Sam welcomed the feelings that came without warning and took his breath away. They made him feel alive. And as if they were alive, like friends who cared, he'd taken to following their advice—which, more often than not, felt like mandates he was obliged to obey.

It had been an emotional mandate that compelled his online search for cocker spaniel puppies. And like previous such mandates it made no sense. Sam knew very little about cockers. They were hardly the breed of choice for the men with whom he'd worked on fishing vessels, oil rigs, salvage barges or rescue boats. And not the kind of dogs, either, whose owners washed high-rise windows or painted bridges or installed roofs—all jobs he'd done.

But whenever Sam had seen a cocker, he'd nearly drowned in the bittersweet flood of longing and hope. So in response to Marge's question, he replied, "It's always been my favorite breed."

"Mine, too. Naturally!" Approval warmed Marge's voice even as she launched into the responsible pet-ownership mini-lecture she always gave. "All dogs are a big responsibility. But cockers require an especially long-term commitment. Seventeen years if you're lucky, sometimes more. Like all living things they need constant care, with intensive care at the extremes of life."

"I understand that. It's a commitment I'm prepared to make."

"Yes, Sam. I believe you are."

"But you're not sure my situation's best for a puppy."

"Only because I've become set in my ways. And here I've always fancied myself a hip old gal. I suppose it's habit as much as anything. In my fifty years of raising cockers, I've always had more families—by which I mean families with children—interested in my puppies than I've had puppies to give away. I expect that will be true this time around as well. In which case, set-in-my-fuddy-duddy ways that I am, I'll probably feel most comfortable sending them off to homes with kids."

"That makes sense," Sam replied. Perfect sense—unlike the emotion that was urging him to insist that, children or no children, it would be best for one of Marge's puppies, for any puppy, to live with him.

"However, Sam, there is one puppy in this litter, a little girl, I might prefer to place with you."

"Oh?"

"She's not socializing as enthusiastically as her litter-mates. Or enthusiastically at all. The problem is she's still very young. Who knows? She might become the most social of the lot. But if she's not . . ."

"I'll take her."

Marge promised to let him know either way and wished him a Merry Christmas, as he wished her.

Then, and for the next four weeks as Sam waited for Marge's call, he prepared for his new puppy, wanting her, naming her, even while he hoped—for her sake—that she'd soon be comfortable in Marge's family room.

Which she would, Sam told himself—then placed online orders for every item a truly welcomed puppy would need. He also puppy-proofed his four-room farm-house . . . including sanding to velvet smoothness every spot in the wood-plank floors from which a splinter might arise.

She *would* become a social puppy, and he *could* call other breeders just in case. He didn't, of course. He'd never abandon the puppy who might or might not be his.

Sam made no calls. But he replayed his conversation with Marge, what he'd said, what he hadn't, and he thought about other calls Marge might make.

She had puppies in Sarah's Orchard, puppies given to families she'd carefully screened. Like a birth parent wanting to be certain her infant would go to a wonderful home, Marge might logically call some of the towns-people she knew.

And what would the good citizens of Sarah's Orchard reply?

That they'd been pretty sure, when Sam Collier had ridden into town on his Harley, that he was a Hell's Angel. The pieces fit: long black hair, black leather jacket, a fierce expression on his face.

Sam had been buying gas, that was all, a brief stop on his way to the coast. He'd felt the wary stares that greeted him and sensed the relief as he roared away.

The neglected apple orchard was two miles out of town. Its For Sale sign, like the trees themselves, slumped in despair.

Sam was traveling fast, speeding toward the sea, when the sadness stole his breath.

Sadness for the forsaken trees.

He skidded to a stop, waited until he could breathe. But intermingled with the sadness was that defiant emotion, hope—which compelled him to return to town.

A dozen years of homelessness, combined with dangerous and lucrative work, enabled Sam to buy the abandoned orchard with money to spare for a haircut, a pickup truck and, most importantly, for the sad trees themselves.

Sarah's Orchard was known for its apples, just as nearby Medford was renowned for its pears. There wasn't a Harry and David equivalent in Sarah's Orchard, however. Instead of one large enterprise, the town's apple industry, such as it was, consisted of small-business owners, each with a particular type of apple-related product.

When Sam arrived in Sarah's Orchard, the apple industry was in trouble. His orchard was by no means the only source of apples, but whatever had caused its trees to give up had affected, although less dramatically, other orchards as well.

The townspeople seriously doubted that Sam's barren trees would ever produce again—especially since it was obvious, given the books he bought from the town's bookstore and nursery, that he knew nothing about the care and tending of fruit trees . . . or for that matter any trees.

But Sam Collier was either a particularly good between-the-lines reader, or a grower with exceptional gifts. The town remained divided over which. There was no dispute, however, about the results—more apples than before and *better* apples.

Sam knew it had nothing to do with him. He'd merely followed the standard advice on pruning, fertilizing, watering, harvesting. The timing had been right, that was all. The ground had lain fallow, the trees in hibernation, long enough. Well rested, the orchard was ready and eager to be bountiful again.

Nonetheless, should Marge happen to ask, any resident of Sarah's Orchard would insist that Sam Collier had both a green thumb and a golden touch. The town's economy had been revitalized thanks to him. Sarah's Orchard was in his debt.

And if Marge happened to talk to one of the chattier townspeople, she might hear that he wasn't a Hell's Angel—though arguably a fallen one. Men admired him, Marge might be told. And women . . . well, it was impossible to look at Sam—or hear his voice, or speak his name—without thinking about sex. It was a harmless fantasy. Sam was too private and too smart to become involved with any woman in Sarah's Orchard.

Sam guessed that Marge, fancying herself a hip old gal, wouldn't be put off by such a report.

The trouble was, with only two possible exceptions, no one would say to Marge Hathaway what Sam most needed her to hear—that if ever a man should have a dog, it was Sam Collier. And what a lucky dog it would be!

But the conversation might not even get that far, because people would insist that Marge must be mistaken about the identity of the man who'd called her. It couldn't have been Sam. He wasn't even in town. In winter, while his apple trees slumbered, he always went away. No one knew where, but they all believed they knew why: to rendezvous with old lovers or meet new ones.

In the beginning, sex had been a major reason for Sam's leaving Sarah's Orchard every December first. Sex and the restless yearnings the Christmas holidays inevitably evoked. The restlessness hadn't diminished over time, but more and more he chose to be alone.

And this year, despite the restlessness—or perhaps because the restless yearning was as much about a wish for a dog as the remembrance of lonely Christmases as an unwanted boy—Sam had stayed home.

People might also tell Marge there was a second reason her caller couldn't have been Sam. If he ever did get a dog, it would be a creature like him, wild and dangerous, part wolf if not pure wolf. And it would be an adult dog, not a puppy. Sure, Sam Collier had a gift for nurturing trees. But that was very different, wasn't it, from the care of a pup?

Whoever had called Marge, these people would say, it hadn't been Sam. No way. In fact it was pointless for her to call him. He wouldn't be back in Sarah's Orchard until early March. And although quite expert when it came to computers, and most generous in offering his expertise to those who weren't, for some reason Sam employed neither a voice-messaging service nor an answering machine.

No one except Sam knew the reason. But it was simple. There'd never before been a phone call he'd regretted having missed.

Sam wouldn't miss Marge's call. If she called.

And now, on December thirtieth, she had.

With a leftover puppy.

That was his if he wanted her.

"I do want her," he repeated. "I can come for her now, if that's convenient. I figure it's about a ninety-minute drive."

"It is convenient, but why don't I tell you a little more about her first?"

Marge's question was a warning. There were things he needed to know before making the drive. Negative things that might make him change his mind.

Sam knew he wouldn't change his mind about the unwanted puppy. But if Marge felt more comfortable revealing everything now . . . "All right."

"Well, needless to say, she hasn't socialized. If anything, she's gotten worse. Mind you, she's a sweet-tempered little creature. A sensitive little creature. The slightest commotion upsets her. And she prefers silence to noise. Even a TV in the background, which is often quite soothing to puppies when the humans in their lives are away, is disturbing to her."

"I don't watch much TV."

"Oh, no? Good. She'll like that. I've had her in our bedroom for a while, away from the chaos. She's calmer there, less afraid, pretty happy entertaining herself and finally eating the way she needs to eat. She didn't eat in the beginning. Too nervous, I guess. But in her own little place in the bedroom—well, she's sturdy now, has the same puppy tummy as her sibs. Her overall health is excellent. Our vet, whom I trust absolutely, says she's physically robust. She's just very timid. Less so with adults than with kids, and it's fair to say she has a definite preference for men. All of which means she might do well with you. Or not. She may not do terribly well anywhere. But she will have a home, Sam. We'll keep her if you don't want her."

"I do want her."

"Well, great! I just had to be sure you knew she's going to need a lot of love and reassurance. Far more than the usual pup. But that's the way with problem children, isn't it? They turn out all right, though, if they get the love they need."

If. Sam felt a long-banished memory straining to be free. He knew what memory it was. The first clear memory of his life. He was six. His baby brother, Tyler, was due to be born in less than a month.

And Sam couldn't wait—until he overheard his mother and stepfather discussing him, *their* problem child.

I don't want Sam anywhere near my son, Vanessa.

Our son, Mason!

Yes, darling, our son. Our Tyler. Who needs *our* protection from Sam.

You really think Sam might hurt Tyler?

I have no idea, Vanessa. But it's not a risk I'm willing to take. There's something wrong with Sam. *Very* wrong. You know it and I know it. Maybe it's time to put him back on medication.

I can't imagine that's the answer, Mason. He's calm now. Even off the Valium, he's calm. And we've *never* seen any violence in him.

Not yet. But the genes are there. I suppose you wouldn't consider shipping him off to his father?

Mason! You know what kind of man, what kind of *monster,* Ian Collier is. He didn't love me, remember? He didn't want me—or Sam.

I remember.

Besides, with luck, Ian's in prison by now . . . or dead.

Still, I can't believe you'd suggest something so cruel. I suppose I should've, though, since you refuse to adopt Sam. It wasn't easy for me, agreeing to talk with Ian, enduring that final abuse, so he'd waive his paternal rights.

I know it wasn't easy for you, darling. None of this has been easy for either of us. But Sam isn't a Hargrove, and Tyler will be. It's Tyler we need to think of above all else.

"Sam?" Marge asked. "Are you there?"

"Right here, but leaving in about five minutes. I should be at your home by four."

2

Queen Anne Medical Center
Labor and Delivery
Seattle
Monday, December 30, 3:45 p.m.

The view from the on-call room where Dr. Kathleen Cahill had lived for the past three weeks was a westerly one, a vista of Elliott Bay and the Olympic Mountains beyond. The winter sky had darkened and deepened as the sun made its descent, painting the twilight heavens lavender—Kathleen's favorite color.

She'd never before paused to wonder why she loved lavender. Kathleen had rarely paused at all. But as she marveled at the sunset, she toyed with the notion that some part of her might have longed for such pastel Seattle evenings, when skies were clear and mothers weren't murdered.

And now she was here. Home. Where the heart was. Where Ian was.

It had been a long journey home—eighteen years during which both she and Ian had been tenacious about keeping in touch with each other . . .

Following her first phone call, they'd talked often, late at night and for hours on end. And, as Ian wanted and needed to do, he told her about Sam.

"He was seven minutes old when they let me hold him. I'd known I wanted to be responsible for my baby, to be the kind of father I never had. But when I held him in my arms, my life had purpose—loving him, protecting him, moving heaven and earth to keep him happy and safe. You must see delivery-room reactions like that all the time."

"Not all the time, Ian. But when I'm privileged enough to witness such an extraordinary moment, I feel great joy for the newborn life."

"And for the baby's parents."

"Yes. Oh, *Ian*."

"What's wrong?"

"Sam died, didn't he? Your precious baby *died*."

"No, Kathleen. Sam didn't die. I lost him, though—not that he was ever really mine."

"Not yours?"

"Not biologically. No. I'd been a blood donor for a while. The blood-bank techs told me how rare my AB blood type was and explained the inheritance to me. An AB father didn't necessarily have an AB child, they said. It depended, among other things, on the mother's type.

46

What *was* certain was the one blood type a child of mine could never be."

"Sam was type O," Dr. Cahill said softly.

"Sam was type O."

"When did you find out?"

"Within a few hours of his birth. I was in the newborn nursery when the routine blood-typing came back. It wasn't an error. Sam really was O, and I really was AB. Believe me, I made very sure—all the while concealing my discovery from Vanessa."

You didn't want to lose your little boy, Kathleen thought. Sam was Ian's little boy by then. He had been since Ian first held him in his arms. Another eighteen-year-old might have been overjoyed by the revelation that would permit him to walk away, run away, from a lifetime of loving another man's son. Not Ian. He'd embraced the responsibility as reverently, as wonder-ingly, as he'd embraced the newborn life.

"Had Vanessa given you any reason to believe she was uncertain about the paternity?"

"No. But as I learned after she left and took Sam with her, she'd known she was pregnant before we ever met."

"And Sam's biologic father?"

"She didn't know, or care. I gather there were a number of possibilities, none of whom appealed to her for more than one night."

"But you did. She chose you. Wanted you."

"I was a pawn in an ongoing game between Vanessa and her parents. She chose me because I was about as unsuitable as they come."

"She also *wanted* you."

Ian thought about the way Vanessa had wanted him. Sexually. Voraciously. It was clear from Kathleen's tone that she meant another kind of wanting entirely—a longing for oneness of the soul. "Sure. For a while. But she became bored, I suppose, ready for something new. The thing is, I didn't see it coming. I believed she was happy with her life. Our life. I guess I just couldn't imagine her being anything but happy."

"Because you were so happy," Kathleen said. "With Sam. Was Vanessa a good mother?"

"Good enough—very good, in fairness, when she decided to be. She didn't want to spend the time with Sam that I wanted to. Every minute I could. But that was fine, or so I thought. While I took care of Sam, she was the social butterfly she loved to be, flitting from one engagement to the next."

"When did she leave?"

"Eight days before Christmas when Sam was four. Her ten-year high-school reunion had been that summer. The festivities began with a picnic at a classmate's Hunt's Point mansion. Vanessa wanted Sam with her at the picnic. She loved showing him off to her friends. He was a remarkable little boy, sunny, happy, beautiful."

"I imagine she liked—" loved "—showing you off as well."

Flaunting her unsuitable live-in lover, Ian thought. The murderer's son. "Yes. She did. I wanted to go to the picnic, anyway, to be with Sam. I didn't worry about him being overwhelmed by a group of strangers. He was very social. But I worried about the lake, the dock, the boats . . . and Vanessa's tendency to become inattentive to Sam when it was herself she wanted to show off most. As things turned out, it was a very pleasant gathering. There were other children and other responsible parents, and I especially liked the way a man named Mason Hargrove interacted with Sam. Mason was undoubtedly showing off as well. He and Vanessa had dated in high school, then gone their separate ways. Mason was working on Wall Street in his grandfather's firm and had just inherited the family estate in Greenwich."

"I'm getting a bad feeling about Mason Hargrove," Kathleen murmured.

"He wasn't a bad man, Kathleen, and I suspect his feelings for Vanessa in high school were a great deal stronger than hers were for him. At the time anyway . . ." He paused. "There was a dance that night. I didn't go. I wasn't working and preferred to have an evening with Sam. Which was fine with Vanessa. She'd shown us off, and there was the relationship with Mason to rekindle. By December their relationship had reached the point where they were ready to get married. I arrived home from a night of work to an empty cottage and a note from Vanessa. We'd had fun, she wrote, but Mason was the love of her life, and she was his. There were some papers she wanted me to sign, as soon as possible. Her attorney had them and was expecting my call."

"Custody papers?"

"That's what I thought they'd be. And I was fully prepared to fight for custody, to beg, borrow, steal the money I'd need to battle the Worthing fortune in court. But when I met with her attorney, I discovered that Vanessa had known the truth of Sam's paternity all along. Sam wasn't mine. All the money in the world wouldn't change that. I couldn't even argue—and would have been way ahead of the times if I'd tried—that it was in Sam's best interest to remain with me. Vanessa was a fit mother, and Mason was a man of exemplary character and background."

"So what did she want you to sign?"

"An acknowledgment that I knew Sam wasn't mine, and that I had no legal custodial claim. There was also an agreement that I'd never make any 'palimony' claims on the Worthing fortune."

"Did you sign?"

"Eventually. But not before using my signature as leverage. I insisted on talking to Vanessa. I had to make sure Sam understood what was happening and was okay with it. He was, Vanessa assured me. She'd consulted with a child psychiatrist in advance and had been advised to take Sam when and how she did. An emotional scene with me, a tearful goodbye, would have created an indelible memory he didn't need. Given his age, the psychiatrist told her, he was unlikely to remember much, if anything, about his life in Seattle . . . especially if happy new memories were laid down as quickly as possible. That's why she and Mason decided to make the move in December, so that Christmas could be Sam's first memory in Mason's home. And it was working, Vanessa said. Sam and Mason had decorated the tree, and there was lots of chatter about Santa. The psychiatrist suggested that in the midst of the excitement of Christmas morning, Vanessa might see how Sam felt about calling Mason 'Daddy.' "

"That must have been difficult for you to hear."

"It was. But I was glad Vanessa had done what was best for Sam, and what the psychiatrist told her did make sense."

"What did she tell Sam about you?"

"That I was her very good friend and had cared about him deeply, but I wasn't his real father. Mason was an even better friend, she explained, who would become his father. She said it confused Sam at first but with repetition, which happened only when he wondered where I was, he was adapting more quickly than the psychiatrist had predicted. It wouldn't be long before Sam forgot all about me."

"Oh, Ian. So difficult for you to hear," she repeated.

"I'm not denying it. But believing this was the right thing to do for Sam made it possible for me to sign the papers. I also agreed not to publicly disclose anything about my relationship with Vanessa or Sam, and, of course, never to contact him. I insisted on two promises from Vanessa in return. On the off chance that Sam ever did remember me, or if he just wanted a little more clarity on the first four years of his life, she'd tell him that even though I wasn't his birth father, I'd loved him as my son and would always be interested in hearing from him."

"Have you heard from him?"

"No. And I've kept my promise not to contact him. And until this evening I've never told anyone, publicly or privately, about Sam or Vanessa . . . or the reason I named the company Rain Mountain."

"Sam was the reason?"

"Yes. On clear days, from our cottage, we had a perfect view of Mount Rainier. It was something we talked about, Sam and I, from the time he was a baby. I'd hold him, and tell him about the mountain and the snow. For the first two years all he did was listen. But he was an attentive listener, and had been saving up words, and when he finally started to speak . . ." *Daddy! Daddy! Daddy!*

Silence fell. An emotional silence for Ian. So it was Kathleen who said, "Rain Mountain was Sam's name for Mount Rainier."

"Yes. It became one of our favorite games. We'd be on the lookout for the mountain, both of us, rain or shine. And when it appeared and I commented on how nice it was to be able to see Mount Rainier, he'd shake his head and say Rain Mountain—" *Daddy* "—Rain Mountain."

"It's a wonderful name."

"Wonderful memories. Ones I thought Sam might remember."

"Maybe he does."

"I don't think so. I never got in touch with him— directly. But when his sixteenth birthday coincided with a time I was thinking about taking the company public, I sent a copy of the prospectus to Vanessa. In addition to photographs of the mountain, there was a history of the company and a little about me."

"You asked Vanessa to give the prospectus to Sam?"

"Only if she believed he'd be interested in seeing it. I don't know if she gave it to him. I never heard back from either of them."

"You said you insisted on two promises from Vanessa?"

"Yes. The other was the promise I'd made to Sam—to get him a puppy for Christmas."

Late at night over the ensuing months, Ian told her about the happiness of his life with Sam . . . and the emptiness when that life was gone.

The loss had lasting repercussions. Ian knew with absolute certainty that he'd never have more children. *More,* for biology or not, Ian regarded Sam as his.

"But you'd be such a wonderful father. You *were* a wonderful father."

"Past tense, Kathleen, where it needs to remain."

"You'll marry, though."

"No."

"But you date."

"Sure. But the women I date know the ground rules going in."

"I'm never going to have children, either."

"Of course you are."

"No, Ian, I'm not."

"Have you never wanted babies?"

"No. Well, I'd never given it any thought before my mother died, and after she was gone . . . losing her affected me the way losing Sam affected you. A pain you don't choose to repeat."

"You'd be a sensational mother."

"Oh! Thank you. I . . . don't know. I'll never know."

"You're going to fall in love one of these days, Dr. Cahill, and everything will change."

Kathleen knew she'd never fall in love. And no one would ever fall in love with her. It wasn't an abstract conclusion, but truth based on fact. Oh, men were attracted to her. She'd inherited her mother's elegant features, her lovely bones. But the beckoning sensuality was only skin-deep. She rarely dated any man more than once and had lost her virginity in a desperate reenactment of what had cost Mary Alice her life.

The stranger Kathleen met in a bar hadn't murdered her. She'd survived the self-punishing madness with a hangover and a surprisingly clear memory of how— even stripped of inhibitions—she'd hated being touched . . . and how disappointed the man had been with her.

"Besides, thanks to you, I'm doing what I've always dreamed of doing. And then some."

"Meaning?"

"I'd known at sixteen that I wanted to deliver babies. But I hadn't realized then that it was possible to specialize in infertility and high-risk OB."

"That's what you're going to do?"

"I hope so. I've recently applied for fellowships in high-risk maternal-infant care. My first choice is in Manhattan, at NYU."

"Then that's where you'll go. Did you apply to any programs in Seattle?"

"No."

"There aren't any good ones here?"

"Yes. There are. Excellent ones. But . . ."

It had to do with her mother's murder, of course, but it was more complicated than a reluctance to return to the city where there'd been such sadness.

Kathleen felt great guilt about what she, Kathleen, had done wrong. She didn't blame herself for Mary Alice's depression. The physician she'd become had an understanding of that.

Dr. Cahill also recognized that her behavior as a sixteen-year-old had been completely understandable—though harmful. Her delay in acknowledging her mother's disappearance had cost the police crucial time. No one had said as much to the grieving daughter. But Kathleen read the newspaper accounts of the search for the killer and listened to the investigators' interviews on TV. The trail was hopelessly cold. As strikingly beautiful as Mary Alice Cahill had been, and as memorable as the rainfall had been on the night of her death, she wasn't remembered—with anything approaching certainty—by the bus drivers who might have picked her up, or the bartenders who might have served her drinks, or the other patrons who might have been in the cocktail lounge where she'd met her killer.

Kathleen's feelings of guilt didn't end with her delay in reporting the disappearance, and, as time went on, her behavior became less understandable and—in her own view—more unforgivable as well.

She'd left Seattle to follow her dream, as if she didn't care about her mother, as if she'd forgotten her. *I'll never forget you, Mom!* Kathleen knew what she should've done—remained in contact with the Seattle police, reminding them often of the lovely woman who'd been slaughtered, helping them care so much about that stolen life they'd never stop searching for her killer.

Maybe it wasn't too late, she told Ian when, one night, she'd confessed her guilt. She just needed to find out who she should meet with and make an appointment and hand-deliver the digitally enhanced photograph she'd had made of her mother's missing locket. But even thinking about a matter-of-fact discussion of her mother's murder caused a breathlessness that felt like panic and a sorrow that precluded speech. . . .

At that point, it had been Ian who felt guilty. It just so happened, and he should have told her, that *he'd* remained in contact with the police. Mary Alice Cahill hadn't been forgotten, and wouldn't be. And if Kathleen would send him the locket photograph, he'd give it to a prosecutor named James Gannon, whom he'd met at a black-tie fund-raiser for Victims of Violent Crimes and who was soon to be heading up a newly authorized cold-case task force—its mission to resolve old cases using advances in DNA.

Ian would meet with James, or he and Kathleen could meet with him together.

Kathleen remained in Boston, where she learned, when Ian called, that barring a confession from the killer, the murder of Mary Alice Cahill would remain permanently open, permanently cold. There wasn't any DNA. There'd been no sex, Ian explained, consensual or otherwise, and no trace of the killer beneath the strangled woman's fingernails. Because, the thought had screamed in Kathleen's head, her mother's fingernails, too, had been chewed to the quick. Kathleen had stopped gnawing her nails. But she clipped them short, for her patients, for their comfort—so short that in the event of her own murder no telltale evidence would be found, no matter how valiantly she fought.

Kathleen had shared with Ian her failings as a

daughter. But not, in all their late-night conversations, had she confessed her failings as a woman.

She should have told him, forewarned him, before they saw each other again—the first time in fourteen years. Kathleen was in New York by then. Her NYU fellowship completed, she'd joined the faculty there.

Ian had flown to New York, on business but primarily to see her, and taken her to dinner at Le Cirque.

They'd made a head-turning couple, the beautiful woman, the sexy man, but the evening was awkward. Stiff and formal. Because of her. Here was this handsome wonderful man, the best human being she knew, and he was looking at her in a way any other woman on the planet—any real woman—would die for. Their relationship could move to an even more intimate plane, his expression told her, assuming that was what she wanted, too.

Kathleen wanted to want intimacy with Ian. They were already so intimate in every other way. If she could just feel the slightest stir of desire . . . She'd recognized it, surely, unfamiliar as it was. But she felt nothing except her own distress. Ian knew the pathetic truth about her now, how strange she was, not a woman at all. An island—no, an iceberg—unto herself.

When he said good-night, she was afraid she'd never hear from him again.

He called fifteen minutes later from his Manhattan hotel.

"Hi."

"Hi. Ian, I'm—"

"The woman whose friendship matters more to me

than anything in the world."

"Thank you. I . . . there's something wrong with me."

"There's nothing wrong with you, Kathleen. And nothing wrong with us. Just ask Plato."

Platonic love was precisely what they had, they decided, and precisely as it was defined: a transcendence of physical desire toward the more purely spiritual and ideal.

Their long-distance friendship survived, grew closer, and seven months ago, Kathleen had made an astonishing admission to her friend.

"I'm going to have a baby, Ian. I want to, after all."

"You're pregnant?"

"Not yet. But I'm going to become pregnant as soon as I can, assuming I can."

"There's no reason to assume you can't, is there?"

"No. Except that I'll be thirty-four in September."

Kathleen didn't need to explain the significance of her age to the man with whom she'd shared so much of her own expertise in infertility. He'd learned as she'd learned, and what they knew, and a generation of women was discovering, was that the chance of conception began declining at a far younger age than was popularly believed. Women who pursued careers in the hope of being financially and professionally established before beginning their families were often devastated when the dreams of having babies were not to be.

By thirty-four, the ability to conceive had already begun to decline.

But as Ian pointed out, "Most of your thirty-four-year-old patients have been able to conceive."

"True. Most have."

"And the baby's father?" *Oh, Kathleen, have you fallen in love?*

"I don't know anything about him yet, and won't ever know very much. I just have to hope he gave truthful answers on the sperm-bank questionnaire."

"You're having a colleague impregnate you with sperm from an unknown donor?"

"An anonymous donor, Ian, who *has* been screened. The sperm bank we use is very careful."

"That seems so . . . impersonal."

"That's the point. And on a more personal level, I won't be asking a colleague to do the insemination. I'll be doing it myself."

"When?"

"I have an appointment at the sperm bank tomorrow, and in two weeks, when it's the right hormonal time— you think I'm crazy."

"No. I've always believed you'd be a good mother. A *sensational* one. And I don't have the slightest doubt you could raise a baby on your own. Single parents do it all the time."

"But?"

"Well, at the risk of sounding a helluva lot more old-fashioned than I've ever imagined myself to be, something about choosing to create a fatherless baby troubles me. A lot."

"It troubles me too, Ian. That's why I was hoping you'd consider being the man in my baby's life. I'll be cutting back on work once the baby's born, maybe not work at all until he or she's in school, so we'd be able to spend large chunks of time with you. . . ."

"Where, Kathleen?"

"Wherever."

"You'd be willing to come to Seattle?"

"Why not? Changing my mind about returning to Seattle seems a pretty small reversal compared to deciding to have a child."

"A small reversal by comparison," Ian echoed. But a monumental reversal in itself. He'd assumed that Kathleen's decision against returning to Seattle would have become even more certain following the revelation that the crime against Mary Alice would never be solved.

But now, as she spoke to him of a baby . . .

"So you'd be willing to come to Seattle," he repeated.

"Yes."

"Would you consider moving here, Kathleen? If not, I could—"

"Yes."

"And letting me be the baby's father?"

"Of course, Ian."

"In every way."

"Every way?"

"Legally, financially, emotionally. Biologically." Ian paused, listening for a gasp a continent away, or a soft murmur of worry, or even a change in the quality of the silence, from serene to wary, at the other end of the phone. He heard nothing. No alarm whatsoever. Kathleen trusted him, believed in him. They were soul mates, not bedmates. She knew, as he knew, that wouldn't change—and that he'd never suggest it should. "We could begin trying, just as you'd planned, in two weeks.

The only difference would be that the donor, the baby's father, would be someone you know well, and who would promise to quit helicopter skiing and any other activity you might determine to be high-risk, and would do everything in his power to stay alive as long as he could—for the baby and for you. Kathleen?"

"Yes?"

"That's not the yes I'd hoped to hear."

"That's because I'm weepy with happiness. *Yes.* Is that better?"

"Much."

"Are we really going to do this?"

"We really are. Did you know that before you called?"

"Not on a conscious level. But maybe I did. Maybe it was what I hoped you'd want to do." *Maybe it was the reason we were destined to be friends.*

It had taken Kathleen one phone call to line up a job in Seattle. As a fertility specialist, she was well aware of the superb reputation of the Reproductive Medicine Clinic at Queen Anne Medical Center. Similarly, her future partners were familiar with her pioneering work in in vitro fertilization with blastocyst transfer —a technique they wanted to make available to the infertile couples in their care—as well as her expertise in high-risk OB.

The match was perfect medically, and even Kathleen's upfront admission that she was trying to get pregnant didn't tarnish the eagerness on both sides. The clinic had a positive attitude toward births among its physicians and staff. How could it not? If Kathleen arrived pregnant, she'd have their blessing to work, or not work, as she saw fit.

Dr. Kathleen Cahill's scheduled start date was January 15. But as of today, December 30, she'd been on call, in the hospital, for the past twenty-one days. And nights.

Plans changed when it came to delivering babies, so her own plans—to spend her first six weeks in Seattle becoming reacquainted with the city . . . and becoming as comfortable with Ian in person and in broad daylight as she was late at night over the phone—had changed, as well.

They'd had almost a week, though, in early December. She'd stayed at the Wind Chimes Hotel, a sky bridge away from his Towers office and condo, and they'd had such *fun*. She wasn't pregnant. Yet. Her failure to conceive in six tries might have worried her if Ian hadn't been so supremely confident.

"Seventh time's a charm," he had told her, as if it was a truth everyone knew. Besides, he'd always envisioned her becoming pregnant in Seattle, not Manhattan. It would happen on their first attempt in Seattle, which— assuming the clocklike precision of her cycle hadn't been reset by her transcontinental move—would be at the end of the month.

Or maybe even on January 1, the day she and Ian were going to move into their new home. The house would be furnished by then, with furnishings chosen by Ian and as yet unseen by her. Ian's selections *could* be delivered as early as December 16, provided—as the floor specialist predicted—that the sealant on the refinished hardwood floors was ready for more than the gentle slip-sliding of stockinged feet.

Kathleen had been feeling so comfortable with Ian, after only one week, that she'd been thinking about suggesting they move in before Christmas. Thinking became deciding as Kathleen headed for Queen Anne Medical Center on the morning of December 7. Ian had meetings till noon, and she'd promised her new partners she'd drop by. This afternoon, over a leisurely lunch at Snoqualmie Falls, she'd tell the man who'd dreaded Christmas ever since Vanessa had taken Sam away that, in their new life, their new home, all future Christmases would be filled with joy. Starting now.

The smile that traveled with Kathleen from the medical center's main entrance to the Reproductive Medicine Clinic on its fourteenth floor vanished the instant she entered the clinic itself.

The waiting room was, of course, a happy sight. Many expectant mothers, each beaming more brightly than the twinkling lights that had been strewn somewhat haphazardly on doorjambs and windowsills.

The clinic staff, by contrast, beamed dimly if at all. A winter virus had been making the rounds since Thanksgiving, forcing its most acutely ill victims to stay at home till the worst and highly contagious time was past. The staffing shortfall was particularly difficult. Seattle was in the midst of a Yuletide baby boom. Babies conceived the day an aircraft carrier had returned from the Gulf were due on the fifteenth, with most of the others likely to appear between the fifteenth and Christmas, and there was a surge in nonmilitary babies as well, thanks to an earthquake that had jolted the Pacific Northwest at approximately the same time.

The baby boom would have been manageable, even with the rotating sick leave, had it not been for the extremely high-risk patient referred to the clinic in late July.

Georgia Blaine was thirty-four. But unlike Kathleen—and Ian—Georgia and Thomas had been trying to get pregnant for eleven years. They'd moved around because of Thomas's job and as a result had consulted an array of fertility specialists in a number of states. They'd been living in California when Georgia received a new FDA-approved ovulation-inducing hormone. Quadruplets, her initial ultrasound confirmed. Quadruplets at least. Subsequent studies as her pregnancy progressed might indicate more.

Georgia's pregnancy was early enough and she was healthy enough that she and Thomas relocated to Seattle, as planned, in July.

The ultrasound performed during her first Reproductive Medicine Clinic appointment revealed seven babies, and by then both her blood pressure and blood sugar were on the rise. She'd required admission on October 19 and had been hospitalized ever since.

In mid-November, shortly before the winter virus struck, it became obvious that Georgia had reached the stage at which she needed one physician—full-time and around-the-clock—whose undivided attention was on her.

The already stretched-thin staff stretched a little more. And they'd almost made it. The hope, which had once seemed a long shot, was to keep Georgia's babies in utero until December 12. Five more days.

Kathleen had volunteered to begin work then and there.

"Do with me what you will!" she'd insisted, and meant it. She'd deliver babies, do routine exams on all the brightly beaming moms-to-be, fetch coffee, draw blood, whatever.

She was a little surprised by her colleagues' choice: that she take care of Georgia. The birth of septuplets was newsworthy. But, Kathleen was delighted to discover, none of her partners felt territorial, much less glory-seeking, about Georgia. In fact, like Kathleen herself, none of them would have prescribed the potent hor-mone—a prescription for multiple pregnancy—to begin with.

All were committed, of course, to doing the best that was humanly possible for Georgia and her babies. And all would be involved when Georgia went into labor.

Kathleen was accustomed to spending consecutive days and nights in the hospital. She'd done it often with her high-risk patients in New York. The typical stay had been three nights, sometimes four, and once eight.

As of this lavender twilight, however, Kathleen had spent three weeks in the medical center on-call room located thirty seconds—less if one ran—from Labor and Delivery.

The room rivaled a guest suite in a nice hotel, com-plete with spacious bath, magnificent view, three-line phone with voice messaging, nineteen-inch TV, com-puter with Internet access, meal delivery, and house-keeping service whenever she requested it.

Kathleen never requested housekeeping. She was perfectly capable of depositing her used sheets, towels, coats, and scrubs in the hamper down the hall, and collecting fresh ones from the linen room on the way back. Kathleen Cahill didn't need a maid—some teenage girl's mother, perhaps, so oppressed by her job she might leave her daughter, despite a rainstorm, desperate for escape.

The memory of her mother, never far away, evoked a sadness that was undiminished by the passage of time.

She embraced the sadness, held it tight before focusing again on the grandeur of the twilight . . . and the happiness of her life with Ian.

It had already begun. No, they hadn't made it to Snoqualmie Falls that afternoon, and there'd been no Christmas together in their new home. But when she'd told him—during the first of their many daily and nightly phone calls of the past three weeks—that was what she'd been planning to suggest, they'd both felt the monumental change.

Their new home. Their new life. Their first Christmas.

Their love was platonic, but it was love.

The twilight sky was grand, and she was happy, and so lucky.

She was smiling when the phone behind her rang.

3

"It's Jen, Dr. Cahill," Georgia's evening-shift nurse said when Kathleen answered the phone. "I'm really sorry to bother you. I know it's only been fifteen minutes since you last checked on Georgia and medically she's rock steady. But she's anxious again and asking for you."

"I'm Kathleen, Jen. And it's not a bother. Ever. I'm on my way."

"Great. Thank you. Kathleen."

Jen met Kathleen halfway between the on-call room and Georgia's room, and as they walked the rest of the way together she finished the apology that had begun over the phone.

"I guess we're all feeling totally inadequate when it comes to reassuring Georgia. You'd think we wouldn't have to call you every time. But you're the only one who can calm her down."

"It's fine, Jen. Really. In fact, I want to take a look at her whenever she's anxious. She's on so many meds that even a slight increase in her anxiety may be our first indication that it's time to think about delivering her."

"I'm pretty sure that's not what's going on now. I mean, it seems to be the same thing, same perseveration, she's been having since Christmas Eve."

Perseveration was a term familiar to health-care professionals who worked on neurology wards, or in nursing homes, where patients might repeat the same question or worry—persevere in doing so—with neither the knowledge they were doing it nor the hope of resolving it.

Georgia's perseveration was situational, a consequence of the antihypertensive meds, among others, she was on. Controlling her blood pressure prepartum was critical. Her thought processes, like her blood pressure, would return to normal once her babies were born.

Georgia was lying on her side, the only way she could lie. The weight of her pregnant uterus would dangerously compress her abdominal blood vessels if she rolled onto her back. The enforced bed rest was taking a toll; her muscles were losing strength and mass.

In her lucid moments, Georgia described herself cheerfully as a beached whale, and even when confused, her basically optimistic personality shone through.

She'd be a terrific mom, and Thomas would be a wonderful dad, and that was good, Kathleen thought, because both parents would be tested.

Kathleen sat beside Georgia and peered, smiling, at the puffy face and worried eyes—which brightened when they saw her.

"Dr. Cahill! You're here. I've been wondering about my babies. How are they doing? Do you know?"

"As it happens, I do know. Your babies are doing great, Georgia. Just great. And so are you."

"Are there really seven babies?"

"There really are."

"I know I'm supposed to be considering a selective reduction, but I can't. I just *can't*."

It was too late, of course, to terminate in utero any of the little lives—to sacrifice two or three to make room for the others to grow. Georgia and Thomas had made the decision not to months ago.

"I know you can't, Georgia." *Neither could I.* "And no one's asking you to. So don't think about it, okay? Because your babies, all seven of them, are doing just fine."

More than fine, Kathleen thought. What had once seemed a farfetched hope, to keep the babies in utero until December 12, had become a reality and then some. They were eighteen days—and thousands of tiny heartbeats—beyond that milestone. And every heartbeat mattered, each a tiny but colossal leap toward maturity, less prematurity, when the infants were born.

Georgia's babies would be premature. No human uterus could support seven fetuses to term. But with each passing second, their ultimate prognosis improved. Already they'd surpassed by two weeks the gestational age at which the world's first surviving septuplets, the McCaugheys of Iowa, had been born.

"Dr. Cahill?"

"Yes, Georgia?"

"I've been wondering about my babies. . . ."

Kathleen offered reassurance again and again, until a smiling Georgia drifted back to sleep. After some additional reassurance, for Thomas this time, Kathleen went to the nurses' station to find Georgia's chart and write a progress note. That complete, but with chart still in hand, Kathleen engaged in a silent, familiar debate about what to do next.

She could return to her on-call room, as she wanted to, or she could do what she *should* do—plunk herself down on a sofa in the staff lounge and chitchat with whoever happened to wander in over the next hour or two. So that, after an hour or two, they'd decide she was so easy to talk to, so much one of them, she'd never again need to remind them to call her Kathleen.

They would, eventually, call her Kathleen. But even at NYU, where she'd been known, liked, respected—for the physician she was—for many years, conversations had come to sputtering halts whenever she came upon social, not medical, discussions . . . as if she'd disapprove of anything remotely personal in the workplace.

She didn't disapprove, of course. It was discomfort her colleagues sensed, *her* discomfort with being the imposter she knew herself to be. Something essential was missing—the womanliness wasn't there. She didn't have the sexual desires women were supposed to have, and although she did very well with her patients, she didn't bond with women who weren't in her care. There wasn't even an easy repartee with the nurses she knew, despite their mutual respect and the closeness with which they worked. The closeness was professional, not personal, because of her; because the sense of sisterhood, that instant connection, was missing as well.

Then there was the other element of womanliness, the ingredient she most feared she didn't have, the instinct that made a woman a mother. What if there was no maternal spark within her? There would be. There *had* to be.

Staff lounge, Kathleen told herself as she closed Georgia's chart. She'd stay there for the next two hours or until Georgia needed her, whichever came first.

Kathleen was nearing the lounge's open door, and could already hear the laughter that she knew was about to stop, when her pager sounded. The digital message read 7649. It was a direct line to the clinic's examination area, an extension used when one of the clinic nurses needed to speak, as soon as possible, with one of the clinic doctors.

The page couldn't be patient related. Kathleen's only patient—Georgia—was in a nearby room in L & D. Someone had probably noticed the changes in her office that had occurred during the holidays and was calling to alert her.

It might simply be avoidance of staff lounge socializing, but Kathleen decided to respond to the page in person.

Respond and confess. She, not some Yuletide mischiefmaker, had rearranged her office furniture on Christmas night. She preferred the desk nestled in a corner, facing the wall.

And when it came to meeting with patients . . . That was why she'd placed the visitor's chairs in front of the window with the courtyard view.

The clinic was two flights up from L & D. Kathleen entered through an unmarked doorway that bypassed the reception area and led directly to doctors' offices, exam rooms, nurses' station and lab.

"Did someone page me?" she asked when she reached the nurses' station.

"Oh! Dr. Cahill. Yes. I did."

"Here I am." *Call me Kathleen.* She didn't say it. Again. She'd said it to Tess twice before. "What's up?"

"There's a woman in the waiting room, self-referred and new to both the clinic and the med center. She called first thing this morning to see if we happened to have an open appointment anytime today. We didn't, of course, but she sounded so anxious that Peter said to schedule her with him this afternoon. But he's gotten really backed up, and Stephanie and Rachel are also way behind, and I remembered you said something about being willing to see patients as long as things were calm with Georgia."

71

"I'd love to see her."

"Really?"

"Really. And now's a perfect time."

"Great. I'll put her in an exam room right away—well, once I get these stat bloods off for Peter."

"Actually, Tess, I'd like to talk to her in my office before she changes. I might as well go get her, too, if you'll tell me her name."

"It's Natalie Davis, and you can't miss her. She has amazing auburn hair, and she's wearing a fabulous coral suit that somehow works with the auburn—and she looks incredibly anxious."

"Do you know why she's so anxious?"

"She says she's pretty sure she's pregnant, and even more sure she can't be."

The beautifully dressed—and beautiful—woman in the waiting room did look anxious.

"Natalie? Hi. I'm Kathleen Cahill. The other doctors are backed up, but I'm free and would be happy to see you."

"Thank you." When Natalie stood, in her high, high heels, she was exactly eye-level with Kathleen in running shoes. "You're caring for Georgia, aren't you? The mother of septuplets? I'm sure I've heard your name on the news."

"We're all caring for Georgia. But yes, at the moment, it's my watch."

Kathleen led the way to her office, found the furniture just as she'd arranged it, and gestured toward the chairs by the window.

"This feels civilized," Natalie murmured.

"I hope so. It'll be better with more comfortable chairs and a coffee table, but this has always seemed the right way to meet."

"I agree." As she settled into a chair and took in the view of the city ablaze with evening lights, Natalie was struck by Kathleen's serenity—which was contagious. For the first time in days, she actually felt a little calm. She was in good hands with this elegant doctor. Serene hands—and empty ones. "Oh, you know, I think I noticed the receptionist put my chart in one of the other doctors' slots."

"I'll find it when I need it. There's nothing in it, is there? Tess said you'd never been here or the med center before."

"There's nothing in it."

"There will be, don't worry. I'll dictate your history and physical after you leave."

"You don't take notes?"

"Not usually."

Just like you wouldn't take notes if you were talking to a friend, Natalie thought. You'd listen carefully—caringly—and remember the important things.

"Tess says you believe you're pregnant and that it's a bit of a surprise?"

"Yes, and yes. I'm not supposed to be able to get pregnant, but in the past week I've done six home pregnancy tests, all positive."

"Home tests are pretty reliable these days. Do you know how pregnant you might be?"

"Two months today."

"That increases the likelihood of the tests being accurate."

"I certainly feel pregnant."

"In what way?"

"I'm more tired than I should be, can take naps at will, and I have morning sickness around the clock." *And I feel joyful, hopeful. Not alone.* "It's the way I felt when I was pregnant once before."

"When was that?"

"Sixteen years ago."

"And you're how old now?"

"Thirty-three."

"And the baby?"

"I lost her—" *killed her* "—at the beginning of the third month."

"First-trimester miscarriages aren't uncommon."

"I know. But it wasn't a spontaneous miscarriage. I was upset. Distracted." *Love you, Natalie?* the disdainful query had thundered. *You're kidding, right? Or are you really that stupid?* "I stepped into oncoming traffic."

"Were you upset about the pregnancy?"

"No. I was ecstatic. I'd also deluded myself into believing the baby's father would feel the same way."

"You were in love with him."

"I was. Worse, I believed he was in love with me."

"You were seventeen."

"True. And he was twenty. But . . . do you want to hear all this?"

"I'd like to, yes. If you'd like to tell me. We may get interrupted. If so, I shouldn't be gone long."

"No septuplets being born today?"

"I don't think so. Which means, except for brief trips to L & D, I'm all yours. You needn't feel rushed on my account—but is there somewhere else you have to be?"

"No. My only plan for the remainder of the day is to go home and take one of those frequent naps."

And in the meantime, there was no place else Natalie had to be, or would rather be, and nothing more important than telling Dr. Kathleen Cahill anything and everything that might help this baby survive.

The medical story was relevant. Obviously. But maybe the emotional one was, too—for herself and the baby. Natalie wondered if the doctor who wasn't taking notes, but listening as a friend would listen, sensed this wasn't something she'd ever talked about before, and needed to.

Because she *did* need to, she realized. She needed, astonishingly, to share with the serene and caring physician the story she'd always been ashamed to reveal. Kathleen wouldn't be shocked, Natalie thought. Nor would she judge.

"I was an emotionally naive seventeen," she began. "But by no means a sexual innocent. Sex was what my group of friends did."

"At what age did you become sexually active?"

"Thirteen."

"Had you started having periods by then?"

"Oh, yes. I started at eleven."

"Did you feel pressured to have sex?"

"No. I really didn't. I enjoyed being popular, and sex was expected with the kind of boys I knew—boys whose vision of the future was the next cigarette, the next beer and, most importantly, the next opportunity for sex. I went along with the sex willingly but not recklessly. Everywhere I looked—my sisters, my mother, my grandmother—I saw lives I didn't want to live. They'd married young because they had to, or believed they did. I had no alternative in mind, just *not* that. I'd overheard one of my sisters complaining that she'd become pregnant—again—despite her husband's use of condoms. When I looked into it, I found that condoms weren't nearly as reliable as we'd been led to believe in our sex education classes at school. Not, in any event, when used alone. That's right, isn't it?"

"Absolutely. When used alone, condoms aren't what you'd recommend to someone you care about, either for contraception or STDs—including AIDS. At a minimum, the sexual partner needs to use a spermicidal jelly, preferably with a barrier as well."

"That's what I did. Diaphragm and spermicidal jelly—the more the merrier. And it worked. I avoided pregnancy and infection at a time when many of my friends were getting one or both. I also remained in school longer than most of my friends. By my senior year in high school I was with a new crowd—one that liked going to parties on the campus of our very classy college on the other side of town."

"Which was?"

"Princeton. What better place to meet Prince Charming? He was so different from any boy I'd ever known. Not only did he foresee a dazzling future for himself, he was confident he deserved it. And equally confident, or so I believed, in his long-term feelings about me. We were star-crossed lovers, of course. Blue blood meets blue-collar. But that made it all the more romantic. And passionate. I stopped worrying about protection. There was nothing to worry *about.* I'd be with him forever."

"You were seventeen."

"And hopelessly romantic—and naive. He was just using me and I didn't have a clue. The fantasy lasted less than three months. He went home for Christmas, to spend the holidays with the family who'd detest me, and I began to feel the way I feel now—pregnant. I must've been about two months along then, too. I was so excited, so eager to let him know. But calling his parents' Westchester County home wouldn't do, and he'd warned me in advance that he wouldn't call me until after he'd returned to campus in the new year. I knew when classes at Princeton resumed. The entire town always knew. Instead of waiting to hear from him, I showed up at his dorm room. Another thing I was never to do. It was January sixth, the Christian feast of Epiphany. I had my own epiphany that day, a far from wondrous one. It began with photographs of his fiancée beside his bed. She was a junior at Vassar and they'd been engaged for a year."

"That must've been devastating for you."

"It was a shock. A free fall from joy to . . . truth."

It's not my baby, Natalie, he'd said.

Of course it is! I haven't been with anyone else.

You expect me to believe that? A tramp like you?

I'm not a tramp! How can you call me that?

Because you are a tramp. A *slut.* What do you think they call a girl who gives it away? If you'd rather be a *whore,* I'll be glad to oblige. *Here*—he'd thrown a wad of money at her—now you've been paid. Do the baby a favor, why don't you, and use the money to have an abortion?

"Natalie?"

"I managed to find my way out of his dormitory. It was early evening, dark and snowing. It was a gentle snowfall, but I remember it hurting my face. Because I was running, I suppose. Or maybe at that point everything hurt. I don't remember running into the street, but that's what I did, directly into the path of an oncoming bus. And I killed her, Kathleen, my carelessness killed her."

"You're being pretty hard on yourself."

"It was my responsibility to keep her safe, no matter how upset I happened to be. And I didn't. I failed her . . . or him. I don't even know that she was a she."

"But you believed she was?"

"From the moment I sensed her presence inside me. Yes." *Just as I believe there's a baby girl inside me now.* "It seemed appropriate that I'd be unable to get pregnant again."

"What was the medical reason your doctor gave?"

"I honestly don't know. I was in and out of consciousness—and in and out of surgery—for several weeks. By the time I was alert enough to understand what had happened, the miscarriage was old news to everyone but me. The focus had shifted to finding out if I'd ever be able to walk. It was one of my sisters who told me I'd lost the baby and that I'd never conceive again."

"Do you know what your injuries were?"

"Broken bones in my pelvis and lower back, and internal bleeding."

"I imagine you haven't used contraception for the past sixteen years?"

"I haven't needed to. There hasn't been anyone."

"Until now."

"Well, until two months ago." It had been a one-night stand—and not even an entire night. Maybe James Gannon would have stayed the night. Maybe not. The issue became moot when his pager sounded and he'd returned the urgent call to Boston, to Christine, the woman he loved. Christine had needed James, and he'd gone to her. "And not since. And no alcohol, either. I *did* have about half a glass of champagne that night."

"That doesn't worry me."

"Really?"

"Not at all."

"That's such a relief."

"You'd like to be pregnant."

"Oh, yes."

"And the baby's father?"

"Isn't in the picture. But I can afford to raise the baby on my own, and I would. Will. Definitely."

Natalie's pregnancy wasn't visible, but her hand resting on her lower abdomen was a gesture Kathleen had seen often, a gesture as old as time, a mother's promise of love to her unborn child.

"I'll need to get your records from the hospital in New Jersey. We'll have you sign a release. Unless—"

"Unless I'm not pregnant." Natalie's hand trembled faintly but did not leave its resting place.

Kathleen smiled. "I have very little doubt about that. Before I send for your records, though, you'll need to decide if you'd like your obstetrical care here or with your usual OB."

"I don't have a usual OB."

"What about routine exams?"

"I haven't had any." It would have felt like grave-digging. That part of her, the baby part, the hope part, was dead. She'd killed it forever, or so she'd believed. But this serene and forgiving doctor was telling her she had a second chance. "I'd like to be seen here, Kathleen. By you." *I trust you with my baby's life.*

"And I'd be delighted to see you. So why don't I ask Tess to show you to an exam room while I find the release form and your chart?"

4

Ocean Crest Ranch
Seaview, Oregon
Monday, December 30, 4 p.m.

Sam dressed up to meet his puppy. The charcoal-colored slacks, button-down shirt and gray cashmere sweater made him look like the Ivy Leaguer his prep-school years had groomed him to be.

Sam also wore a Rain Mountain parka, an Ian Collier creation—like Sam himself. Sam hadn't purchased the parka. It had been a gift from the Apple Butter Ladies, a duo in their seventies who'd taken to using apples from Sam's orchard for their delectable treat.

The Apple Butter Ladies were also the two possible exceptions to the skepticism that would have greeted

Marge's assertion that it was Sam Collier of Sarah's Orchard who'd called about adopting a puppy. The Apple Butter Ladies might even have offered a ringing endorsement. They marched to their own eccentric drummer, and had lived long enough, thank you, that they weren't shy about expressing their opinions.

The ladies had been particularly forthright when they'd given Sam the parka. It was less menacing than his black leather jacket, more suitable for the apple farmer he was. And Rain Mountain's top-of-the-line offering wasn't really *that* fluffy. It folded to a nicely compact bundle, yet afforded the maximum protection against the elements, the consequence of magical fibers . . . the sort of alchemy, the Apple Butter Ladies apparently believed, that Sam would understand.

Besides, they added, the color reminded them of the "deep, dark green" of Sam's eyes. The two women might call themselves relics now, but they'd turned some heads in their day. They knew a good-looking man when they saw one—and didn't have the slightest hesitation in admitting it.

Sam wore the parka for the Apple Butter Ladies, despite the fact that putting it on meant cloaking himself in a bittersweet emotion that made no sense . . . as if he longed for the father who hadn't wanted him in the first place and had abandoned him without a backward glance.

Ocean Crest Ranch was marked by a brightly painted sign and a pair of cocker spaniels carved out of driftwood. Their living counterparts, beautifully groomed and wagging their tails, trotted up to greet him when he reached the house. A black Lab welcomed him, too, his smiling muzzle whitened with age, and a flock of laughing children, scampering in the yard in the fading rays of sunlight, announced his presence with a chorus of soprano voices.

"Grandma! Mr. Collier's here!"

A sense of wrongness swept through Sam. It wasn't fair to take a puppy away from this happy place—except that the leftover puppy had already removed herself.

Marge could have been an Apple Butter Lady, Sam thought as she came outside.

The assessment was affirmed when she spoke. "My goodness, Sam Collier. No lucky woman's managed to snag your heart yet? I'll bet it's not for lack of trying."

Sam's heart wasn't available for snagging. Or so he believed as Marge led the way through the cheery chaos of her home to the relative silence of the master bedroom.

But there was his puppy, strawberry-blond with dark brown eyes. Until she spotted the intruders in her private little world, she'd been playing in her playpen with a stuffed squeaky toy—a fox, Sam decided, with an especially large tail.

Seeing Sam and Marge, the puppy dropped her toy, backed into the corner of the playpen and flattened herself onto a yellow-gray blanket. Sam wanted to reach for her, an urge he forced himself, for the moment, to resist. He knelt at the playpen's opposite corner instead.

She was so small, so young, so terribly afraid—and trying so very hard to make herself invisible.

"Hello there," he whispered. "You're not coming out

of your corner, are you? Wouldn't consider it. Too scary. Well, that's okay. I understand."

Sam did understand. He'd been a frightened young creature once, an unloved and unwanted little boy who hid in his room, hunkered down, far from the circle of love. *Leave me alone.*

And what had Sam feared? What had kept him from venturing out? Confrontation with what he already knew: that there was something dreadfully wrong with him. Something dangerous, even.

And Sam's most fervent wish? *Touch me. Hold me. Love me.*

Sam could resist no longer. Leaning over the playpen railing, he extended his hand toward the cowering puppy.

"What if I just put my hand here, beside your fox, not too close but also not too far?" The puppy neither advanced nor retreated. Sam thought he detected the slightest tilt to her golden-red head. "I think I'll just rest it here for a while, if you don't mind, and if you feel like coming out to visit, that would be fine, too. Or not."

Silence fell. A standoff between curiosity and fear, hope and terror.

Leave me alone.

Love me.

"Keep talking to her, Sam. She likes your voice."

As soft as Marge's whisper was, it jarred him. Lost in his personal time warp, he'd forgotten she was there. But as he heard the echoes of his own voice, he felt uncomfortably exposed.

He'd ventured a little too far out of his own private corner. Swiftly, reflexively, his hand withdrew.

At that point, the puppy began making a frantic, squeaking noise.

Hold me. Love me. Daddy! Daddy! Daddy! The thought, and its emotion, staggered him. Where had that come from? Sam had no memory of calling any man *Daddy*. It seemed impossible that he ever had. It must have been part of his boyhood wish, the most desperate part of all, hidden until unmasked by this puppy's cries.

Sam must have picked her up, for surely the tiny puppy hadn't leaped, hadn't flown, from her playpen corner to him. It happened so quickly he really didn't know. Maybe she'd met him halfway. Maybe not.

But here she was, in his hands, her heart racing against his fingertips, and now, sensing the solidness of his chest, beginning a furtive ascent. She found footing in the cashmere and up she went, to his shoulder, where she burrowed into the space between his sweater and the Rain Mountain parka.

It felt so personal, as if this baby animal truly needed him. But Sam knew it was instinct at its most fundamental. Self-preservation. She'd needed a new place to hide and it just happened to be on him.

"What do you think?" Marge asked.

Puppy needs home. It was an emotion more than a thought—and it became even more emotional as his heart pumped the greater truth. *Home needs puppy.*

His voice was a hoarse whisper. "I think she and I should head for Sarah's Orchard before it gets any darker."

"I agree. Let me just grab her blanket, her fox, the bag of goodies I have for you."

The bag itself, a Christmas tote, was an enchantment of pastel reindeer and turquoise Christmas trees. Marge described the contents as they made their rapid journey through the house. It was obviously a difficult journey for the puppy, as fast as it was. She trembled in terror.

Sam held her closer, tighter, and forced himself to pay at least some attention to Marge's words. The puppy's vaccination record was in the reindeer bag, and several booklets on the care and nurturing of puppies, and a few days' worth of food, with instructions about the proper amount of water to add. And, to make her new environ- ment as familiar as possible for the anxious puppy, her food and water bowls, as well.

Sam's puppy had an impressive pedigree, Marge said. Champions galore. She wasn't yet registered with the American Kennel Club, but it was just a matter of letting Marge know. She'd submit the application and send him the papers when the registration was complete.

"She doesn't have to be registered, of course, unless you plan to show her."

"Not a chance."

When they reached Sam's pickup truck, Marge patted the puppy. "Take care, sweet thing. And keep in touch, will you, Sam? I'm only asking because I'm so sure the two of you will do just fine."

"I hope so."

"I *know* so."

Sam had ordered the smallest crate available from one of the online suppliers. It was designed, according to the description, expressly for puppies.

The ocean-blue crate had seemed too small to Sam

when it arrived, and that impression recurred when he'd secured it with the passenger side seat belt onto the front seat of his truck.

But that had been before he met his puppy.

The crate was huge, compared to the puppy, with ample space for her blanket and her favorite toy.

Marge's prediction that Sam and his puppy would do just fine was tested even before they left Ocean Crest Ranch. Definitely not fine, from the puppy's standpoint, was the specter of being transferred from her sweater-and-parka cave to her safely secured crate.

Her brown eyes darted with alarm and her legs paddled furiously against the air.

Sam very nearly returned her to his shoulder. But . . .

"You're safer here," he explained. "In your crate. And see? Your blanket's here, and so's your friend the fox. And I'll keep my fingers right here, too. Okay?"

It was okay enough that she settled down on the blanket and off they went.

Her crying began less than a mile later. Sam found a good place to pull over, a scenic outlook abandoned on this winter twilight, and when he opened the crate, she came to him, rushed to him, climbing up to his shoulder even as he lifted her.

"It's okay, little one," he murmured as she cuddled. "You're okay. I'm right here, and everything's going to be fine. I'll be honest with you, though. We can't drive this way. Too dangerous. So don't even *think* about trying to talk me into it. How about if we hang out like this for a while and chat until you're in the mood to sleep? Then, while you're asleep, I'll drive us home.

Does that sound good to you? I hope so. It sounds pretty good to me."

The sunset over the Pacific painted the sky lavender with pink fringes. Magnificent, Sam thought, and even more magnificent mirrored off the glassy surface of the tranquil winter sea. It was the ocean that drew him, always had. Were it not for this puppy, *his* puppy, he'd be atop the water now, sailing wherever the wind and waves wanted him to be, until it was time to return to his awakening trees.

Never again would Sam spend endless months lost at sea. There was a time, not so long ago—an hour ago?—when the realization would have evoked the restless torment of a wild animal forever caged.

And now?

A squeak close to his ear, not frantic but purposeful, gave him his reply.

"You're probably not much of a sea dog, are you? Well, that's okay. But you're a listener, aren't you, and I'd stopped talking for just a little too long. So, let's see. We could discuss your name. I thought Holly might be nice. You're a Christmas puppy, after all." And Holly was the name emotion had chosen for him, for her, and with a certainty as powerful as the impulses that had compelled his online search for cocker spaniel puppies and brought his Harley to a skidding stop beside an orchard of forlorn apple trees.

Sam hoped the puppy liked her name, and the farmhouse, and the orchard, and the only world she'd ever know—the world he'd choose, or not choose, to show her.

He was responsible for every aspect of this tiny creature's life, from her very survival to the happiness—or sadness, fright, loneliness, uncertainty—she'd experience during her years on earth.

Was he willing to accept that responsibility?

He already had.

Did it scare the hell out of him?

Oh, yes.

"I'll do my best for you, Holly. I promise."

He moved her gently from his shoulder to his chest, a transfer that this time—safe haven to safe haven—alarmed her not at all. And, as he felt the beating of her heart, he wondered about the father—*Daddy! Daddy?*—he'd never known. Had Ian Collier ever held his helpless infant son like this, heart to heart, and if so, had it scared the hell out of him, too?

Ian had been eighteen when Sam was born—half as old as Sam was now. Had it been too much, too overwhelming, for the orphaned son of a killer? Was that why Ian Collier had so easily, so callously, abandoned his wife and child?

Perhaps, Sam thought. Perhaps.

Or maybe Ian Collier's passion for the mountains eclipsed even Sam's passion for the sea—a passion so consuming that Ian couldn't give it up, wouldn't give it up, even for his baby boy.

Ian raised his face to the night sky, closed his eyes, and inhaled the always exhilarating fragrance of snow. It was all he could do on this perfect winter night not to shout his happiness to the heavens.

And if he did, and his fellow skiers, many of whom recognized him, concluded he was a lunatic? It wouldn't matter. Nothing so trivial—nothing at all—could diminish his joy.

He was marrying the woman he loved, who loved him, too. Kathleen wasn't *in* love with him, and Ian was very much in love with her. But Ian Collier had indulged in more than his fair share of sexual passion. True, he'd never known, and would never know, the wonder of making love with the only woman he'd ever loved—but spending his life with that woman was the greatest wonder of all.

It was also an astonishing surprise.

After their reunion in New York, when the platonic nature of their relationship had become so excruciatingly clear, Kathleen's best friend waited patiently for her to fall in love. Ian wanted that joy for her, and he steeled his heart to smile—for her—when she shared the happy news.

But she'd always maintained that falling in love was an impossibility for her—and when she'd had happy news to share, her dream of a baby—it was to him that she'd come.

Ian opened his eyes, smiled at the starry heavens, and felt like shouting anew. The urge was quelled by breathlessness.

Altitude had never affected him before. His system had always been more acclimated to the thin air of the mountains than the bounty of oxygen found by the sea. But he'd been at sea level since June, finding their home, making it ready, and forsaking entirely the ski season in the southern hemisphere. Ian didn't view his summertime trips to the Andes as high risk, any more than he regarded as dangerous his ski adventures by helicopter in the backcountry of British Columbia.

Risk was conferred by the skier, not the venue. Ian skied the most treacherous terrains because he was skilled enough to do so, and he did so safely. Not everyone did, however, and there were enough horror stories of avalanches wiping out entire ski parties that—rather than reassuring Kathleen it couldn't happen to him—he'd simply canceled his trips and for the past six months hadn't ascended any higher than Queen Anne Hill.

But today, at Kathleen's suggestion, he'd driven to Crystal. Their plans were in place, and Georgia's babies weren't ready to be born. Besides, according to the "pass report" she'd seen on the morning news, the conditions were perfect for the night skiing he loved to do.

Ian's gaze fell from the heavenly splendor to the splendor closer by. The snowy slopes glittered with their own galaxies of sparkling stars, ice crystals shimmering in the man-made light. It was familiar, this universe of light and snow, but it was more luminous—his whole world was more luminous—because of her.

5

Reproductive Medicine Clinic
Queen Anne Medical Center
December 30, 5 p.m.

Kathleen had been called to L & D just as Tess prepared Natalie for the exam. Kathleen had popped in to let Natalie know there'd be a brief delay, then left to reassure, once again, an anxious Georgia.

That reassurance hadn't taken long, but Kathleen had been waylaid by a medical center administrator who was anxious, too. An extremely capable executive, he'd worked himself into a bit of a panic about Georgia's babies. He wanted what was best for the septuplets, of course. But Queen Anne Medical Center's reputation—and future prominence—was also at stake. Here was a chance to leap onto the world stage. The world's media was already in place. The administrator wanted to be sure that the leap would be a graceful arabesque, not a catastrophic tumble.

Kathleen had endless patience for Georgia's perseveration. Not so for the repetitious questions the administrator felt compelled to ask. Was Kathleen absolutely certain, he'd queried more than once, that each and every member of each and every team—seven in all—knew exactly what his or her role would be during those critical moments when the babies were born? And yes, he had heard her when she'd told him she'd be able to tell enough in advance of Georgia's impending delivery to

91

call in all the teams from home—but mightn't it be better to have them housed within the medical center, just in case?

And so on. And so on.

"Sorry!" Kathleen apologized when at last she returned to the clinic exam room.

"Don't be," Natalie replied. "I'm fine. Blood work drawn, release form signed." And in receipt of lots of literature for the mom-to-be.

Natalie hadn't delved into the pamphlets, nor had she leafed through any of many magazines for pregnant mothers. Instead, she'd reclined on the exam table, eyes closed, heart open, calm.

Her pregnancy was real. Everything was going to be all right this time. *This time.* The two words became a joyous mantra, soothing and certain, until a ripple of fear churned through the calm.

This time was so much like last time. She'd conceived in late October, become aware of her pregnancy at Christmas, and now, too soon, the sixth of January loomed ahead. The anniversary of her baby's death was commemorated every year, in her heart, in her dreams, in the dread that settled over her.

The dread was there already, trying to smother her in its billowy folds. But she wouldn't be distracted. This time. January 6 would come and go, and the tiny life inside would flourish.

Natalie would be so vigilant with this baby.

As would the physician who was, even now, conducting a most meticulous exam.

It was a systematic exploration, from head to toe, with

abdominal and pelvic exams left until last.

"You had a ruptured appendix."

"Yes, I did. But I'm amazed you can tell." Natalie knew very well what her abdomen looked like: a puffed and puckered quilt crafted from scars.

"It's an older scar."

"I was six, and it *did* rupture. You can tell that from the scar?"

"I can at least make an educated guess. Based on the raggedness of the edges, and the width of the scar itself, it looks as if the wound wasn't surgically closed—which it wouldn't be if the rupture had been complicated by infection."

"That's probably exactly what happened. I was pretty sick."

The abdominal exam complete, Kathleen began the pelvic with a bimanual palpation of the uterus, ovaries and fallopian tubes. Except for asking Natalie to tell her of any discomfort, Kathleen was silent. She knew Natalie's obstetric and gynecologic history—as much, at any rate, as Natalie could provide.

Kathleen's touch was firm yet gentle, and nothing hurt. Physically. But as Kathleen's hands—one inside, one on top—sandwiched whatever there was in Natalie's right lower abdomen, and lingered there, and lingered, Natalie felt a sharp stab of fear.

"I bet you're a great poker player," Natalie murmured.

Kathleen didn't look up. "I'm not really a gambler. Why?"

"You're feeling something, but I can't tell from your expression if it's bad or good." And Natalie knew it could be very bad. She'd done her research on false-positive pregnancy tests. Rarely, but terrifyingly, the seemingly happy result could be caused by tumors secreting hormones that were similar to the ones produced during pregnancy.

"It's *not* bad, Natalie, and I'm sorry for worrying you. I'm feeling scar tissue, that's all, from the appendiceal rupture, the accident, maybe both. What I'm not feeling, though, is your ovary. If it weren't for what your sister told you about being unable to conceive, I'd have guessed it was removed when your appendix was. But I suspect it was removed when you were seventeen, and that when the doctors told her about it, she concluded that meant no more babies in your future." Kathleen smiled. "I can definitely confirm one future baby. Your uterus is enlarged, consistent with the eight-week gestation you describe."

"And it feels normal?"

"Perfectly." Except for the missing ovary, and the resultant scar tissue, the pelvic exam was fine. Untrapped by a web of scars, Natalie's pregnant uterus had ample room to grow. Unless something unexpected showed up in Natalie's labs, or in the medical records that were being sent, Natalie would be one of the healthiest and lowest risk patients Kathleen had managed in many years. Before doing the speculum exam, Kathleen pinned between her fingertips an almond-sized structure on the left. "Do you feel anything when I apply a little more pressure here?"

"Yes. A twinge."

"Have you felt similar twinges before?"

"On occasion."

"What I'm palpating is your left—and entirely normal—ovary."

"And the twinges?"

"Also normal. They occur during ovulation, when the ovarian follicle ruptures to release the egg. Some women feel them every cycle, some intermittently, some never."

So the twinging was an alarm, Natalie mused, a signal from the ovary that it was the opportune time to conceive. Natalie didn't recall an ovulatory twinge either before or after she'd made love—had sex—with James.

But twinge or no twinge, she was pregnant.

Kathleen completed the exam, after which Natalie sat on the exam table, legs dangling, while they talked.

"You obviously had a lot of trauma to your pelvic bones. I don't anticipate that being a problem, space-wise, during your pregnancy. As to whether it's best to deliver you vaginally or by C-section, we'll just have to see where we are when the time comes."

We will see. Where *we* are. It was a promise, Natalie realized. Kathleen would be right there with her—with them. "Okay."

"Do you have any residual pain from your accident?"

Natalie smiled. Sparkled. "My traumatized bones aren't too pleased when I spend all day on my feet, and my sciatic nerve sends me some fairly negative feedback from time to time."

"Wearing heels can't help."

"No. But I only wear them when I have to."

"Which is when?"

"Whenever I'm with a client. I sell real estate. A certain dressiness goes with the territory—or should. It underscores the specialness of looking for a home. I do wear flats when I drive and—Kathleen? What is it?"

"Not it, you. You're the Natalie I've heard so much about from Ian Collier. The real estate agent extraordinaire."

"Well, I don't know about that, but I did work with Ian to find a home he wanted to buy."

"*The* home he wanted to buy." The home of dreams, Kathleen thought, where dreams had flourished, then vanished, and where new dreams would be born—the Seattle landmark once known as the Worthing estate. It still was the Worthing estate to some, even though the last of the Worthings to live there, Vanessa's parents, had sold it thirty-two years before. "I know Ian pretty well. He's so grateful to you for making it happen."

"I really didn't do much."

"Except approach the owners to see if they wanted to sell."

"It never hurts to ask, and it was definitely meant to be. The owners were planning to sell, but they'd been told they needed to do a cosmetic fix-up before putting it on the market. I'd have given them the same advice, since prospective buyers can't always see beyond old carpets and graying walls."

"But Ian could."

"Oh, yes. Although," Natalie added, "I got the feeling he'd have bought the Worthing estate sight unseen. Have you been inside since he's fixed it up? I know he was going to do that right away."

"I have been inside, and it's beautiful."

"But he hasn't moved in yet. I live nearby and I've noticed that the only light on in the evening is the one on the front porch."

"He's moving in on the first."

"You really do know him, don't you?"

"Yes," Kathleen murmured. "I do."

"He's a wonderful man."

"He is, Natalie. A wonderful man who'd love to have you at his wedding in the home you helped him buy."

"His *wedding?*"

"And mine. Ian and I are getting married at seven in the evening on New Year's Day."

If the revelation of the Ian Collier-Kathleen Cahill nuptials was shocking to Natalie, she was far too lady-like to let it show. In fact, she seemed to approve.

"*Now* I understand why Ian wanted that exact property. In addition to being one of the more romantic estates in all of Seattle, and having probably the best view of Mount Rainier, the location's ideal for you—a two-block walk from work to home."

"Everything about the property's ideal, Natalie. For both Ian and me."

"This is great!"

"You mean it."

"Of course I do, Kathleen. It's so easy to see the two of you together. So perfect!"

The wedding was going to be small. The judge and her husband, the two required witnesses. "Let's each invite a witness," Ian had suggested when it had become clear Kathleen was going to be living at the hospital for a while. Kathleen knew what he was doing, of course—

encouraging her to develop friendships with her new colleagues. "Guilty," he'd admitted when she asked him about it. When she'd made a confession of her own— "It's not that easy for me, Ian"—he'd told her not to worry. He'd take care of it.

But Ian would be delighted to have Natalie at the wedding. So would Kathleen. She felt surprisingly comfortable with Natalie, as if she had it in her to form a sisterly bond, after all. But maybe it was something else entirely, a bond forged the moment Natalie made the decisive, and no doubt uncomfortable, high-heeled trek up the white brick driveway to the Worthing estate to see if the current owners might like to sell. Natalie had become, at that moment, a much-appreciated part of Kathleen and Ian's future plans. "The ceremony will be at the house, and after that we'll all go to Canlis for dinner. We'd love it if you'd join us."

"Are you sure?"

"Very sure. You could even be my witness—if you'd like."

"I'd *love* to be."

"Thank you! Why don't you come over about six-thirty, if that's convenient, so we can show you the house? Oh, and there's a dress code. No heels allowed."

Like the Worthing estate, Natalie's apartment was within easy walking distance of the medical center. One walked down the hill, however, to Natalie's building, and up the hill to the mansion Ian Collier had purchased for his bride.

Natalie walked the four blocks carefully, in the center

of the sidewalks, and traversed the crosswalks with even greater care. She didn't glance at the cityscape below, nor did she permit herself any thoughts, much less emotions about her pregnancy. And she was stone-deaf to the screams of pain as the steep descent, made in heels, wreaked havoc on her bones.

Once inside her apartment, her baby safely home, emotion took over. As did pain.

The pain carried her to the bed where the baby had been conceived, and as the pain subsided with rest, emotion carried her far away—to the seventeen-year-old girl with the crushed pelvis and the shattered heart.

She hadn't given up, that devastated girl. She'd fought hard to survive, a battle waged as much against the ravaged heart as the crumpled bones. She'd felt so guilty she couldn't understand what was preventing her from doing what she both wanted and deserved to do: curl up and die.

Her family certainly wasn't blocking the path between Natalie and the grave. And neither, at a conscious level, was she.

The doctors believed Natalie would survive, that she could walk again, and with even more work her limp might, for short periods of time, almost disappear. With prolonged walking, however, or even standing, the pain and the limp would inevitably recur.

A career counselor had visited Natalie's bedside early on. An essential part of any successful rehabilitation program, the counselor informed her, was to establish realistic goals for reentering "the real world."

Now was the time for Natalie to begin thinking about

possible careers—yes, now, even though it would be many months before her discharge from rehab. She'd need a job that required a minimum of walking, of course, and depending on how self-conscious she'd feel about her limp, she might want something that required only limited interaction with people she didn't know.

Natalie tried to comply with the counselor's advice. But failed. During the rigorous months of physical rehab, she simply didn't have the energy to do anything between sessions except lie facedown in her bed and listen to the TV.

Listen . . . and hear . . . and learn about the news, history in the making, and the voices that told it.

There was a sameness in the way the voices spoke. A universal pronunciation, Natalie realized, so nonabrasive and accent free it was readily welcomed into kitchens and living rooms throughout the country—and identical to the blue-blooded diction of her Prince Charming.

Do you *hear* yourself, Natalie? he'd asked with disgust. Your accent is a *joke.* The only thing more pathetic is the trashy way you dress.

From her bed, facedown, Natalie began her own Eliza Doolittle transformation. She perfected her speech, facedown, and when it finally became possible for her to lie on her back and see the television screen, she studied the wardrobes necessary to complete the image of a lady.

She'd buy such tailored clothes eventually. After she was released from the hospital and found a job. Natalie still hadn't done any career-planning, which was just as well. The criteria changed as her doctors watched her walk and walk and walk without limping—with what she described as "tolerable" pain—and stand flat-footed without any pain at all.

Another thing changed during the endless months of rehab. A small fortune flowed from the city to Natalie, by way of her parents, the consequence of a lawsuit brought in Natalie's name but without her knowledge.

She would have objected had she known. The accident was entirely her fault. The suit against the bus driver—meaning the city—was both frivolous and cruel.

But there were eyewitnesses on Natalie's side, her parents' side, passengers on the bus who were prepared to testify that the driver had been going way too fast for the ambient darkness and falling snow.

The city settled out of court, an "undisclosed but substantial sum" that she heard about on the news.

The revelation merely widened the rift between Natalie and her family. The gap had always been there. She'd made no secret of her determination not to marry a boy she didn't love because of a night of reckless sex in the back seat of a car. Not, in short, to follow in the footsteps of her parents, her sisters, and—with the exception of the college boy who'd used her but disdained her—everyone she'd known.

The gap became an abyss following the accident. Natalie's foolish liaison with the wealthy student, in which she'd dared to reach beyond her grasp, was itself an expression of contempt for the way her parents and sisters lived.

Her parents regarded the settlement as partly hers but mostly *theirs*. They'd tried their best with their ungrateful daughter, and now she was damaged goods.

They gave her a small portion of the settlement—just enough to enable her to leave New Jersey, as she wanted to, and start over someplace new.

Natalie chose Seattle for no other reason than that it sounded like a nice place to live. As for the legendary rain?

Cozy, she discovered. Not depressing at all.

Natalie found work as a receptionist in a real estate office and, liking it so much, loving it, decided to become a Realtor herself. Once licensed, she was promoted from receptionist to entry-level agent, apprenticing with the most experienced agents during the week and taking phone duty in the office on weekends.

It was on a drizzly, cozy phone-duty weekend that a couple dropped by in search of a home. They had no specific home in mind, just wanted an agent who could acquaint them with the possibilities—high-end possibilities, it turned out. Software experts from California's Silicon Valley, they'd accepted senior management positions with Microsoft.

Over mugs of hot chocolate, and with maps and listings in hand, Natalie showed them neighborhoods they might want to consider, and sample properties available in each, then suggested the agent she believed would best fit their needs, a woman who specialized in high-end properties on the Eastside and knew the Microsoft community very well.

The couple didn't want another agent. They wanted Natalie. As did other Microsoft recruits. The word on Natalie Davis got out, a ripple effect that made her one of an elite cluster of high-end specialists in the city. As a result, she became the listing agent for the Winslow home in Broadmoor—which was how she and James Gannon had ended up in bed two months ago.

6

Broadmoor Country Club
Seattle
Friday, July 7
Eighteen months ago

"*Way* overpriced," Natalie embellished when it was abundantly clear that Christine Winslow agreed.

Christine's parents, whose home it was, were cruising for the summer. Christine had insisted they go. She'd handle everything, she assured them, with shore-to-ship communiqués as needed.

Christine's first move after bidding her parents bon voyage was to contact the "fabulous" real estate agent she'd been hearing about from her friends. The house had been on the market a while, listed with another agency, and in Natalie's estimation—and Christine's— significantly overpriced.

"Where would you price it?"

"Somewhere between two-point-two and two-point-four. My guess is that its eventual selling price will be right at two million two hundred thousand. That's only a guess, of course, based on my impression of the real estate market over the past few months."

"That's actually higher than I would have guessed," Christine said. "But great, let's go for it."

"Okay. We need to decide on the asking price. If we set it a bit higher than our hoped-for selling price—something like two-point-four—that leaves negotiating room. But we can also set it at two-point-two and make it clear to agents and buyers that that's the price we believe is fair. And firm."

"Let's do that. Why play games?"

That was Natalie's preference as well, and for the same reason.

So the listing was hers, and, because of Christine, the entire process was pleasant . . . and unpressured. Money hadn't been a Winslow family issue since before Christine's great-great-grandparents were born. And Christine's parents had already purchased—with a personal check—a lakefront condo on Carillon Point. The condo was lower maintenance than the Broadmoor estate, but far pricier.

Christine, who was almost exactly Natalie's age, was the real thing, an authentic lady, her graciousness as innate as her patrician beauty. Christine liked showing the home with Natalie, assuming Natalie didn't mind. She didn't, of course. Christine was the perfect hostess to prospective buyers, informative and low-key. She loved her girlhood home and was delighted to have a chance to share it with whoever happened by.

It sometimes felt as if the lady and the ladylike imposter were friends. But that was because of Christine. Her radiance embraced without prejudice. For Natalie, such warmth and welcome was a remarkable place to be. The lonely part of her, a far larger part than she'd previously acknowledged, secretly hoped the lovely home would languish on the market—with frequent showings—for quite a while.

Natalie even imagined confessing the wish to Christine. *This is so much fun. I hate to have it end.* And without the slightest difficulty, Natalie envisioned Christine's smiling reply. *Then let's way overprice it again, Natalie! Why not?*

Natalie didn't confess, and with its new price, and the always brisk summer-in-Seattle market, a month later Natalie had in hand a full-price, contingency-free cash offer.

"Already?" Christine raved when Natalie called her with the news. "You really are the real estate wonder you're rumored to be."

"It's not me, Christine. It's the beautiful homes I'm lucky enough to represent."

"Too modest, Natalie! But thank you. Now what?"

"We find a time that's convenient for you when I can present the signed offer."

"What time's convenient for *you?*"

"I have a showing at four in the Highlands, but other than that . . ."

They met at the Village Starbucks at two.

The offer on the house was nice. But Christine had far more thrilling news to share.

"I'm engaged! Can you believe it?"

"Of course!" What man wouldn't want to marry Christine? Natalie hadn't even known Christine was involved with someone special. Why would she know? The fact that Christine was loved, and in love, wasn't something she'd flaunt any more than she'd flaunt her wealth—or the spectacular diamond she now wore. It wasn't the ring that made Christine Winslow flushed with happiness. It was the engagement to the man she loved. "When?"

"Night before last, and you can probably tell I'm still floating. I'd hoped he'd ask me—someday. But I had no idea it would be so soon. It's not too soon, mind you. I'd have said yes to James Gannon if he'd proposed the night we met . . . that enchanted evening nine weeks ago."

"James Gannon." Natalie saw a crystal-clear image of dark brown hair, ocean-blue eyes, and still waters that ran far deeper, and were far more turbulent than anyone else—meaning the media—perceived them to be. "The King County prosecutor?"

"You mean the incredibly sexy, unbelievably romantic, stunningly talented King County prosecutor? Yep. That's him. My *fiancé*." Christine sighed. Then frowned. "I'm going to tell you something that's not widely known yet and that needs to be kept secret until James makes the announcement himself."

"I won't say a word."

"I know *you* won't, unlike others who *might*." Christine was referring, with fondness, to her many less discreet friends. "James is leaving the prosecutor's office."

"But—"

"There are plenty of good—James says 'terrific'—prosecutors in the office, and James should have as much right as anyone to make a guilt-free quality-of-life decision. Shouldn't he?"

"Absolutely, Christine. I'm just surprised it's a decision he'd make." Natalie knew, as all of Seattle knew, that money wouldn't have been a factor. James, too, came from very old wealth. It wasn't something he advertised, of course. But when a reporter was tipped to the fact that throughout his eleven-year tenure in the prosecutor's office James had donated his entire salary to victims of violent crime, James Gannon's very old wealth was very new news. Still, what James gave most of all to victims of violence was his tireless passion for justice on their behalf. And now he was giving that up— and Natalie was sitting across from the reason he was doing it. "He's leaving the prosecutor's office because of you."

"As romantic as that might be, and as incredibly romantic as James is, the truth is he'd made the decision before we even met."

"A quality-of-life decision, you said."

"But it's not the work per se. James has enough energy—or should I say stamina? Anyway, he's not afraid of hard work. In fact, he thrives on it. But you're familiar with the kind of cases he handles, the worst of the worst. Rape, murder, torture. That's all he's seen— twenty-four-seven—for the past eleven years. He knows it's a skewed reality, the ugliest possible view of humankind, but simply knowing that isn't enough any-more. He's ready to see the goodness again, spend time in that world and close the door on evil."

I'm *so* glad. Natalie's surprisingly impassioned thought didn't stop there. I just hope it's not too late, that he hasn't already seen too much. "He'd never go back, would he?"

"To the prosecutor's office? I don't know. I hope not!

It's not even the horrific reality that worries me most. James couldn't become jaded or cynical if he tried. But it's *dangerous* to spend your life prosecuting the bad guys."

"Dangerous?"

"Death threats are a regular occurrence. True, most are without substance, but it only takes one crazed killer with nothing more to lose. I mean, if divorce attorneys can get killed by unhappy clients . . . Anyway, it's just another reason I can't wait till he's officially out."

"Does he have a new job in mind?"

"Not only in mind, but all lined up. Beginning the Monday after Thanksgiving, James will be the in-house counsel at Rain Mountain."

"Talk about a change in job description."

"An ideal change. He'll be working side by side with Ian Collier, whom he already knows very well."

"I remember reading that James is an expert skier." Natalie also remembered where she'd read that particular tidbit—in an *Emerald City Insider* article entitled "Sexy, Single and Sleepless in Seattle." The magazine, renowned for hyperbole and innuendo, had also described James Gannon as an "unrepentant playboy" while making only passing allusion to his "stellar" prosecutorial career. "He and Ian ski together?"

"When they can, which is not as often as either would like. That's not how they met, though, how they became friends. Ian had an interest in a cold case, an unsolved murder, and met with James to discuss what progress had been made. I don't know any details about the case, or the reason for Ian's interest. James didn't say. I do know he had little hope to offer, even with the advances in DNA."

"That must have bothered James."

"A lot. Still does. It would even if he and Ian hadn't become friends. But thankfully they have, and James has a fabulous job just waiting for him. In the meantime, besides tying up loose ends at the prosecutor's office, he's preparing to move from criminal law to contracts law by reading volumes of relevant statutes, precedents, all the fine print he can find."

"Impressive."

"That's James. If he's going to do something, he's going to give it his all—which means, of course, that the result will be sensational. I know you're going to like him, Natalie."

Going to? Natalie couldn't imagine she'd have the chance to find out. "I'm sure I would, Christine. But I'm not certain we'll ever meet."

"Of course you will! I'd like to have him review this purchase offer for starters, if that's all right with you. Great," Christine said as Natalie nodded her immediate assent. "Then, beginning soon, you and I have to start looking for a home for James and me. We're thinking about getting married in May. If we haven't found our dream place by then, we can live in his condo until we do. It's very nice, in the Wind Chimes Towers, but a downtown condo is not where we plan to raise our family. . . ."

During the next few months, as she and Christine toured the Emerald City's most magnificent homes, Natalie learned more about the man Christine was going to marry. Christine never mentioned James's wealth. Never would. But she talked about his family in Menlo Park, how close he was to his sisters and parents, and that he always wore his pager—for them—even when he wasn't the prosecutor on call.

James was the youngest of the family. The golden boy. He'd remained close to his northern California home, attending Stanford as an undergraduate, then Stanford Law, until his move to Seattle shortly after receiving his law degree. His family had been supportive of his decision to relocate—although bewildered by it.

He'd made the decision seven years earlier, during his first visit to Seattle, and as far as they could tell, he'd never questioned it since. And it wasn't even as if that first visit had been so phenomenally wonderful that it cast the Emerald City in an unrealistically idyllic light. Quite the opposite. Made during Christmas break of his freshman year, what was supposed to have been a ski trip in the Pacific Northwest had been a washout. James, his roommate and two other freshmen from their Stanford dorm had spent the soggy week at a fraternity house in the city, watching the rain.

His fellow travelers had been disgusted by the unrelenting downpour that had ruined their plans. But James's enchantment with Seattle hadn't been dampened.

It would be a nice place, he'd decided then and there, to settle down and raise a family—as he was now about to do with Christine.

Because of Christine, Natalie discovered. James Gannon's plan to follow the happy footsteps of his parents and sisters down the aisle and into the nursery had been substantially altered by his years spent prosecuting the monsters who preyed on children.

His awareness of the lurking perils had made him decide not to have children of his own.

But *that,* Christine confessed to Natalie, had changed. "I've always wanted children, and James wants my children, our children, and all you and I have to do is find the perfect home."

Christine and Natalie screened potential properties, while James put the finishing touches on his prosecutorial career, and when they found homes Christine wanted him to see, Natalie scheduled evening showings.

So Natalie and James did meet. And he was every superlative the adoring media—and his radiant bride-to-be—had bestowed on him. Larger than life. Sexy, handsome. A gentleman.

Natalie still saw the churning depths she'd imagined when she'd first seen his photograph. The evil he'd seen—known, spoken to face-to-face—was flailing in that shadowed sea. The memories of evil would never be drowned, Natalie realized. A man like James couldn't possibly forget the things he'd seen. No loving, caring human could.

But James could be happy, was happy, with Christine.

The happy couple was polite and gracious despite their joy. They didn't exclude her, as other couples had done, behaving as if she was a servant who wasn't really there.

At ten in the morning on November 17, Christine and Natalie found the perfect home. Both knew it right away, and the moment he saw it, James would, too. The Magnolia Bluff home had just come on the market, and was overpriced, and it was extremely unlikely it would sell while Christine was in Houston, fulfilling maid-of-honor duties at a sorority sister's wedding that she'd agreed to over a year ago. Besides, there was a fail-safe. Natalie could ask the listing agent to let her know of any other particularly interested buyers—in which case James could make an offer, if need be, while Christine was away.

Christine communicated all that to James, via cell phone, while Natalie drove her to the airport for her one-fifteen flight. James was agreeable, of course, though he wouldn't mind seeing the home before he bought it. He'd call Natalie later to set up a time.

"Tomorrow evening?" she suggested when he phoned two days later. "I could try for this evening, if you prefer, though the listing agent likes to give the owners at least two hours notice."

"Tomorrow evening's fine, Natalie. But we could also arrange for a time earlier in the day."

"Would that be better for you?"

"I thought it might be better for you," he told her. "These evening showings must make for pretty long days."

"Don't worry about me! I'm used to working into the evening."

"Christine said you were going to ask the listing agent to call you if there's other serious interest in the property."

"I already did."

"And you believe she'd tell you?"

"Oh, yes. I've known her for years."

"Let's not set up a showing for me then, unless you hear from her and there's some urgency in making an offer. You know Christine will want another look when she returns, and I can see it when she does."

"Oh! Okay. If you change your mind, just let me know."

Natalie didn't want to obsess about James's reason for having already changed his mind about her showing him the house. But since her subconscious seemed determined to mull it over anyway, she spent the following evening analyzing it to death. She'd felt hurt by his dramatic about-face. *Hurt.* How paranoid was that? As if James Gannon's decision, any decision he might ever make, actually had something to do with her.

Paranoid *and* grandiose, Natalie admonished herself. Yes, she could deconstruct the conversation to make it appear that he'd changed his mind based on something she'd said. To wit, the issue of an evening versus daytime showing. But that made no sense.

Okay, no rational sense.

What did make sense, and could allow her to dismiss the entire incident, was that James was frantically busy tying up loose ends in the prosecutor's office—as Christine had said he'd be. Far too busy, even, to accompany his fiancée to the wedding in Houston. And there was no rush to see the house. Besides, there was something more romantic, and more appropriate, about seeing his future dream home for the first time with his future bride.

In the end, James Gannon never saw the home on

Magnolia Bluff—although Natalie did arrange another showing for Christine. She'd returned from Houston on the Sunday before Thanksgiving, the same day Grant Monroe arrived in town.

Randomly assigned to be roommates at Stanford in their freshman year, James and Grant had maintained a friendship ever since. A professional relationship had developed as well. A scholarship student at Stanford, Grant had gone on to earn a Ph.D. and subsequently a tenured professorship in criminal psychology at Harvard. He'd written four books on the psychopathic mind and collaborated on many others. As a result, nationally recognized expert Dr. Grant Monroe testified frequently at murder trials, for the prosecution only—including once for a homicide prosecuted by James—and he was regularly called upon by stymied law enforcement agencies when a killer was at large.

Grant's spur-of-the-moment Thanksgiving-week trip to Seattle was warmly welcomed by James and Christine. They'd been encouraging him to visit, anytime, for months—especially since the upcoming serial-killer trial in Louisiana meant he'd be unable to attend their wedding in May.

By Thanksgiving Day, James would be clear of the prosecutor's office and he wasn't due at Rain Mountain until Monday, so the timing, as of Wednesday evening, was ideal.

Until then, Christine would show Grant the sights during the day.

And the sight Grant most wanted to see?

"The home we're going to buy," Christine said when

she called Natalie to arrange the showing, "whether James sees it beforehand or not!"

7

Magnolia Bluff
Seattle
Monday, November 24
Thirteen months ago

The men who'd been assigned by computer to be freshmen roommates at Stanford's Branner Hall had pursued different careers but with an identical goal: to make the world a safer place by helping put the most heinous of criminals, the psychopaths who brutalized without remorse, behind prison bars.

Grant and James looked alike, too—at first glance. Tall, dark, stunning. But Natalie felt that, unlike James who fought to keep his personal demons hidden from view, Grant was visibly haunted by horrific images. They were readily apparent in his long-lashed brown eyes. Seductive eyes, Natalie realized, beckoning eyes. Eyes that spoke of deep wounds that only the right woman, a most special woman, could hope to heal.

Grant didn't want that woman to be Christine. Natalie saw his torment, and his temptation, while they explored the dream house James had yet to see . . . would never see. Natalie saw that, too, and knew the truth before James did. Even, perhaps, before Grant or Christine.

Neither wanted to succumb to the attraction they so clearly felt, and which would lead, if followed to its passionate conclusion, to the betrayal of the man who meant so much to them both.

But the betrayal was going to happen.

Natalie only hoped they had the kindness, and the courage, to tell James face-to-face, and soon.

Natalie never learned how kindly or courageously Grant and Christine confessed to James that they'd fallen in love. But she did learn that the confession had come quickly.

On the Monday after Thanksgiving, James called Natalie from his new office at Rain Mountain Enterprises to tell her that he and Christine wouldn't be buying the Magnolia Bluff house, or any house, after all.

There was apology in his voice, as if he'd let Natalie and the home owners down. It was the same gentleness, she thought, with which he would've conveyed a devastating verdict—not guilty—to a victim's loved ones. He would've blamed himself, as he blamed himself for losing Christine. He'd loved her. Given his all. And it hadn't been enough.

"I'm sorry, James."

"So am I."

Christine called Natalie, too, a week before Christmas and from the Boston home where she—Mrs. Grant Monroe—now lived.

"I hate what we did to James. But what Grant and I have . . . it's intoxicating, Natalie, and so powerful it sometimes frightens us. It's as if neither of us has a choice. We have to be together. If I'd married James, knowing how I felt about Grant, it would've been an even greater betrayal. James deserves a love like this. *Everyone* does."

Six months later, at the end of June, Ian Collier asked Natalie Davis if she'd help him find a house.

"I'd be delighted to."

"That's great. Thank you. James Gannon tells me you're the best."

Until the referral by James Gannon, Natalie's acknowledgment to the person who'd recommended her had always been immediate. She'd either phone or write a thank-you note and send Godiva chocolates and Cristal champagne.

She'd phone James, she thought, then reconsidered. Nothing about James was usual, including her overreaction to his referral. James had suggested her to Ian. Period. It shouldn't feel to Natalie the way it *did* feel— almost as thrilling as if James himself had called to say he'd been thinking about her.

In a moment of stark clarity, Natalie forbade herself to thank James until after she'd been successful in finding a home for Ian. And when that had been achieved, she postponed even longer. Eventually, with disgust, she confronted the reason for her delay. It wasn't fear of excessive effusiveness on her part, but rather of James's disinterested reply—which would shatter in one brief conversation the fantasy she'd been harboring—that her thank-you to James would be a beginning, not an end.

The sooner she pulverized such foolishness, the better.

She needed to acknowledge James for precisely what he was: an ex-client, and not even a satisfied one, who'd been kind enough to send her more business. An ex-client, in short, to be treated the usual way.

After purchasing the chocolate truffles and vintage champagne, she wrote a quick and rather restrained note: James, Thank you so much for referring Ian. Hope all is well. Natalie.

She entrusted the package to her usual courier, who promised to deliver it within the hour, and made a simultaneous promise to herself. She wouldn't count the minutes of that hour, by the end of which James could have received the thank-you gift and reached for the phone. . . .

Natalie didn't count the minutes. But she felt the metronome beat of time, steady and sure, leveling the remnants of her fantasy.

When James called eight days later, it was an apology once again. He would've thanked her sooner, should have, but had decided to wait until his return from a business trip. Now that he was calling, and if the idea appealed, he'd like to take her to dinner.

The idea definitely appealed, and they arranged a time. On the agreed-upon evening, James arrived at her apartment with the Cristal, chilled, in one hand, and the chocolates, unopened, in the other.

Natalie's surprise had surprised him a little. Her gifts were too good, he explained, not to share.

It hadn't been her intent that she and James share the chocolates and champagne. She'd simply done what she'd done for every other client—who'd almost always been couples like James and Christine should have been. And of the ones who'd been single and unattached, none had been straight, sexy, thirty-six-year-old males. Therefore, none had interpreted the champagne and chocolates in the way an eligible man logically would: as a bold and unambiguous invitation to romance. *Sex.*

And James Gannon's reply to her unwitting gifts of seduction? And to her unintentional promise of champagne and dessert with passion in between?

The reply glittered in his deep blue eyes. *I accept . . . with pleasure.*

Natalie could tell him the truth, her foolishness in not realizing he would misunderstand. *Or* she could remember that she was no longer a naive seventeen-year-old with a fairy-tale problem, but a woman fully grown and quite capable of keeping her fantasies in check.

She could even pretend to be precisely what he believed her to be—a sophisticated businesswoman who indulged her passions from time to time.

Although she didn't have any champagne flutes . . .

"I found these at Pike Place Market," she said as she retrieved two elaborately painted wine goblets from a kitchen cabinet. "Festive, I thought."

"Very festive."

James poured the expensive champagne and, after a gentle clink of goblets, wandered the short distance to her living room window to study the view of Queen Anne Medical Center.

"Have you lived here long?"

"Since moving to Seattle fourteen years ago. It's really a unique location," Natalie embellished as a gulp of champagne hit her empty stomach, warmed her veins and sent bubbles of giddiness racing to her brain. More giddy bubbles. The first batch had started dancing euphorically when she'd seen the desire he'd made no attempt to hide. The joyful dance, in turn, compelled her scarcely ladylike swallow. "One of the few properties in all of Seattle without a glimpse of mountains, sound, bay or lake."

"You're renting?"

"I am." Seattle's top-selling high-end real estate agent had a staggering amount of money languishing in the bank. "I know I should buy a condo, or even a house. But . . ."

"You're cozy here."

"In my tiny one-bedroom apartment with its hospital view? Yes. Very cozy."

"I can see why. It's nice. A comfortable nest."

A nest that was suddenly very small with him in it, and distinctly uncomfortable . . . in a restless, giddy way.

"Thanks," she said as her restlessness sent her to her living room credenza in search of the Orca whale-motif coasters, never used, but which she was pretty sure were stored there.

She hadn't quite reached the credenza when he spoke. "You're still limping."

She stopped cold. Ice-cold. The champagne warmth had vanished, and even the swallow she took before answering did nothing to restore it.

"Limping?" *Still* limping?

"Aren't you?"

She looked at him then, drawn by the concern in his voice. "Yes. I guess I am. I can't believe you noticed. I didn't realize it was so apparent."

"It's not *so* apparent, Natalie. And I'm sorry if I've embarrassed you."

"What did you mean *still?*"

"You were doing it a year ago, weren't you? At least when you had showings at the end of the day?"

"Is that why you wondered if I'd prefer an earlier time to show you . . ." *the dream house for the dream marriage that was not to be.*

"The home on Magnolia Bluff?" James smiled. "Yes. That was why. I've had enough sports-related injuries to know that the weight-bearing ones get worse the more you stress them. I thought you were limping because you'd sprained an ankle and were playing hurt. I was right, wasn't I? You were playing hurt. But the injury wasn't, isn't, acute."

I thought you'd sprained, he'd said. Not *we* thought. James had noticed her limp. Christine hadn't. "I had a run-in with a bus when I was seventeen. The bus won."

"That's too glib, Natalie. Tell me more."

"I . . . wasn't paying attention, and it was snowing, and I walked right into its path."

"And you were quite badly hurt."

"I needed a number of surgeries. I have lots of scars."

"What about pain?"

She sensed that James wasn't asking about the ache that made her limp at the end of the day. He understood the kind of trauma she must have sustained—the damage that must have been done to her pelvis.

So he was asking if it hurt her to have sex . . . to make love.

Natalie didn't know, of course. Hadn't envisioned ever

finding out. There'd never been pain—with sex—for the promiscuous teen she used to be. And no pleasure, either, save for the fleeting gratification of feeling wanted.

She stepped out of her heels and smiled. "Voilà. No more pain."

James set his full and festive goblet on the windowsill, crossed the carpeted floor, and, upon reaching her, placed a tender hand on her champagne-flushed face. "I'm glad."

"So am I." Glad and soaring anew, a euphoria evoked by his caress, not the giddy dance of bubbles.

"May I ask you another possibly embarrassing question?"

She nodded slowly against the heat of his hand.

"Do you usually send champagne and chocolates as a thank-you for referrals?"

"Yes."

"Ah." His hand fell away and he glanced at his watch. "Why don't I call The Thirteen Coins and find out how soon they can seat us?"

"All right. If you like."

"I think you know what I'd like, Natalie."

"That's what I'd like, too, James." *You.*

"You're sure that's not just the champagne talking?"

"Less than half a glass? It's *helping* me talk, I suppose. But it's not telling me what to say, or what I want to say." Natalie met smiling eyes, intense with desire. "I miss your hand."

"You don't have to."

His hand, warm and strong, returned to her face. Where it belonged. It felt so right, so perfect . . . and not enough.

"Both hands," she whispered, greedy, needy.

"Your wish," he said softly, "is my command."

James cradled her lovely face, until needy and greedy, too, he became restless to explore, to weave his fingers in the auburn hair he'd never touched and travel uncharted paths of wonder from eyes to lips to neck to shoulders. His lips followed, tasting, cherishing. James felt himself becoming at once lost in the journey, and found.

Natalie, too, lost herself in their loving. She, too, felt lost . . . and then found.

She hadn't known it, but she'd missed him, all her life. His touch, foreign yet familiar, was welcomed joyfully, boldly and without fear.

They made love in her night-dark bedroom, but his lips learned all there was to learn about her scars, caressing the damaged flesh as lovingly as he caressed the rest of her. All of her.

There was no pain. And, to Natalie, it felt as if pain would be vanquished forever, conquered by his fierce tenderness . . . and the ferocious pleasure his touch evoked.

"Are you okay?" he asked eventually.

"Okay?"

"Did I hurt you?"

"*No,* James. Did I do something that made you think you had?"

"*No,* Natalie." His voice smiled and she heard his relief. "I've just never been so consumed by the moment . . . or, more accurately, by the woman."

"Oh." *Oh, James.*

"Care to translate?"

"Neither have I . . . been so consumed . . . by the man."

"Good," he murmured, kissing her neck then moving away.

Natalie missed him immediately. With a sharp grief almost immediately assuaged.

He'd simply been rearranging things—his heavy muscles, her delicate bones—to create a nest for her in his arms.

"I was going to call you, you know," he said when she was cuddled close. "Months ago."

"You don't have to say that."

"I'm not saying anything, Natalie, that isn't true. It's important you believe that. Believe *me*."

"I do believe you, James." Believe you. Believe *in* you. "Something happened that meant you couldn't call?"

"I could have called, but didn't. I'd made the mistake of deciding to wait until the dust settled."

"At Rain Mountain?"

"No. In Boston."

"Oh." *Oh, no.* "Dust swirling around Grant and Christine?"

"You might say that. Four and a half months ago, in mid June, a woman with whom Grant had been involved before Christine was murdered."

"Murdered?"

"She was being stalked. Grant knew. They'd remained friends despite his marriage to Christine. She'd confided in him right away. Among the other usual recommendations, he'd encouraged her to alert the police. She didn't.

Just kept telling herself—and Grant—that the threat would go away. She should have known better. She was a professor at Harvard Law School with a specialty in criminal law."

"The threat didn't go away."

"No. On that night in June, she heard a noise outside her window and thought she saw a man in the shadows. She phoned Grant, who told her to call 911, and that he was on the way. Her body was still warm when Grant arrived."

"It was Grant who found her?"

"Therein lies the beginning of the swirling dust. She'd been stabbed, had no pulse, wasn't breathing. It was too late. He probably knew that before giving her the first breath. But he made an effort to resuscitate her anyway."

"He had to try," Natalie whispered. "Had to do *something.*"

"He did try, kept trying, was still touching her, covered with her blood, when the police reached the scene."

"She . . . what was her name?"

"Paris Eugenia Bally."

"She, Paris, *had* called 911."

"During the attack, I gather. The 911 operator heard the struggle. No voices, just sounds."

A chill rippled through Natalie. A shiver deep within. James curled her closer, warming her, and as his lips brushed her temple, he murmured, "Sorry. Why don't we talk about something else?"

"No. I'm fine." And so safe, she thought. So lucky . . . unlike Paris, the victim of the kind of violent crime James Gannon had fought so hard to avenge. "It's just

125

that when you said the 911 operator overheard the struggle, it rang a bell."

"Tell me."

"Well, it's similar to what happens in Hitchcock's *Dial M for Murder.* Ray Milland listens to what he believes is Grace Kelly being strangled to death. But at the last moment she grabs a pair of scissors and stabs her assailant. You've seen it, haven't you?"

"If so, and with apologies to Mr. Hitchcock, I don't remember."

"You might have seen the remake, though. *A Perfect Murder* with Gwyneth Paltrow and Michael Douglas?"

"I definitely haven't seen that. But it's the same story?"

"Basically. There are contemporary high-tech touches—cell phones and so on—and for some reason a change in murder weapons. I guess they decided a modern wife, who works as a translator at the UN and lives in a luxury penthouse in Manhattan, wouldn't spend her evenings clipping old newspaper articles about her husband's once-illustrious tennis career. Hence, no scissors handy."

"So what does she reach for instead?"

"A butcher knife. And, in the new version, Michael Douglas listens on his cell phone—one of two that he's juggling—to what he believes is Gwyneth Paltrow being bludgeoned, not strangled, to death. It's pretty awful to watch the struggle, but I wonder if just listening to it, and letting your imagination provide the visuals, is even worse."

"I have a feeling it is. The 911 operator who overheard

the murder in Boston was apparently quite shaken up."

"It's also pretty awful for Grant to have discovered the murdered body of someone he'd known and tried to help."

"It had ramifications beyond his discomfort."

Therein lies the swirling dust. "The police *didn't* suspect Grant."

"Did. And, I think, still do. Statistically, the person who reports a murder, or is found kneeling over the corpse, is most likely to have committed the homicide."

"But Grant was summoned to the scene by the murder victim—Paris."

"That's right. And he has a witness. Christine was home when Paris called. She saw Grant's concern."

"That's not proof that Grant had nothing to do with the crime?"

"Not unless Christine also heard Paris's side of the call. Even then a wife's exculpatory statement would have to be balanced against the weight of other evidence."

"Like Grant's being covered with blood? He has a perfectly valid explanation for that."

"Yes, he does. And I feel sure if that's all the police had, he'd have been ruled out as a suspect by now."

"But he hasn't been."

"No. He's been neither cleared nor named."

"So they must have something more. Like his fingerprints on the knife?"

"It wasn't a knife, Natalie. Paris was stabbed to death with her own scissors." As Natalie gasped, he added, "Paris had a passion for sewing."

"How often are people murdered by scissors?"

"Not very."

"But it *is* right out of *Dial M for Murder*, isn't it?"

"So much so that unless the dust settles soon—meaning Grant's cleared and the killer's in custody—I think I'd better take a look at the Hitchcock classic as well as the remake."

"I have both on DVD. We could watch them . . . I can't say it."

"Can't say what?"

" 'Now.' I'm feeling too cozy. Too lazy." She started to rouse herself. "The TV's right here, and the DVDs are in the closet, so I can easily—"

"Next time."

Natalie curled back into her nest, and into the promise of his words. There'd be a next time, and a next, and a next.

"I can't imagine either movie being relevant, anyway. Certainly nothing a killer with a brain would choose as a blueprint."

"The murders weren't perfect, after all?"

"No. Is there such a thing?"

"As a perfect murder? I honesty don't know. Macabre as it sounds, we devoted a remarkable amount of college time to proposing murder scenarios we believed might work."

"You and Grant?"

"Sometimes it was just the two of us, but usually it was a larger group. And, given the competitive nature of Stanford undergrads, some fairly clever—if horrific—plots were devised."

"Perfect plots?"

"There were a few, at least in the abstract, in which none of us could identify the inevitable mistake."

"Inevitable."

"That's what Grant thinks now, based on years of research into the criminal mind. The same aberrant thought processes that create a psychopath would, he believes, preclude the possibility of his fashioning a perfect crime. It's not a matter of intellect. Many psychopaths are exceptionally bright. But their behavior gives them away. Even when they try to behave as they believe a normal person would, they can't. Their perception of 'normal' is intrinsically flawed."

"So a psychopath doesn't get, can't get, that a normal husband wouldn't sell his missing wife's car before her disappearance has been ruled a homicide."

"Exactly. The psychopath can't see what's wrong with that. It's a lack of vision, by the way, that's tremendously helpful to the police."

"You said you honestly don't know if there's such a thing as a perfect murder."

"It would require a psychopath so aware of his defective behavior, and so tuned into what normal behavior should be, that he could behave in a convincingly empathic way—which, almost by definition, a psychopath can't."

"And a normal human being wouldn't murder in the first place."

"Not the kind of calculated killing we're talking about. No." James traced a finger over her naked shoulder. "This isn't the world's happiest topic."

"No, but it's real. And important." And maybe James needed to tell her about the murder a continent away that had entangled him in a relationship he'd been trying to forget. *Need me, James.* "Were Grant's fingerprints on the scissors?"

"He says no. He touched Paris, but not the scissors."

"What do the police say?"

"The police aren't saying anything."

"They don't have to, I guess, until someone's under arrest?"

"Even then, what the police have uncovered is known only to the prosecution pending an evidentiary hearing or mandated pretrial disclosures to the defense."

"But you could—no, never mind."

"I could what, Natalie?"

"Nothing. I mean, you couldn't, *wouldn't*—"

"Make a few clandestine calls to the prosecutors in Boston?"

"Yes. But *please* forget I even started to say it. I know you'd never do anything as unethical as that—anything unethical at all. Will you forget it? Please?"

"What I'll remember," he said softly, "is that you knew I wouldn't do it. Christine didn't."

Meaning Christine had asked James to make the improper calls. For Grant. And at the expense, once again, of James, jeopardizing his career this time, not his heart. Not only his heart.

"Christine must be terribly upset," she said. "Not thinking clearly."

"She is upset. But in a righteously indignant—and clear-thinking—kind of way. How dare the police so much as question the innocence of the man she loves?"

The man she loves. "You're so calm when you say that."

"There's no other way to be. Christine chose Grant. Married Grant. What's past is prologue, to quote the Bard. And this night, this present, is very nice."

This night, Natalie echoed in silence. This present. Which no one can take away, no matter what the future has in store. "Did Grant also want you to talk to the police and the prosecutors?"

"No. And he wasn't very happy when he found out Christine had."

"Still, he must be upset that the police are unwilling to rule him out."

"He's more intrigued than upset. He knows he's innocent and trusts that the system he's always worked with will ultimately proclaim him to be. But he'd really like to know what the police have, or think they have, that points to him."

"He has no idea?"

"None."

"But he and Paris had been involved."

"Past tense. The relationship ended when Grant met Christine. Paris wasn't pregnant with his baby, or anyone's baby. That's the sort of leak even the best police departments can't seem to prevent. To the extent that Grant's upset, it's because of Paris. He feels guilty for what happened to her. She asked for his help, and he let her down."

"She didn't follow his advice."

"He feels he should've been more forceful. More insistent. She's the primary reason he's eager to be cleared as a suspect in her murder. Once that happens, he'll be free to work with law enforcement to solve the crime."

"The same law enforcement that's refusing to clear him?"

"Grant knows they're doing what they have to do and respects it. And them. The respect is mutual. Grant's been instrumental in assisting Boston Homicide in a number of cases. Bygones will be bygones once he's cleared. They'll be delighted to have his help, and Grant will be happy to give it."

"Has Grant told the detectives everything he knows?"

"He has. He's cooperated fully, without a lawyer in sight. The police know what Grant knows, but it's not reciprocal. Grant knows nothing about the forensic evidence found at the scene—and the clue that's inexplicably pointing to him."

"A clue left by the killer to intentionally mislead the police?"

"That's what Grant believes. It's the only thing that makes sense if the police really have the evidence against him they apparently believe they have."

"So . . . what's happening now?"

"We're all in limbo. Waiting."

"For?"

"My best guess? For Grant to be arrested. Frankly I expected it would've happened already and we'd be well on our way to getting a peek at whatever the prosecution has."

"And well on the way to providing Grant with everything he needs to solve the crime."

"That would be the plan."

"Too bad one of his friends at the police department doesn't just give Grant a little peek now. It would be wrong, I suppose, although . . ."

"Although?"

"Well, you certainly hear about police sharing incriminating evidence with suspects as a means of getting the criminal to confess. The police can even lie about what they have, can't they?"

"Absolutely. But they wouldn't lie to Grant. They know he'd spot it right away. But he keeps hoping someone on the force will decide to tell him the truth. He believes, and I agree, that it's unlikely to happen until after a formal arrest."

"So he'd just as soon be arrested? To get the show on the road?"

"It would certainly give us something to do besides wait."

Us. "You'll be his attorney."

"No. I won't. Even before his involvement with Christine, I wouldn't have been."

"Friends don't defend friends against murder?"

James smiled. "Something like that. I've also never done defense work. This wouldn't be the time to learn."

"But you've been waiting. In limbo." *Not calling me.*

"I promised Grant and Christine that I'd go to Boston if he was arrested. As a friend. Period."

"An incredibly good friend—a forgiving friend."

"And a different friend than I'd have been a year ago. There are boundaries now, ones Grant and Christine know I'm not going to cross."

"Such as?"

"Keeping secrets, withholding confidences. It's not something I'm willing to do. But I will go to Boston. I've been expecting to, or I would've called you sooner, and we would've discovered this."

"This," she whispered as his lips found hers. "You."

"You," James echoed. *"You."*

It began again, the fierce and tender loving, the foreign made familiar and the familiar ever new.

When his pager sounded—and consumed by each other as both of them were—their only response was to laugh.

"Ian," he predicted as he reached toward the pager on the nearby floor. Assuming Ian had found time to go to his safe-deposit box, he and James were going to meet before the formal workday began to review Ian's existing will and discuss the changes the soon-to-be married man wanted to make.

But the text message on James's pager wasn't from Ian.

"It's Christine. Grant's under arrest." James sighed. "I should call her. I think my cell phone's somewhere over—"

"Here." Natalie handed him the receiver from the portable phone beside the bed. "Use this."

"Thanks."

Five months before, Christine had witnessed Grant's end of a frantic phone call from Paris Eugenia Bally. Now, in the darkness, Natalie listened to James's response to a similarly desperate plea.

And she heard, in the darkness, his gentle reassurances

to the woman who'd betrayed his love.

"We knew this was coming, Chris. . . . Yes, we did. It's for the best. It will move things along, get Grant cleared. . . . Of course I'll be there. . . . Yes, I'll leave tonight. Was Grant able to line up the defense attorney we'd talked about? . . . Good. Have you called your parents? . . . You should call them. They'll want to be with you. And why don't you call Meg, too, and June, and maybe Beth? . . . There are plenty of hotels in Cambridge—what? I don't know about that. . . . All right, I will, for a while. We'll see . . . okay. Take care. I'll see you soon."

James replaced the receiver and sat on the bed.

"You have to go."

"I do. And I may be gone for a while. Grant's always said that if the prosecutors really had good enough evidence to issue an arrest warrant, it would have to mean he'd been framed."

"By the stalker, who'd seen him with Paris, and gone into a jealous rage."

"That's one scenario. Maybe the most likely one. But Grant's concerned it might have been more elaborate—and psychopathic—than that. His testimony has helped put a lot of truly evil men behind bars. His worry is that one of them set this whole thing up to get even with him, to murder a woman he cared about . . . and send Grant to prison for her killing. If that's the case, the killer won't murder again as long as Grant's in jail."

"So he's not going to ask to get out on bail?"

"The last time we discussed it, he said no. It's an issue he'll take up with his defense attorney, but my guess is that no one's going to change his mind. Grant doesn't want to put anyone else he knows at risk. It may be a moot point, anyway, depending on how he's charged. First-degree murder isn't necessarily a bailable offense, particularly if the prosecution has aggravating factors it plans to cite."

Natalie's brain was already reeling from the conversation she'd overheard. The affection in James's voice when he talked to Christine. The reminder to call her parents, and her three best friends, the women who would've been bridesmaids at her wedding to James.

Then there was the discussion of hotels—and Christine's obvious wish, to which James had clearly acceded, that he stay in the couple's home, not a hotel.

The couple's home, where only Christine would be—and where James had agreed to be, too. For a while.

"How long?" The question simply escaped.

"Will Grant be in jail? It depends on how quickly the defense and prosecution can agree on what comes next. The defense will request an evidentiary hearing. I have no idea how soon that can be scheduled, and how much legal maneuvering might get in the way."

"But . . . a while?"

"A while." James stood but reached in the darkness to touch her face. "I'd better go. This *was* nice. I'll call you when I can."

Natalie heard from him ten days later, a short call made at two in the morning Boston time. He sounded distracted, exhausted, and the quietness of his voice made it clear he was somewhere that his normal tone would have been overheard—a guest bedroom, perhaps, across the hall from the master suite where the bride slept without her groom.

"I'm going to send you a package, if that's all right."

"Of course."

"It mustn't be opened, Natalie."

"I never would!"

"I know. But if I send it to the real estate office, will someone else?"

"Probably not. But if I know when it's coming, I'll just plan to be there when it arrives. Or I can plan to be here. Either is easy."

"Thank you."

"You're welcome!"

They discussed the options, decided on a UPS next-day delivery to her home, and that was that, the reason he'd called.

"James . . ." Natalie heard herself, needy, greedy, although it was James who was so ravaged. "It's not just one long party in Boston, is it?"

Her teasing was answered by a soft, surprised and grateful laugh. Then a solemn confession. "It's all more difficult than I thought it would be."

Natalie wouldn't permit herself to define *all*.

"I'm sorry," she whispered, as she had almost a year ago, when he'd lost Christine.

And just as James had replied to her then, he said, "So am I."

8

Cambridge, Massachusetts
December 30, 9:30 p.m.

James stood at the living room window of Grant and Christine Monroe's home. Snow fell in lacy wisps illuminated by lamplight, pristine ballerinas on a brightly lit stage that reminded him, as they twirled and glowed, of night skiing at Crystal.

It was an image that held immense appeal.

James Gannon wanted to stand at the top of the steepest ski slope he could find, point his skis straight down and just . . . let go. He'd never actually done that. But he knew it was possible, and survivable. Such indifference to danger had been an Ian Collier trademark in Ian's most risk taking days.

James had been only six at the time, but as a teenager and a racer, too, he'd seen tapes of Ian's fleeting but stunning downhill career. Ian's career, and his devil-may-care approach to skiing—and life—had ended with the accident at Kitzbühel. James had seen that tape, too, and wished he hadn't.

Ian remained an expert and aggressive skier, but because of Kathleen, and the future they'd planned, Ian had given up all risk taking.

It wasn't a sacrifice, James knew. A happier Ian than James had ever known before had spent a thoroughly enjoyable summer overseeing the cosmetic improvements to the Worthing mansion, followed by a thoroughly engrossing autumn deciding—amid the myriad Rain Mountain decisions to be made—on the furnishings for the newly spackled, painted and carpeted rooms.

As the snow fell in Boston, James reflected on the day Ian had come to his office on Kathleen's behalf to learn what was known about the murder of her mother. Ian had come, appropriately, to James, who'd just been given oversight responsibilities for all cold-case homicides in King County.

James hadn't volunteered for the job. He'd been handpicked. The homicide detectives had wanted him. James's prosecutor colleagues also endorsed his selection. Of all of them, James was most adept at establishing rapport with families of victims. The surviving loved ones, victims too, trusted James to do his very best. He, of all of them, would be believed by grieving families when he had no choice but to tell them their loved one's murder would never be solved. And he had the compassion, and the patience, to do it well.

James's role was especially important in cases that were irretrievably cold. The survivors needed to be reassured that the police and the courts had done all they could do. From experience James had learned the soothing things to say.

James had also learned—over the years and with each passing year—the toll his job was taking on him.

He was becoming emptier, even as he fought to make the real victims whole.

The evil he encountered was slowly but surely hollowing him out—and taking up residence in the empty space?

Never. And yet James wondered what he'd do if someone he loved was harmed. Especially, he tormented himself, if that someone was a child. One of his sisters' sons or daughters. Or one of his own.

Would he really be able to stand aside and let the justice system work? And what if the judicial process failed? If the child killer—or molester—went free?

It amazed James that more grieving parents didn't take the law into their own hands. He wasn't at all sure he'd be able to impose such laudable restraint on himself. But maybe that was because, as a prosecutor, James saw far more of the horror than parents—or juries—were permitted to see.

James saw it all. The unabridged horror. It was the prosecutor, after all, who edited the evil that would be shared with the parents or presented to the court. James Gannon was a ruthless editor, and an expert one, deleting every grisly detail that could be cut without compromising the outcome of the case. Imprisonment was key, and with a maximum sentence.

James's record, so far, was unblemished. He'd won for the victims, living and dead, every measure of victory the law allowed. But more and more the triumphs felt as hollow, as empty, as he did himself.

He should take some time off, he'd thought as he awaited Ian Collier's arrival that day.

James had, of course, already carefully reviewed the Mary Alice Cahill file. And during that review he'd discovered that he'd been in Seattle, hoping to ski but watching the rain fall instead, when the murder occurred. James and his three rained out companions had stayed, in fact, in a fraternity house less than a mile from where the mother's journey toward death had begun.

The New Year's Eve discovery of her nude and strangled body beside the road near Snoqualmie Pass must have been front-page news. But James and his college friends had spent their soggy vacation oblivious to the murder. James had returned to California with his decision to one day live in Seattle. And if he'd known of the crime near the washed-out ski slopes? The future prosecutor would've been all the more determined to move to Seattle and do everything in his power to keep the city the wonderful place he sensed it could be.

James knew why he'd been unaware of the murder. He was an eighteen-year-old on holiday with his friends.

He learned from Ian Collier why Mary Alice Cahill's teenage daughter had also been unaware—because of her fear, her terror, of the horrific truth. James also saw Ian's love for the obstetrician who was awaiting the results of their meeting.

Because of that love, because Ian was almost as touched by the murder as Kathleen, James edited what he revealed to Ian as carefully as he would've done if he'd been meeting with Kathleen herself. He'd emphasized the reassuring aspects, such as they were. Mary Alice had died quickly. She hadn't been raped. Ian knew she'd been found, nude, in the pouring rain. But he didn't know, and James didn't tell him, what the police had decided to conceal—that her body had been posed grotesquely, obscenely . . . and so uniquely that had the killer murdered again, and left the same pornographic signature, it would've been as good as the DNA they didn't have.

There was no point in revealing that. The crime-scene photographs were in all the law-enforcement databases. To date, there'd been no similar crime.

James had accepted, with gratitude, the digitally enhanced photograph of the locket, and asked Ian to thank Kathleen, to tell her it might help.

"Where are you going?"

The familiar voice behind him drew James from his reverie. He heard the question, answered it in silence. To meet the woman whose mother's murder I'd hoped to avenge but could not, and witness her wedding to the man who'll spend the rest of his life giving her the happiness she deserves. And, after that wedding, I'm going to find the steepest ski slope I can.

"James?"

Any moment the headlights of his taxi would illuminate more brightly the ballet of snow. He was still watching the snowfall. Hadn't turned. "You know where I'm going, Chris."

"To Seattle. For Ian's wedding to Kathleen. I also know your flight's not until ten a.m. tomorrow."

"It's a flight I don't want to miss."

"So you're leaving now?"

"To spend the night at an airport motel."

"You really want to get out of here, don't you?"

"It's snowing." He turned to her at last. "It's going to snow all night. The roads will be a mess in the morning."

"That isn't what I meant, James. And you know it."

"It's been a difficult time for everyone."

But for Christine most of all. With each passing day, less and less remained of the vivacious woman James had known. She was living on nervous energy, a sustenance so meager—and so punishing—that the golden girl was fading away, her battered system on the verge of giving out . . . giving up.

She would rebound, James had told himself—and assured her desperately worried parents and friends. The ordeal behind her, she'd become herself once again. Radiant, confident . . .

Until then, she needed their unwavering support. And when Christine's friends and family wavered and needed encouragement themselves? It was James they turned to—as Christine did.

She relied on James, trusted James, and it was James to whom she posed the same litany of unanswerable questions day after day, night after night. When will Grant be cleared? Why is it taking so long? How can the police and prosecutors have made such a mistake? What if—oh, James—what if they never find the monster who really did this?

James answered the impossible questions as best he could. And with all the patience and gentleness he could muster. But his patience was running thin. He'd been battered, too. And he had questions of his own, tormenting ones, stabbing without mercy through his exhausted brain.

"Very difficult," he repeated, prompting her.

As focused as she seemed, he knew her concentration came in tiny spurts.

"Yes, very," she agreed. With a burst of energy and

emotion, she continued, "But especially for you. Because of us. I've been so unfair to you, haven't I? Asking you to stay here with me. I'm *sorry,* James. I've just needed you here so much."

"I'm fine being here, Christine. I want to help."

"But we haven't really talked, have we? About us."

"We don't need to. You fell in love with Grant. There's nothing more to say."

"You hate me, don't you?"

"No. I don't hate you."

"But . . . oh, James, are you still in love with me?"

The question angered him, and his patience finally snapped. He was framing a coldly furious reply—until he saw something new, and at the same time old, on her haggard face. She wanted his love, hoped for it, wished for it, and not as a collector's item, a treasure to be placed on a shelf, but as the vibrant thing it once had been.

James didn't doubt what he saw. At this moment, as he was about to leave, that was her desperate wish.

He summoned every ounce of patience he could find, and dredged from the harshness of his exhaustion the remnants of gentleness as well.

"No," he told the woman who would have been his bride. "I'm not. But I care about you, Chris. I always will."

Silence fell, a soundlessness broken only by muted footfalls in the bedroom overhead. Christine's parents were here, and Meg and June were staying in a hotel near Harvard Yard. Christine wouldn't be alone.

And James needed to get away, to begin on this snowy

evening the journey that would take him to the marriage of a friend—and a ski slope in the Pacific Northwest.

When the cab arrived, and he was on his way, James identified a more immediate need. Scotch, and lots of it.

James Gannon wasn't much of a drinker. But on this night, his first of absolute privacy in the past two months, he craved a blurring at the edges of his mind, a respite from the knife-sharp questions assembled there . . . just a little peace, and only for a while.

Kathleen tried, as much as possible, to adapt her sleep to Georgia's, the same way a new mother, a pragmatic one, slept whenever her baby did.

It had been impossible in the beginning. During the day, when Georgia enjoyed her deepest sleep, Kathleen had had too much else to do. They'd all believed the septuplets' birth was imminent then, and even though intrapartum and postpartum responsibilities had been carefully considered and meticulously assigned, Kathleen spoke personally with each member of every team, reviewing their specific tasks one by one. Because there were aspects of the plan she didn't like, she needed to discuss, with an assortment of decision makers, the alternatives she preferred.

There were also frequent calls from the media that someone—Kathleen or her overworked colleagues—needed to handle. Kathleen handled them all.

The flurry of activity calmed as December 12 came and went, and Christmas neared. And, although it was increasing again, and Kathleen was busy throughout the day, Georgia's sleep pattern had changed.

Her daytime sleep was fitful. Brief, frequent naps. And at night, from midnight till dawn, she was predictably wide-awake and anxious and needing Kathleen.

But there was a stretch from six to midnight when Georgia slept.

And so did Kathleen.

Georgia was asleep by six tonight. But Kathleen didn't even try until after seven.

Seventh time's a charm, Ian had told her with such certainty Kathleen believed it was true. Tonight was that seventh time.

And it would be charmed. There were so many auspicious sevens.

Georgia's seven babies. Seattle's seven hills. The seven o'clock hour of her wedding to Ian.

At the stroke of seven, alone in her on-call room, Dr. Kathleen Cahill inseminated herself for the seventh time.

There was a minibar in the hotel room at the airport.

But James didn't so much as glance its way.

During the snowy cab ride from Cambridge to Logan, he'd acknowledged a need far greater than Scotch—and more dangerous than a straight-down schuss of Everest . . . and with the intoxicating promise of peace.

It was only eight o'clock Seattle time, but he'd obviously awakened her.

"It's James."

"James," Natalie whispered. "Where are you?"

"Still in Boston. You were asleep."

"Just dozing." *Dreaming. Taking care of our baby.* "Hi."

"Hi. Would you like to go back to sleep?"

"No. I'm fine! Wide awake and rested. Really."

"Okay." The soft reply was relieved. Grateful. "I'm sorry I haven't called you."

"I imagine you've been very busy."

"It's more than that, Natalie. There's just never been a good time, a private time, until now."

She almost didn't hear his explanation—never a good time, a private time—because the explanation she feared thundered so loudly in her head. Christine and I are back together, he would say. She realized she made a mistake. She was infatuated with Grant. But it wasn't really love. Grant knows, and he's all right with it, and we've told him we'll both stay in Boston—and Christine won't proceed with the divorce—until he's free. But I wanted you to know, Natalie, and to tell you again that what we had that night was very nice, and Christine knows about it and—

"Natalie?"

"I'm here. Awake." And hearing the echoes of what he'd actually said. "But this is a good time to call? A private time?"

"It is. Finally."

"Oh, good." She was in her bed, where James had been, and if she held the phone tight and close, it felt, in the darkness, as if he was there now. "Does that mean there's good news? They've caught the real killer?"

"I'm afraid not. There's not really any news."

"So you're waiting for the hearing on the sixteenth?"

"You've been following the case."

"Of course I have. I check the Boston papers online

if it's a night when Grant's attorneys aren't on either *On the Record* or *Trial Talk*."

"A rare night?"

"They're on a lot. I hadn't realized quite how well-known Grant was—is—or how highly regarded by law enforcement nationwide."

"So it's not just his defense attorneys talking."

"No. There's usually a fair and balanced panel of lawyers, both for the defense and the prosecution, and forensic psychiatrists, FBI profilers, homicide detectives. You haven't watched?"

"The stress level surrounding Christine and her supporters is high enough without adding speculation by assorted pundits. I am interested in what his attorneys are saying, though."

"Pretty much what you told me. Grant's innocence is a given. As is the integrity of the lawyers acting on behalf of the commonwealth of Massachusetts. So the only way they could've filed murder charges against an innocent man was if they'd been duped by evidence they believed was overwhelming—but which, in fact, had been planted by an extremely clever psychopath—who'll be unmasked as soon as Grant gets a look at what they've got."

"How do the pundits respond to the defense theory of an elaborate frame?"

"They split along the legal equivalent of party lines. The defense attorneys endorse it. The prosecutors don't. But the viewers are virtually unanimous in their support."

"How do you know that?"

"The shows keep running tallies of the calls and e-mails they receive. The defense pundits maintain that bodes very well for an acquittal if the case ever comes to trial."

"And the prosecution pundits?"

"They don't really disagree. Attractive defendants always fare better with juries, they say."

"That's certainly true."

According to the TV pundits, Grant's appearance, combined with his reputation, was his ace in the hole. If worse came to worst, Grant could take the stand in his own defense—and prevail.

"How's Christine doing?"

"Not terribly well."

"And Grant?"

"Well enough—except for being worried about Christine."

"Are you worried, James?"

"About Christine?"

"Or anything."

"I guess I've always been more of a problem solver than a worrier. Is that funny?"

"No."

"I heard a laugh."

"Problem solving instead of worrying is just so quintessentially male."

Now he laughed. "Do you have a problem with that?"

"A problem with problem solving? Or with your quintessential maleness? No. I don't believe I do. With either."

"Good. I do have a worry."

"Oh?"

"I'm concerned that my morning flight won't be taking off on time—or even at all."

"Flight? Are you—" *coming home to us?* "—heading this way?"

"Hoping to. Snow permitting." James glowered at the winter wonderland beyond his window. Beautiful and ever-deepening, it was a worry, and a problem he was powerless to solve. He hadn't simply needed to get away. He'd needed to get away *to her.* "I'm not sure when I'll arrive in Seattle. But, snow permitting, in time for a seven-o'clock wedding New Year's night. Would you like to come with me?"

"To Ian and Kathleen's new home?"

"Ian's obviously invited you, too. I didn't know, but if I'd thought about it for half a second I would have. Ian really wanted that property. He never told me why, but there was no mistaking how important it was to him. And you made it happen."

But it wasn't Ian who invited me. It was Kathleen . . . just moments after confirming that I was pregnant with your child.

"Are you drifting back to sleep?"

"No. I was just remembering that it was actually Kathleen who invited me."

"You know Kathleen?"

"Not really. We just happened to meet. She knew I'd been involved with Ian's purchase of the estate, and she invited me to the wedding for the same reason you thought Ian would have."

"What did you think of her?"

150

"Kathleen?" *That I trust her with our baby's life.* "You know her, don't you?"

"I know of her. From Ian. And I've seen a photograph Ian has of her." And many photographs, too, of her mother, obscenely posed and looking so much like the beautiful daughter who was left to grieve. "But we've never met."

"Oh, well, she's wonderful, and obviously loves Ian very much, and she's the reason, I think, it was so important to Ian to buy the old Worthing estate. He wanted it for her. You'll like her, James. I can't imagine anyone not liking Kathleen Cahill."

"I know I'll like her. I already do for making Ian so happy." *I just wish I could have helped her.* "So may I escort you to the wedding?"

"Yes. Thank you. Kathleen suggested arriving at six-thirty for a tour."

"That's fine by me."

"Snow permitting," Natalie said. "Maybe you'll have on-time flying and be home tomorrow."

"If so, Natalie, and you're free, no, wait, tomorrow's New Year's Eve."

"And you have plans."

"I thought you might."

"I do. I'm going to be right here, all evening, hoping you'll drop by."

Crystal Mountain Resort didn't have a run named Seventh Heaven. If Ian had wanted to ski such a run, he could've gone night skiing at nearby Stevens Pass. And perhaps he would have, had he known this would be the night Kathleen would be trying for the seventh time, the charmed time, to become pregnant.

Or perhaps not. Seventh Heaven was an expert's run, a perilous descent along cliffs and between trees, and if, when, the shadowed slope became sheet ice, as it sometimes did, even the best skier could take a punishing spill.

Crystal's Green Valley, by contrast, offered an exhilarating descent but not a treacherous one. Perfectly groomed and cliff free, the popular "in bounds" run held, for even an intermediate skier, negligible risk.

Ian loved skiing Green Valley, always had. During his ski patrol days, when his sentry duties were through, he'd swoop down the vast snowscape of moguls, taking their troughs and peaks one by one.

So it was safe, familiar Green Valley Ian skied now. Glittering Green Valley beneath the lights, a pristine brilliance to match the purity of his joy.

Other skiers, recognizing him, paused to marvel at his grace. Those with cameras—and in aftermath of Christmas there were quite a few—made digital recordings.

So when the accident happened, it was captured in living color and from many angles. Those closest to the midair collision heard the unspeakable sound of skis hitting flesh, their razor-sharp edges slicing muscle, the high-velocity steel shattering ribs.

Unspeakable. Indescribable. And faithfully preserved on the microchips in their videocams . . . along with the frantic screams that followed.

It's Ian Collier!

Who knows CPR?

He's bleeding to death!

Where's the ski patrol?

Is he . . . alive?

Oh, no. Oh, please. Help him! Hurry! Please!

There were the sounds, too, of cell phones being opened, powered up, digits pressed.

And another sound. A wordless wail. Not human, that keening to the starry sky. It couldn't be human, those who heard it thought.

But the howl was very human. A cry of despair from a thirteen-year-old boy who believed he'd killed his hero.

And from that hero?

Not a sound.

Unless you counted one too hushed to be heard—the whisper of snow crystals melting in a sea of blood.

Kathleen had read, somewhere, that it was possible to influence dreams. It was simply a matter of falling asleep thinking about whatever it was you wanted to dream.

It wasn't all that simple to do. You had to keep your mind from drifting to other thoughts and be so focused on what you'd consciously chosen to dream that the dreams that might have been, the ones your subconscious mind had been busily preparing, would be summarily trumped.

Kathleen had tried the technique before, and without success. Other thoughts, worries, had drifted in before she'd drifted off.

But on this all-important night, this seventh-chance

night, she'd locked onto a thought and hadn't let it go. *You will be so lucky, little one, to have Ian as a father. The luckiest baby in the world. All you have to do while I sleep, while I dream, is find a home inside me.*

Kathleen was dreaming of Ian, and their baby, when the Air-Lift Northwest helicopter flew over her on-call room and landed on the helipad adjacent to the emergency room.

Kathleen kept sleeping, kept dreaming as Ian was rushed into Trauma Room A.

The trauma team was waiting for him, alerted about what to expect—massive blood loss, splintered ribs, shock—and fully trained in what to do.

They knew which lines to start, what blood to send, which specialists to call. The OR staff was similarly savvy. As were the doctors and nurses in the Surgical ICU.

But no one, not one soul in the hospital where Kathleen Cahill had lived for the past three weeks, knew to notify her. . . .

9

Sarah's Orchard
Tuesday, December 31, 4:30 p.m.

It was eight-thirty by the time Sam and Holly completed what should have been the ninety-minute drive from Ocean Crest Ranch to Sarah's Orchard. They'd made the journey safely, with Holly secure in her crate, and they'd made it calmly, thanks to a need for sleep that eventually eclipsed her determination to resist—and thanks as well to the perfect bed for her dreams: Sam's Rain Mountain parka. *Holly's* Rain Mountain parka, he'd amended as he watched her snuggle onto it, sigh and promptly fall asleep.

Sam believed the Apple Butter Ladies would approve.

"Here we are, Holly," he'd said as he opened the farm-house door. "Home."

The next twenty hours had been a free-floating medley of rest and play, discovery and milestones.

Her first noisy drink of water. Her first, and noisier, meal.

Her first encounter with the lawn beyond the kitchen door. The grass, like the apple trees, was in its midwinter hibernation. It hadn't grown since its final mow, a medium-length trim, in early November. But the emerald blades were thigh high on the puppy. She was that small. And what Sam had believed would be a soft carpet for her proved a difficult terrain.

But she was an intrepid puppy, with him at her side, and after a brief conversation of squeaks and reassurances, the lawn was hers.

Holly slept on top of him during her first night in her new home, her tummy warm on his chest, her nose cool on his neck. She was a good little sleeper when her batteries needed recharging. She awakened every three hours or so, but fell asleep again upon her return from outside.

Sam carried her during their nighttime trips to the lawn, and for the first few trips during the day. Sam liked carrying her, holding her. Loved it. But Holly needed to explore her new world on her own, so they did that, too, her every brave step and sniffing discovery made with the certainty that he was close by.

Holly was brilliant, of course. The smartest puppy ever to set paw on the planet.

Sam told her as much the first time she awakened from a nap and trotted to the kitchen door.

"What a good girl you are," Sam said as he followed. "What a *smart* girl."

At the sound of his voice, Holly stopped, looked up, and tilted her head.

"And are you a happy girl, too? A little happy, at least?" *I want you to be happy.*

As if in reply—no, it was her reply—her tail moved left, then right. Her first, if tentative, wag.

Which became, as she did, bolder and more confident throughout the day.

She played. They played. And when she slept, atop her parka in the crate, or on an already favorite throw rug on the floor, or on his always welcoming lap, Sam read his puppy-ownership booklets as he waited for her to awaken.

And when Holly was awake, Sam talked to her. Constantly. Her tilting head and wagging tail insisted that he do so.

She wasn't particular about the subject matter, seemed endlessly interested in any topic he chose.

Sam told her about the orchard, and the Apple Butter Ladies, and that it was time, didn't she think, to sell his Harley? They discussed the wind, the clouds, the birds, the sky.

It was all new to her, a bounty of wonderful discoveries.

And, for Sam, it was all new and wondrous, too.

When she crashed, on his shoulder, at four-thirty, Sam booted up his computer and went online, to the *Mail Tribune* Web site, to see what the rest of the world had been doing in the now twenty-six-and-a-half hours since Marge Hathaway had called.

He realized that he expected only happy news on this New Year's Eve—as if the entire world had tumbled to, and surrendered to, the monumental yet simple joy of letting one's life be controlled by a puppy.

The *Mail Tribune* online carried both local and national news. Its headline—Ian Collier Expected To Recover—spanned both.

Sam clicked on "related links," the archived headlines, beginning late last night, that chronicled a story in which recovery had not always been the anticipated outcome.

Tragedy At Crystal Mountain.

Teen Skier Distraught. Fears Death Of Hero.

CPR Administered On Slope.

Condition Critical; Survival In Doubt.

Med Center Switchboard Deluged With Concerned Calls.

Rare Blood Type Won't Determine Outcome, Doctors Say. But Donations Welcome.

Were it not for Holly, Sam Collier would have gone online last night. And if he'd seen that death appeared imminent for the father he couldn't remember? Would he have raced to Seattle to be with Ian when he died?

Sam didn't know.

He'd once planned a reunion with his father, a get-together set in motion ten days before Sam turned sixteen. The first step was to learn where Ian Collier was, assuming he was still alive. Sam's mother had reiterated to eleven-year-old Sam the words he'd overheard at six: with luck, the man-monster, who was totally incapable of love, would be in prison—or dead.

Even if his father was dead, Sam might pay him a visit, to rage at his grave . . . if it could be found.

From his boarding school in New Hampshire, Sam dialed the first number from the long list of potential phone calls he was determined to make before conceding defeat.

The initial call was the simplest and the least likely to be fruitful, or so he believed.

At the time, twenty years ago, area code 206 encompassed the western half of Washington state. But since the directory assistance operator wanted him to name a city, Sam asked, first, if there were any Seattle listings for Ian Collier.

There were two, she told him, but both for the same man. One was residential, the other business—the main number, she noted, for Rain Mountain Enterprises.

Rain Mountain. The unfamiliar name evoked such emotion that Sam swiftly hung up. He'd felt the bittersweet flood of longing before—at Christmas, or whenever he saw a dog—but never like this. Not with this breath-stealing hurt and this heart-racing hope.

Rain Mountain meant nothing to Sam. No memory he could recall. But he knew, as surely as he'd known anything in his almost sixteen years, that the Ian Collier at

Rain Mountain was the Ian Collier he had vowed to find.

And rage at.

He redialed directory assistance, got both numbers, but tried the Rain Mountain one first. He was interested, he told the receptionist who answered, in learning about the company.

It was on the verge of possibly going public, a grandmotherly voice in public relations informed him. She'd send him a copy of the prospectus if he'd give her his name and address.

His name. She didn't react to it, except to wonder if he spelled Collier with one *l* or two, and, when he told her two, she commented pleasantly "just like Mr. Collier," and went on to transcribe the address Sam provided, his mailbox number at the boarding school.

Sam realized he was waiting for her gasp of comprehension. Wait a minute! You're Sam Collier? Mr. Collier's son? I can't believe it. *He* won't believe it. He's been searching for you for years!

After the phone call ended, without such a gasp, Sam's own comprehension was incisive and sharp. Ian Collier hadn't needed to search for his son. The boy who'd spent his childhood hiding in the lonely sanctuary of his room hadn't been hidden at all. Sam had always been just a phone call away. As close, and as far, as Ian was.

Sam's usually empty boarding-school mailbox contained two items on his sixteenth birthday—one from each parent. The card from Vanessa would include a check, more sizable than her usual amount, he guessed, since a sixteenth birthday was supposed to be special. Sam always got money, lots of it, when his birthday or

Christmas rolled around. It was what a mother gave, what his mother gave, to the son she couldn't be bothered to know.

Sam would open the card later. On his way to the bank.

His priority was the large white envelope with the Rain Mountain Enterprises return address. He opened it in his dorm room behind a closed door. A locked door.

He lifted the flap carefully so as not to tear it.

Sam knew he'd seen photographs of Mount Rainier. In third-grade geography, probably, and four years later, definitely, when he and his boarding-school classmates had been required to learn in excruciating detail the landmarks, economy and history of all fifty states.

But Sam knew he'd never seen photos like the ones in the prospectus, photos that showed the mountain when it glowed gold at dawn or pink at twilight—or when, beneath a shimmering blue midday sky, the snow glittered white and pure.

The pictures evoked emotion, as did each and every printed word, especially those that were direct quotes from Ian himself.

The orphan, the murderer's son, had been a penniless boy in a city where million-dollar views belonged to everyone and where, in every direction, there were mountains to see.

The mountains were distant, though, as if someone had painted magnificent murals at each horizon—the Olympics to the west, the Cascades to the east, Baker to the north, Rainier to the south.

It was the orphan's skepticism that compelled him to hitch a ride, at age thirteen, with a van of skiers headed for Crystal. He didn't "believe the mountains, close up, could be as magical as they seemed from afar." They'd be disappointing. Not a big deal. An illusion that could be exposed and thereafter ignored.

But Ian Collier found "majesty, not mirage" in the snowcapped splendor. A majesty to be marveled at, and be part of, not to challenge or conquer. That was why he became a skier and not a climber. He wanted to be "at one with the grandeur, not at war with it."

The prospectus, and Ian's own words, made him sound like a dreamer, not a monster . . . of course. That was exactly what a puff piece on the company's owner would do.

And, for those in the know, like the monster's forsaken son, Ian Collier's true and despicable colors shone through in what had been conspicuously omitted from the glossy pages. Ian's four-year relationship with Seattle heiress Vanessa Worthing wasn't mentioned. Couldn't be. Future stockholders might want to know the details, and any hope of taking the company public would be dashed. Investors wouldn't readily hand over their hard-earned money to a man who'd been so unkind to his little boy, so mentally cruel, that the child had needed to be medicated, tranquilized, for a full two years after his mother—also a victim of Ian's psychological abuse—found the courage to leave.

There'd been a benefit, Vanessa had explained, to the tranquilizers Sam had received. They induced an amnesia of sorts, mercifully blocking out the four years with Ian, as well as the subsequent two years spent trying to recover from the torment. Sam didn't know how merciful it really was. Maybe if he'd been aware of his surroundings during the first two years of his mother's marriage to Mason Hargrove, Sam wouldn't have awakened so abruptly, at age six, to the harsh reality of a stepfather who wanted him about as much as Ian had, a mother whose hatred of Ian made it impossible to feel lovingly toward his son, and a baby brother, soon to be born, from whom Vanessa and Mason would keep Sam far away . . . and to whom, Sam would witness from afar, they'd be the wonderful parents they'd never been to him.

Sam spent his sixteenth birthday finalizing the plans for his reunion with his father. He made other plans, too, and left school the following day.

Left forever.

On his way to the bank, he mailed a letter to the address in Greenwich, Connecticut, that was his mother's home, Mason's home, Tyler's home—but never his. It was a polite letter. He didn't blame them for not loving him. But he wanted them to know that in addition to dropping out of the New Hampshire boarding school, he was dropping out of the life he'd lived since awakening ten years before. Sam didn't describe how much he'd hated that life of privilege and loneliness . . . and homelessness. He simply wrote, in the comforting truth of well-worn clichés, that it was time for him to move on, to find himself. And, in the event that they might worry, he assured them he'd be fine.

Then, after closing out his account at the bank, where he'd deposited every birthday and Christmas gift he'd ever received, Sam Collier bought himself the first real present of his life, something he wanted very much. The motorcycle wasn't the Harley he'd buy one day, but it would easily get him to Seattle by Christmas—and what better time to drop in on his father?

Christmas was six weeks away. Plenty of opportunity to rehearse every angry word he wanted to say. Sam shouted his angry words from atop his speeding motorcycle, and gulped them as he sobbed his rage in the forests where he slept, and finally he laughed the contemptuous words, laughed them—and he made a U-turn a hundred miles west of Naperville, Illinois.

To hell with Ian Collier.

To hell with the past.

Sam had a lifetime ahead of him, his life, to live as he pleased.

Sam Collier found escape in the sea, and peace in the company of dogs. Fleeting escape. Fragile peace. He'd had to keep moving, searching, until the emotions that came without warning and demanded to be heard compelled him to stop.

And here he was, in a four-room farmhouse in the middle of a landlocked orchard that was closer to Seattle than he'd ever imagined he would be. Here he was, wondering whether he would have rushed to his dying father's side if he'd read about Ian Collier's accident at a time when Ian's survival had been in doubt.

And, if he had, if he'd gone to Ian, would it have been in the spirit of reconciliation or the remembrance of rage?

The question was moot. Ian Collier was expected to recover. Still, as the baby creature nuzzled against his shoulder, he had his answer. Reconciliation, not rage.

But the issue was moot. To hell with Ian Collier. To hell with the past. It was hardly necessary—quite the opposite—for Sam to watch the press conference scheduled to begin at Queen Anne Medical Center just moments from now. The update on Ian Collier's condition would be carried live on Seattle TV—and in Sarah's Orchard, or anywhere else, it could be viewed online.

Seattle's KOMO-TV Web site also had links to articles about Ian Collier. Rain Mountain's Rainmaker—A Biography Of Ian Collier. Rain Mountain Scholars Pay It Forward. Ian Collier Purchases Historic Queen Anne Estate.

It would also be quite unnecessary for Sam to read those articles. But he might, after the press conference, or some other time while Holly napped.

Sam's present focus was readying his computer for the television feed. He adjusted the video portion first, enlarging the picture to full screen, making it sharp and clear. KOMO 4 TV's regularly scheduled programming had already been preempted by college football, a postseason bowl game.

The press conference was beginning—or at least the hype was—with dramatic graphics and "Breaking News."

Sam still hadn't adjusted the volume. He'd intentionally had it on mute. But as the feed shifted from prerecorded graphics to a live shot of the Seattle skyline, his left hand gently touched the sleeping Holly as his right hand brought an unfamiliar voice, that of a female reporter, into their home.

"It's okay," Sam reassured her as she stirred. "You're safe, Holly. You'll always be safe."

Sam patted her as he murmured. Holly yawned, stretched, curled—and returned to dreams.

Sam's left hand remained where it was, on her silky coat, as he fine-tuned the volume and listened to the reporter's words.

She was standing outside, backlit by the glow of an immense sign that read Emergency Entrance. In the distance, beneath a sky as clear as in Sarah's Orchard—the same night sky arcing between medical center and farmhouse, father and son—the Space Needle shimmered its holiday splendor in twinkling lights of red, green, gold.

"We're awaiting a press conference on the condition of Rain Mountain owner Ian Collier. We'll take you inside as soon as it begins. First, however, we're going to show you some new video of the accident itself, taken by one of our viewers but not previously aired because Ian Collier's prognosis seemed so grim. And although his condition has markedly improved, and we understand that a complete recovery is expected, we want to warn parents that the footage, which includes audio, is graphic and somewhat disturbing, even for adults. So you may want your children to leave the room for the next ninety seconds. Okay, again, this is amateur video, unedited, taken last night at Crystal Mountain."

Watching a tape of a near-fatal accident wasn't something Sam Collier would ever choose to do. He'd seen enough traumatic injury in person, when he'd put himself in a position to help—in maritime rescues—and when he'd simply offered what assistance he could, the time a co-worker fell from the upper reaches of a wave-rocked oil rig, or another was crushed beneath a palette of improperly off-loaded slate.

And when the injured victim was his father . . . With a little more warning, Sam might have chosen not to watch. And maybe he was in the throes of that choice when the video began, with grandeur, not with trauma.

The man, his father, swooped down the mountain with exquisite grace and breathtaking joy. Ian Collier wasn't alone. Another skier, expert, too, but without Ian's grace, skied nearby. It was a stunning pas de deux, each dancer skiing as if he were the other's shadow in a side-by-side synchrony of leaps and turns.

Perfect. Until the apprentice threw in a complicated step the master wasn't expecting, a mid-leap crisscross, which became a high-speed collision—complete with an excruciating clarity of sound.

Help him! The silent scream was Sam's as adrenaline surged within, equipping him for this battle as for past battles. Armed, dangerous, willing—with no place to go.

"You can see why we decided against showing the accident video until now." The reporter's face replaced the horrific cliffhanger and her voice provided as soothing an antidote as was possible to the echoes of shattering bones and cries of terror. "We've also with-held the identity of the other skier. And because he's a minor, a thirteen-year-old, we'll continue to do so. I was able to speak with his mother earlier, although she declined—for her son's privacy—an on-camera inter-view. Although physically uninjured, the boy's under-standably distraught. He's obviously an exceptionally good skier himself, and his hero, whom he's idolized since putting on his first pair of Rain Mountain skis, is Ian Collier. Ironically, it was that hero worship that caused the tragic accident. There's apparently a tape, which we're trying to get, in which Ian Collier and another skier, an Olympic gold-medalist, are skiing in tandem, as in the footage we've just seen, and crisscrossing whenever the skier on the left gives a specific hand signal and the other skier nods in reply. The teenager believed that's what he and Ian Collier were doing. And on the film we've shown, as well as others taken from different angles, it's clear the boy did give a hand signal, and it looks as if Ian acknowledged it with a nod." The reporter paused, touched her earpiece, then resumed, "I've just received word that the press conference is about to begin, so I'll throw it to Keith, who's already found a front-row seat in the auditorium inside."

The next voice didn't belong to the KOMO reporter named Keith, but to the only press-conference participant on the auditorium stage not wearing a white coat. He introduced himself as the hospital administrator. He stood at a central podium, flanked on either side by people Sam assumed were the doctors and nurses who'd been most involved in Ian's care.

"I'd like to begin by thanking all of you for coming this evening. It's a fabulous New Year's Eve, isn't it? Ideal weather for the Space Needle fireworks, which is a great way to celebrate Mr. Collier's remarkable progress. I'm going to turn the proceedings over to Dr. Rob Traynor, our trauma chief, who'll introduce the rest of his all-star team and update you on their patient's condition. After that, we'll open the floor to questions. Dr. Traynor?"

The trauma chief did introduce his team of nurses and surgeons. But he didn't mention all the white-coated health-care providers on the stage. A tall dark-haired woman remained unidentified—an oversight, Sam decided, that didn't bother her in the least.

Sam watched the mystery woman as Dr. Traynor described the trauma Ian had sustained—fractured ribs, contused lungs, through-and-through laceration of the major artery in his arm. It was the severed brachial artery that had posed the most imminent life-threatening danger. If a witness to the accident hadn't sprung into action, cinching a belt above the bleeding site, Ian Collier wouldn't have had the opportunity to experience the all-star care.

As it was, he'd reached the medical center in time and was in the operating room six minutes later. The torn artery was repaired, and sharp pieces of his shattered ribs were removed, and . . . "When I spoke with him ten minutes ago, he said to give everyone a warm hello." With that, Rob Traynor's recap was finished, and the reporters' questions began.

"So he's . . . with it?"

"Completely with it. He sustained no head injury or spinal cord injury at all."

"No neurological injury, you mean?"

"I didn't say that," Dr. Traynor replied. "Not surprisingly, the deep laceration to his arm severed a few nerves. But the deficit is relatively minor and likely to improve."

"He had a concussion, though, didn't he? He was unconscious at the scene."

"He was *semiconscious* at the scene, and when he lost consciousness en route to the medical center, it was due to a combination of his dangerously low blood pressure and the overall shock to his system. His brain's just fine."

"You said he told you to say hello. That means his endotracheal tube has been removed?"

"A couple of hours ago."

"Is he in pain?"

The trauma surgeon smiled. "As he himself just informed me, it only hurts when he breathes."

"Is he still in intensive care?"

"He is, and we plan to keep him in the unit overnight. He's been moved, however, from the Surgical ICU's critical-care area to one of our telemetry rooms. He'll be on a cardiac monitor while he's there, but otherwise it will feel to him as if he's on a regular ward, not in the ICU."

"Is there something wrong with his heart?"

"Not a thing. Monitoring the heart is simply an excellent, noninvasive way of monitoring the entire patient."

"And he *is* out of the woods?"

Sam's unidentified woman had been listening to trauma chief Traynor as intently as Sam had been. She hated hearing about the trauma, Sam decided. Ian's trauma. Even though it was a retrospective recounting, and she knew the outcome was good, she hated that Ian Collier had been forced to endure such pain.

Sam hadn't imagined he'd see a smile from her. But with the trauma chief's—Ian's—quip about hurting only when he breathed, a smile appeared.

It was a beautiful smile, intelligent and serene, and it held until she sensed—as Sam sensed—the slightly too long delay in Dr. Traynor's reply.

She looked at the inexplicably silent surgeon, and saw, as Sam believed *he* saw, the shadow of worry as the heretofore articulate doctor seemed to fumble for words. Maybe the surgeon, like most physicians, was simply cautious in making categorical predictions . . . especially when the patient in question was still in intensive care.

The hospital administrator was far less circumspect.

"Out of the woods and out of the hospital soon," he replied as he returned to the mike. "Very soon, if he has anything to say about it. Any more questions?"

"Since Ian Collier has no family, and there are rules about who's permitted to visit patients in the Surgical ICU, was anyone with him last night?"

"We like to think all our patients feel they're with family when they're here." It might have been a practiced answer, but the administrator's passion made it seem genuine. The man with no family, except a long-forsaken son, had been in caring hands. "And in the case of Mr. Collier, any number of our staff know him personally. As a matter of fact, the newest member of our medical center family, Dr. Kathleen Cahill, has known Mr. Collier ever since her selection as a Rain Mountain Scholar eighteen years ago."

The administrator gestured to Sam's mystery woman. So, mystery solved? In part. She was now a mystery with a name, and an eighteen-year acquaintance with the father he'd never known.

More than an acquaintance, Sam thought.

A relationship. It was she who'd been at Ian's bedside throughout the night. He was sure of it.

"And," the hospital administrator continued, obviously satisfied with what he viewed as an ideal segue, "as many of you know, Dr. Cahill is also the obstetrician who's spent the past three weeks monitoring our mom-to-be of septuplets, Georgia Blaine. I asked Dr. Cahill to be here this evening to update you on the other Queen Anne Medical Center story that's making news. Dr. Cahill?"

The administrator had been beckoning to her as he spoke, so by the time he was ready to yield the podium microphone, Kathleen Cahill had made her way from the edge of the stage to its center.

"Good evening," she said. "Georgia's doing well, in large part because of the trouper she is, but also because she knows that every extra moment the babies can be nourished in utero translates into fewer hours, perhaps fewer days, of mechanical ventilation and other supportive measures once they're born."

"Thanks to Dr. Cahill," the hospital administrator stepped forward to interject, "the septuplets have had three weeks of extra moments."

"It's not thanks to me." She didn't speak into the microphone, nor did she face the room of reporters as she spoke. Her displeasure wasn't for show; it was very real. "Georgia and Thomas—"

"I see we have questions," the administrator interjected again. "Let's begin over here. Keith?"

"Do you have any idea, Dr. Cahill, when the septuplets will be born?"

It was *the* question, Sam thought. And one to which every reporter in the room undoubtedly expected a cautiously vague reply. *Time will tell. Babies arrive when they arrive.*

But Kathleen Cahill surprised them.

"Between five and seven hours from now."

"Have the teams been alerted?"

"Yes."

"You said you expect the babies to be born sometime between ten-twenty and twelve-twenty," a reporter was saying. "Does that mean you might consider delivering some just before midnight and the others after?"

Kathleen didn't reply at once. Sam wasn't sure she would. She certainly didn't have to. Her expression was eloquent, her pale blue eyes shimmering ice.

"The decision will be based solely on what I believe is best for the tiny lives already destined to enter a world in which they'll have to fight to survive. I'll do whatever I can to give each and every one of them the very best chance."

Good for you, Sam thought. *Good for you.*

10

Queen Anne Medical Center
Surgical ICU
New Year's Eve, 6 p.m.

Kathleen hadn't known, until the press conference, that Ian's endotracheal tube had been removed. She'd been at Georgia's bedside, or within seconds of it, all afternoon.

And before that, from two in the morning on, she'd made the five-minute—and four-flight—trip from Georgia to Ian countless times.

And before *that*, Kathleen had slept, dreaming wondrous dreams, until midnight, when the call came from L & D that an especially anxious Georgia needed her. Kathleen had spent the ensuing two hours with Georgia, calming her, even though she knew there'd be increasing anxiety for Georgia—and for Kathleen herself—in the hours that lay ahead.

Georgia's body would sense its need to bid godspeed to its cargo. Kathleen had to determine when that need became a necessity for both Georgia and the babies. There wouldn't be an obvious signal. Among Georgia's carefully selected medications were ones that blocked the usual signs and symptoms of labor, and labor itself.

What remained was the invisible, immeasurable symptom Georgia was beginning to display—the anxiousness that was part eagerness, part fear. Kathleen had to decide when that eagerness reached its most hopeful zenith and deliver the babies then. Rushing the delivery would cost the little lives vital extra moments of in utero nourishment they might have had. And delaying it beyond the zenith, because she failed to discern that crucial peak?

Eventually the life support within the womb would shut down, and if the babies were still there . . .

They wouldn't be. Kathleen's determined vow was laced with her own heightened blend of eagerness and fear. The septuplets could depend on her to know when the perfect time came to make the swift, safe transfer from life support in the womb to life support in the world.

That time was still hours away. The need to deliver was impending but not imminent. All Kathleen had to do was pay attention. Subtle though the indicators would be, they would be there. And she would spot them.

At two in the morning, with Georgia relatively calm, Kathleen had made what she'd believed would be a quick trip to the staff lounge. She'd needed a little nourishment herself. She was feeling . . . queasy. Nerves, she told herself. As glorious as her dreams, and as confident as Ian's prediction that the seventh time would be a charm, it wasn't possible that she'd be experiencing morning sickness already.

But if, *when,* she experienced it, she'd welcome the queasiness with joy. And salt crackers. Which she was in pursuit of then. Salt crackers had been available in every staff lounge she'd ever entered—as predictable as the abrupt silence that so often greeted her.

But it hadn't been silence that greeted Kathleen in the L & D lounge at two a.m. It had been sadness and eulogy—a rehearsal for what was expected to be the death of Ian Collier.

He'd been out of surgery for three hours by the time Kathleen first learned of the accident. Three hours during which she hadn't been with him and he wasn't responding the way he should have. The surgeons had done all they could. The artery had been repaired, the bone chips—potential daggers—meticulously removed, the fractured ribs stabilized and realigned. And his lungs, bruised and battered by the direct blow they'd received, were oxygenating surprisingly well, and expanding, courtesy of the ventilator he was on.

But his blood pressure was wobbly, despite the volume replacement he'd been given. Continuous-drip pressors were required to keep his diastolic reading in an acceptable range. He wasn't awake, either. The lack of consciousness couldn't be ascribed to lingering anesthetic effects and should have been stimulated by what had to be the enormous pain of his shattered ribs. Ian's pain would remain unmedicated until his mental status improved.

Kathleen had dashed to the ICU.

"I have to see Ian Collier," she announced to the first person she encountered when she got there.

That person, a third-year trauma resident, either understood that Dr. Cahill wasn't requesting permission to see the patient—she was going to see him—or assumed she was yet another in the long line of consultants the trauma chief had called.

Without a word, the resident led her to the glass-walled cubicle. Without a pause, Kathleen walked right in.

And without a clue to the identity of the determined physician with the haunted blue eyes, the white-coated sea of surgeons parted for her. Their dying patient's response to the sound of her voice was instant—eyes open, the hint of a smile—and, as one, they withdrew.

No one returned to Ian's cubicle until Kathleen emerged an hour later. She'd been paged to L & D, and needed to be on her way, but not before giving an order to the trauma chief himself. Ian could sleep, she told him, if he'd authorize some morphine for his pain. And as long as Dr. Traynor would be making medication

175

changes, he might want to rethink the dopamine drip. Ian's blood pressure was fine on its own.

She wanted to be paged immediately if Ian's condition deteriorated at all.

Kathleen wasn't paged, not once, throughout the day. And she would have been despite the fact that Queen Anne Medical Center's trauma chief, unused to receiving orders from anyone, much less an obstetrician, had bristled at her imperious approach. But Rob Traynor knew a miracle when he saw one. If he'd needed the miracle worker, if his patient had needed her, he'd have personally gone to L & D to find her.

But Ian had been fine. Sleeping. Improving. Miraculously.

A spectacular recovery that was stoked by the brief but frequent visits from Kathleen.

No one overheard the words she whispered to Ian Collier. But everyone noticed that she whispered but didn't touch—as if Ian would recognize her voice but not the feel of her long slender fingers on his flesh.

Kathleen had no idea if Ian heard her words. After her two-in-the-morning visit, when he'd awakened just long enough to prove it was safe for him to be medicated to sleep, he'd slept through every visit. It wasn't a terribly restful sleep, Kathleen thought. Even with the morphine, a maximum dose, he grimaced in pain.

Kathleen whispered the same words, over and over. "I was sleeping when they brought you to the hospital. Dreaming. And incubating, I think. I really do. I'm sure that last evening, the seventh try, was the charm you knew it would be. It's as if I feel the new life already. Our *baby*. It's the only plausible explanation for my feeling of joy even though you're lying here. It's the baby's joy, Ian. Knowing you'll be his or her daddy."

Kathleen hadn't been able to visit Ian during the afternoon or before the press conference. There'd been too much to do with Georgia and for Georgia—a calling in of the troops, a final review of logistics, although Kathleen's best guess still put the delivery several hours away.

Kathleen discovered, at the press conference, that there'd also been a lot going on in the SICU throughout the afternoon. A wide-awake Ian must have communicated his desire to have the endotracheal tube removed. Such a desire, however fervent, wouldn't have been honored unless and until he'd demonstrated his ability to adequately ventilate his lungs despite protests from his broken bones.

Ian had obviously passed that test, and he'd been transferred from his glass-walled cubicle to a telemetry room. His heartbeats, in the form of strong and steady neon-green blips, were still being monitored, but his room afforded other luxuries: phone, TV, Space Needle view.

Following the press conference, Kathleen heard his voice as she approached his room. He was on the phone when she reached the doorway. She paused there, would wait there, until he beckoned her in. He would, she knew, once he sensed she was there.

Kathleen wasn't in a rush to have Ian notice her. She needed a little time to diagnose, and then conceal, her discomfort at seeing Ian in bed. She hadn't felt the discomfort before, when she'd whispered words of hope to the man who lay motionless, unconscious, with a tube down his throat. Because, she realized, he'd borne so little resemblance to the vital man she'd always known, and was seeing now. In bed.

Ian was dressed far more modestly now than he'd been throughout the night. His flimsy hospital gown was hidden entirely beneath a robe that was—like all QAMC robes—many cuts above the standard-issue striped-seersucker garment provided by every other hospital in which Kathleen had worked.

And therein lay the problem. Ian Collier didn't look like a patient. He looked like who he was, Rain Mountain's powerful and charismatic CEO. Oh, he was away from his office. But there was always work to be done— overseas calls that sometimes, after hours, he chose to make from the comfort of his bed.

After hours. Before hours. Ian Collier's empire had outposts around the globe. For all Kathleen knew, every day began and ended with such calls. She didn't know. But very soon, she'd learn firsthand what Ian did, how he dressed, in the privacy of his home . . . their home.

She'd become comfortable with what she learned. By surrendering to the sexual desires that were there, after all? No. She had no such desires. Not for Ian. Not for any man. Her discomfort was a reminder, as if she needed one, of the womanliness she was missing.

Okay. Diagnosis made. Reconfirmed. And, Kathleen told herself, her discomfort was understandable. Their relationship was platonic. Seeing each other in bed, wandering into the other's bedroom for a friendly chat, wasn't something platonic friends would do, were expected to do. Was it?

Of course not. And, in addition to the fact that it was she who was doing the wandering, her destination was a hospital room, not a bedroom.

There. Problem solved. And awkwardness concealed.

She was ready. Ian could catch a glimpse of her anytime.

She was surprised he hadn't already. She was well within his peripheral vision.

But Ian was preoccupied, Kathleen decided, with the terribly important conversation he was having with a distraught thirteen-year-old boy.

"You're a terrific skier, Corey. Far better than I was at your age. . . . You're right. You have made a study of me, haven't you? I only discovered the mountains at thirteen and didn't put on my first pair of skis until the following year. You'll be better at eighteen than I was. . . . Yes, when I was the forerunner for the downhill course. Mark my words . . . No, Corey, the collision was entirely *my* fault. You gave the signal for the crisscross, and I nodded in reply, and then my mind simply wandered. But we'll do it again sometime, okay? And I won't mess up . . . Yes. I do mean it. . . ."

Ian turned his head, saw Kathleen, beckoned her in with a smile. "Great. I have a little recovering to do, but once I've done that, I'll see you in Green Valley. In the meantime, remember that you did nothing wrong . . . Good . . . Happy New Year to you, too."

Ian replaced the receiver without losing eye contact with Kathleen.

He knows this could feel awkward for me, she thought

as she met his slightly worried gaze. She pulled the chair near his bedside a little closer, sat, and smiled away his worry. "Hi."

"Hi. And good for you."

Kathleen really didn't want to discuss her conquest of the awkwardness she'd felt.

"That's exactly what I was going to say to you."

"I'm referring to the press conference," Ian said.

"Oh. You didn't think it was too Wicked Witch of the West of me to nix the fun—drama, whatever—of a few babies born one year, a few the next?"

"I got no Wicked Witch of the West feelings at all."

"That's nice of you to say, especially since I was the one who suggested yesterday's trip to Crystal."

"It was a wonderful suggestion, Kathleen. Not your fault I had one bad run."

"Or your fault, either. Was it?"

"I honestly don't know."

"You're such a nice man, Ian. Don't deny it. I overheard you tell Corey you were to blame."

"It was something I thought he needed to hear."

"Enough that within, oh, seconds of being extubated you made it your mission to get the name and number of the boy who, last I heard, was in seclusion at a location other than his home."

"It was an easy mission. The nurses have been fielding frequent calls from his parents, checking on me. I just asked them to let me take the next call myself."

"Very nice of you. Truthful or not. Do you remember anything about the run?"

"I remember everything, up to and including both the

sound and the feel of being hit. My memory gets a little murky after that. I heard shouting, I know, before passing out."

"So what do you remember about skiing in tandem with Corey?"

"Nothing. I have no memory of Corey, no awareness of Corey, at all. Maybe my mind really did wander. It's certainly been meandering ever since."

"You've been sleeping."

"That hasn't stopped my subconscious from meandering. Worrying."

"About what?"

"About not having told either you or James where to find the documents you'd need in the event of my death."

"Which we didn't need."

"But would have if I'd died."

"You didn't die. You're not *going* to die."

"I certainly don't plan to. But I've made plans, Kathleen, just in case. There's a prepaid contract with a funeral home and I've chosen the cemetery where I'd like my ashes—"

"I'm not listening to this!"

"How grown-up is that?"

"As grown-up as I intend to be."

"May I at least tell you where the relevant documents are?"

Kathleen sighed but smiled. "I suppose."

He smiled back. "Thank you. The funeral and burial information is in the bottom drawer of the filing cabinet in my office, in a folder labeled 'Miscellaneous.' The keys to my safe-deposit box are there as well, and so is a document giving James power of attorney for all matters, personal and corporate, pending probate of my estate."

"Okay. Great. Now I know."

"I want you to know a little more. The will that's in the safe-deposit is my current will. It's ten years old and needs to be revised. I wanted to discuss the revisions with you first. And with James. I'd planned to have the new will signed before Christmas."

"But James had to go to Boston, and I've been here with Georgia, and revising your will is something we can do anytime in the next forty years or so."

"I think we'll do it sooner than that. Although . . ."

"Although?"

"Well, as I've been lying here, worrying, I've convinced myself it wouldn't be the end of the world if I died with the old will in place."

"It would be the end of the world if you died. Period. Which you're *not going to.* But now that I know where the relevant—I mean totally irrelevant—documents are, may I ask you something?"

"You may."

"Did your subconscious meander to any happy places?"

"Oh, yes. To us. Our life. Our baby."

"Good," Kathleen whispered. She wanted to shift their conversation from death to life, and from worry to hope. But that wasn't really fair to Ian. He'd had a serious confrontation with his own mortality and needed to talk. "But I'm feeling a little more grown-up at the moment, so if you'd like to tell me about the funeral arrangements or—you've chosen a cemetery?" *Oh, Ian. What a lonely thing to have done.*

"And purchased a plot with a spectacular view of the mountains. It's a beautiful place, Kathleen, and the process wasn't the least bit grim."

"It wasn't?"

"Not at all. My goal was to find a peaceful spot for whoever might decide, after my death, to drop by." *A peaceful place, Kathleen, for you.*

"To drop by," Kathleen repeated, "to visit you."

"To remember me. Wherever I go after death has very little to do with where my ashes happen to be. At least that's what I believe. We talked about this once, when we talked about your mother."

"Yes," Kathleen said. "We decided she was close by, in my heart, in my memory, and always would be."

"And?"

"She is. Always."

"So that's what matters. Not what's done or not done to the mortal remains."

"But you've already made the arrangements."

"Because I've seen such turmoil when grieving loved ones are left to guess—and second-guess—what decisions the deceased would have wanted them to make. That's why I decided to take that unnecessary torment off the table."

Kathleen nodded. In practical terms, Ian was absolutely right. "Sometime in the next forty years or so, you can show me the place you've chosen."

"It's a date." And sometime in the next forty years or so, I'll tell you there's room beside me in that peaceful place. I purchased room for—Ian didn't permit himself to finish the thought. He could be matter-of-fact about his own death, but there was pure emotion when it came to hers.

"Ian? Is there something else?"

"There is something else. It's not a worry, really. And it predated the accident. I've been thinking—a lot—about Sam."

"That's not surprising, is it? We'll be living where you lived with Sam, where you loved your little boy so much, and we'll be raising our babies there."

"It's not surprising," Ian conceded. "But my thoughts about Sam have been more . . . constant, and more ambivalent, than I should allow them to be."

"Ambivalent?"

"Sam's a principal beneficiary in the will I have yet to revise, and could have revised, regardless of where you or James happened to be. But didn't."

"Because the revision would have included taking Sam out?"

"It's time."

"Not if you're ambivalent. Not if you have even one slightly ambivalent thought." And, Kathleen realized, Ian had very mixed feelings about removing from his will the very reason—Sam—he'd created Rain Mountain, and named Rain Mountain and, as a result of the company's success, had needed a will in the first place. It wouldn't be the end of the world, he'd just told her, if his unrevised will remained in place. She wholeheartedly agreed. "What Sam meant to you, Ian, what he *means* to you, will never go away. And shouldn't. It

184

makes no more sense to take him out of your will than to block him from your memory. In fact . . . maybe it's time to get to know him again. Do you have any idea where he is? Or what he's doing?"

"No."

"All the more reason not to make drastic changes until you do. It shouldn't be too difficult to track him down. An Internet search for Sam Worthing Hargrove would probably do the trick. Even more direct, however, would be a call to Vanessa—which I'd be delighted to make."

Ian saw the ferociousness in Kathleen's eyes, her fury with the woman who'd given him a son and taken that beloved boy away. "And share your opinion of her while you're at it?"

"Only after she's told me everything I want to know."

"Calling Vanessa would be the right place to start. For Sam's sake. We know she explained to him who I was—and wasn't—when he was four, and agreed to reiterate the facts when he was older if he was curious about me in any way. Most likely, he wasn't. Most likely, and best for him, would be no memory of me at all. Sending the Rain Mountain prospectus to Vanessa on his sixteenth birthday certainly didn't elicit a reply."

"You have no idea if she even showed it to him. Besides, that was twenty years ago. Sam was a teenager then, and a grown man now. Two years more grown-up than yours truly." Kathleen plotted as she spoke. She was going to find Sam Worthing Hargrove. And if on talking with Sam, perhaps even meeting with Sam, Kathleen decided a reunion would be happy for Ian, then a reunion there would be.

"Let's talk about tomorrow," Ian suggested.

"Okay. I'd say this room will do very nicely."

"Not as nicely as the living room at the house."

"Ian, I don't think so."

"The septuplets aren't arriving tonight?"

"They're arriving."

"After that, for all purposes, you're off the case. You can go home, get married, take a few weeks off—can't you?"

Kathleen's smile promised that she planned to do all those things. "I don't believe I'm the problem."

"I've been hurt worse than this and raced downhill the following day."

"Is that so?"

"Close enough." His expression became serious. "I want to be married in our home, Kathleen. Tomorrow evening, at seven, as planned. I want that very much."

Our new life, in our new home, on the first day of a brand-new year. That had been their joyous plan . . . their solemn pledge.

Which, she vowed, they would keep.

"So do I," she said with finality. "And that's when and where it will be. I have a witness, by the way."

"You do?"

"Did you doubt it?"

"Never. Anyone I know?"

"As a matter of fact . . ." Kathleen's pager sounded and she stood as she read the message. "I'll tell you later. I'd better get downstairs."

"Show time?"

"I wouldn't have said so. My guess is we're still a few

hours away. But I have to see her to be sure. I may not be able to come back until the babies are born—whenever that is."

"Like a few before midnight and a few after?"

"Oh, probably!"

"Don't worry about me, Kathleen. I'll be fine. I'm going to have a great view of the Space Needle fireworks, so if you happen to be free . . ."

Ian didn't complete the sentence. Didn't need to. Kathleen knew and shared his wish. And if she happened to be free, she'd be with him, at midnight, to celebrate the glorious beginning of their glorious new year.

11

Sarah's Orchard
New Year's Eve, 8 p.m.

Of the two Apple Butter Ladies, sisters-in-law Clara and Eve, it was Clara with whom Sam usually spoke.

And it was Clara he'd called now. She'd answered midway through the first ring.

"Don't you tell me, Ryan MacKenzie, that you've changed your mind! Don't you *dare.*"

"I wouldn't dare," Sam replied to the laughing, scolding seventy-eight-year-old voice. "But it's me, Clara. Sam. Not Ryan."

"Sam?"

"Collier."

"I know which Sam!" Clara MacKenzie's voice had a new target now—and it held the same fondness for Sam as it had for her twenty-two-year-old grandson. "For heaven's sake! What I don't know is where you're calling from. It's a very good connection, though, isn't it? Whatever exotic port it happens to be."

"I'm here. At the farmhouse. Calling to wish you Happy New Year."

"Why thank you, Sam. How nice of you. Happy New Year to you, too! Is everything all right with you? It's unusual for you to be back in town so soon."

Sam had already decided not to confess, if he could possibly avoid it, that he'd never left. No need to let Clara worry that he'd spent Christmas alone. "Everything's perfectly all right. I was also going to ask you about your Christmas sales, but if you're expecting a call from Ryan—"

"I'm not. He'd just called to say that he and Susie are going to spend the night in Sacramento instead of driving all the way here. They got a late start, and the New Year's Eve traffic's already bad. I told him I thought it was a good idea to stop, but when the phone rang about ten seconds after he'd hung up, I was afraid he'd changed his mind because he didn't want me spending New Year's Eve scandalized by images of him and Susie in the same motel room. *As if!* As they say."

"Who's Susie?"

"Oh, that's right, you haven't heard the news. My grandson's in love. Can you believe it?"

"Actually, I can." And as he thought about Ryan MacKenzie, who'd spent his summer days working at Sam's orchard and his summer evenings computerizing his grandmother's business, Sam decided it was probably the real thing. "Do you like Susie?"

"Haven't met her! But they'll be here until January tenth. Everyone else adores her, though, and there's already talk of a June wedding—and of the newlyweds settling right here."

"Ryan loves Sarah's Orchard."

"He does, doesn't he? My only big-city grandchild who prefers our little town. I'm not sure what he plans to do in Sarah's Orchard. Nothing that has anything to do with his sociology degree, I'm sure. I wouldn't be surprised if he talks to you about working more than just summers at the orchard."

"I'll give Ryan all the work he wants. He's always been my best employee."

"And mine. Speaking of which, you asked about this year's apple butter sales. In a word, fantastic. Our best year ever. We have about three jars left. They'll be gone, too, by the end of Ryan's visit. One of these days, Eve and I will have to go into production again. At the moment we're taking a break."

"A well-deserved one."

"I'll admit it's been a fun, carefree Christmas. But we do enjoy making the apple butter. Isn't it nice to enjoy both work and play—when work is play?"

"Very nice," Sam said, and realized, as silence fell, that they were nearing the end of things to say. The conversation had already lasted longer than he would've predicted when he'd made the decision to call. He'd felt like wishing someone a happy new year. There was no one he knew better than Clara—whom he barely knew at all. He'd wished her Happy New Year, and she'd been surprised but pleased, and it was time to say goodbye, and yet . . . "I have a puppy."

"How wonderful, Sam! Tell me more."

"She's a cocker spaniel. I've named her Holly."

"Well," Clara MacKenzie said, "I hope she knows what a lucky puppy she is!"

Natalie had seen James Gannon in love. With Christine. She knew the way such happiness looked on his handsome face.

Natalie also knew what James's desire for *her* did to his dark blue eyes.

And she'd known, without seeing, the sadness when he'd called to say that he and Christine wouldn't be buying Magnolia Bluff after all.

And she'd heard his exhaustion, and imagined dark circles, during their long-distance conversations last night and several times today.

All but one of today's phone calls had been long-distance. And despite his frustration—and hers—that his departure time kept being pushed back, it gave them the unhurried opportunity to discuss everything Natalie knew about Ian, the accident itself and his ever-improving progress.

The real estate agent with the hospital-view apartment got frequent updates from the critical-care nurses who lived across the hall. Natalie's neighbors hadn't known of her relationship with Ian Collier. But once she'd explained that the injured CEO was not only a client but a friend—James's friend, she'd embellished silently—they'd been happy to keep her informed . . . especially since, following the two-in-the-morning visit by an obstetrician named Kathleen Cahill, the news had been happy indeed.

Natalie heard James's relief as she shared the good news about Ian, and more relief when the airline posted a departure time that at last was real. And in the one call that wasn't long-distance, she heard a smile to match her own. James's snow-delayed flight had just snuggled into its gate at Sea-Tac, and as its weary travelers prepared to disembark, a hundred cell phones were powered up.

James wanted to stop by his condo first. It would be nine-thirty by the time he got to her apartment. If that was okay—not too late?

Perfectly okay, Natalie told him. And she thought but didn't say, No time's too late, James. Not for you.

But when her doorbell chimed at nine-thirty on the dot, and she opened the door to a James she'd never seen, the silent thought screamed, It *is* too late—for James. He's too far gone.

She'd expected to see exhaustion. What she saw was more like death. He'd lost weight. And as Natalie knew well, James Gannon hadn't had an unnecessary ounce on his entire body to begin with.

James had lost color, too. Virtually all color had fled his skeletal face. Even the dark circles she'd imagined weren't there. Which meant what? That his heart had stopped beating? Or, more likely, he'd left it in Boston with Christine.

Natalie wanted to touch his colorless face and warm his icy lips with hers, and love him, love him, until the torment vanished. And as for the heart he'd left in

191

Boston, he didn't need it. She'd give him hers. She already had. He just didn't know it.

He would worry about the consequences, for her, of giving such a generous gift. He'd worry because he was—barely—living proof of giving one's heart to someone who didn't reciprocate in kind. Natalie's reassurance would only add to his torment. But he *had* given her a heart. It beat deep inside her, and, as tiny as it was, it pumped sheer joy—a fuel so powerful it could keep both mother and daughter alive . . . and flourishing.

"Natalie?"

"You're here," she murmured to the corpse on her doorstep.

"Looking a little the worse for wear. I hadn't realized quite how bad until I saw myself in a mirror at my condo. I guess I hadn't really been paying attention in Boston."

You had more important things to do. But also important to him, and the apparent reason he'd insisted on stopping at his condo, had been showering, shaving, changing before coming to her. Showering, shaving, changing. Monumental tasks, and acts of politeness. James was a gentleman, always.

"You look . . . awful."

A glimmer of life, of laughter, touched his haunted eyes. "Too awful to come in?"

"Oh! Sorry." She made a sweeping gesture. "Please."

"Thank you."

"Can I get you something to drink?"

"No, I'm fine."

Natalie, already en route to the kitchen, spun around.

"Excuse me?" She said it lightly, teasingly. She had to keep the glimmer alive, keep him alive. And if that required feigning a merriment she didn't feel, she would. Natalie's gaiety, as false as it was, also provided a wall between what she wanted to do—touch, love—and what James needed her to do. Whatever that was . . .

"I don't need anything to drink."

"I have an unopened box of Godiva chocolates—"

"I'm fine, Natalie. Better just being here . . . with you."

As James spoke the soft and solemn words, the glimmer in his eyes became quite bright and glittering and pure, *pure* blue.

"James." Natalie touched his translucent face. "Tell me what you need—what I can do."

James encircled her delicate wrists with fingers that were bones. "What I need," he echoed quietly. "I wish I knew. I know what I'd like—to go to bed with you, to be lost in you . . ."

"Would that be so terrible?"

A slight smile moved the hands that rested on his clean-shaven cheeks. Natalie's fingertips touched bone, the patrician ridge beneath his troubled eyes. "Not terrible at all. But not the answer."

As his smile disappeared, Natalie felt the taut rippling of the muscles of his jaw. "What is the answer?"

"Good question. Unfortunately, it gets me back to 'I wish I knew.'" James took her hands from his face, held her wrists, handcuffed in bone, between them. "I'm sorry, Natalie. I probably shouldn't have come."

Natalie heard the "probably" and clung to it, drew strength from it. His hands still encircled hers—and drew strength from touching her? Natalie doubted it. And yet . . . he seemed reluctant to let go.

"I could fire questions at you," she said, her voice carefully light. "Who knows? Maybe one of them would lead to the answer. I mean, we've already established that my last question was good."

James let go. Stepped back. "Fire away."

"Okay. Maybe we should sit?" The suggestion was as much for her as for him. She knew the first question she was going to ask, the obvious one. She needed to be sitting down when he confessed the truth.

James smiled. "Sure."

Where to sit wasn't a dilemma in her small living room. She had two love seats, facing each other, with a coffee table in between. Natalie hadn't put the chocolates on the table but wished she had, especially when she saw the way James was looking at what she'd placed there: the overnight package he'd sent for her to keep.

"I thought you might want it."

James answered by lifting his troubled gaze from the box to her. "Something else I wish I knew. So, Natalie, ask."

"Well, it seems that whatever's—" *caused you such anguish* "—bothering you has to have something to do with the past two months in Boston."

"Can't argue with that."

"So it must have something to do with Christine."

"Or Grant."

Or Christine and Grant.

"I know what's bothering me, Natalie. I just don't have the answer."

"But talking about it might help."

"It might. It's very difficult to acknowledge to myself, much less admit out loud."

So he hadn't told anyone. How could he in Boston? But he was in Seattle now, home now, and he was going to tell her. Trust her. *Tell me what you need, James. What I can do.* He'd already told her what he needed: to speak the painful truth aloud.

He hadn't spoken it yet. Was reconsidering, perhaps, the fairness of transferring such torment to her. *Too late, James. Way too late.*

"You're still in love with Christine."

The words drew him from his conflicted thoughts. "What did you say?"

"You're still in love with Christine."

"I can't believe you think that."

"But . . . aren't you?"

"Still in love with Christine? No, Natalie. I'm not. I worry about her. I care about her. But I'm not in love with her. I'm beginning to think you weren't listening to what I said."

"When?"

"In bed." His voice was deep with remembrance. And deeper with desire. "So much for Shakespeare."

"I was listening."

"And?"

"I remember you said the past is prologue."

"But?"

"That was when the past, Christine, was three thousand miles away."

"It doesn't matter where she is, or where I am. I'm not

in love with her." James smiled, and desire glittered anew. "Really, Natalie. I'm not."

It was impossible not to believe him. There wasn't a chance she'd try. And if only this astonishing moment could last.

It couldn't.

James needed to tell her something. Something else.

And Natalie needed to hear.

"What's troubling me is Grant."

Natalie followed his gaze to the box on the coffee table.

"What's in there?"

"A nine-by-twelve manila envelope Grant hid beneath floorboards in his bedroom the day before his arrest."

"And inside that?"

"I don't know. I haven't looked. I do know what it's purported to contain."

"Which is?"

"Crime-scene photos and souvenirs from thirty-plus murders, all unsolved and on file at the FBI. The killings span many years, twenty states, and until shortly before Grant's arrest were determined to be unrelated. Which they still may be. But when an FBI profiler took another look at the data, he saw something that suggested the murders could be the work of a single killer."

"That hadn't been considered before?"

"If so, it had been dismissed. All the victims were women, but the similarities ended there. They ranged in age from eighteen to fifty, and from very rich to very poor, and in physical appearance were more different than the same. Additionally, the cause of death varied from murder to murder."

"Serial killers tend to have fairly firm preferences, don't they? Both in the victims they choose and the way they kill them?"

"That's certainly the conventional wisdom. And I don't know—Grant doesn't know—what it was that suggested a link to the profiler at the FBI."

"The profiler didn't tell Grant?"

"No. He wanted Grant to look at the data cold, to see if he came up with the same conclusion. That's the way Grant wanted it, too."

"The criminologists I've seen on television have been pretty unanimous in their opinion that Grant's as intuitive as any profiler they've ever worked with. Plus he's got the hard science to draw on, his extensive research on the psychopathic mind."

"Grant's one of the best. Some would say *the* best."

"Including Grant?"

"No. He gives best-profiler honors to the fellow who's asked him to consult on this case."

"Who must also hold Grant in high regard—so much so that he asked for Grant's input at a time when Grant was under suspicion himself."

"Grant was grateful for the vote of confidence and intrigued with what might be an atypical—even unique—serial-killer case. He doesn't know if it is. The package arrived at his office the day before his arrest. He told me he'd glanced at the photos but didn't have a chance to study them."

"You said there were souvenirs as well?"

"Replicas, provided by the families, of personal items

the killer took from his victims."

"Like jewelry."

"That's the most usual."

"And in this case?"

"Grant didn't tell me. I'm not sure he even knew. He realized his arrest was imminent. Both leaks and rumors had increased dramatically. Grant worried about break-ins at his office by the tabloid press."

"So he took the profiler's data home."

"After first offering to return it to the FBI. In another vote of confidence, the profiler told him to put it in a safe place and look at it when he was released from jail. Grant says the crime-scene photos are among the most disturbing he's ever seen. Since he didn't want Christine finding them, he put them beneath the floorboards. It was a hiding place he'd used before. This wasn't the first time he'd been sent materials on unsolved murders he felt were too sensitive to leave at work. He hadn't shown Christine the hiding place, and seriously doubted the police would find it. They hadn't during their previous two searches. But he'd feel better, he told me, if the envelope wasn't there. He asked me to remove it from the house and send it somewhere safe. Which I did. Without telling you what was inside."

"You knew I wouldn't open it. I'm just as glad I didn't know." Natalie stared at the box, still wrapped in its overnight packaging, and felt a chill as she thought about the horrors inside. Or not. "You said Grant told you what it's *purported* to contain."

"You do listen to me, don't you?"

"Every word. And what's worrying you is that Grant

lied to you about the contents." It wasn't just a worry, Natalie knew. It was a torment. Not the sort of thing caused by a little lie between friends—particularly when James had already forgiven Grant a far greater betrayal. The theft of Christine. So if this was a lie, it must be a monstrous one, a gargantuan betrayal. "What do you think is inside?"

"Another question to which the answer is 'I wish I knew.'"

"Did Grant ask you not to look?"

"No."

"So you could."

"And will."

"But you're not in any hurry to."

"I'm torn between wanting to rip it open right away—and never open it at all."

"If you believed he was telling you the truth, you'd open it right away."

"No. If I believed what he was telling me, I'd never open it. I wouldn't have to."

"You've already said you will open it."

"That's right. Which means I don't believe him. The trouble is, he could be telling the truth about what's in the envelope and I'd still have my doubts."

"About what?" Natalie asked, even though, this time, she knew.

And this time she'd do what James wanted and needed her to do: listen to the unspeakable admission he had to make.

"Grant's innocence in the murder of Paris Eugenia Bally." There. He'd said it. And he suddenly felt peace—

because of Natalie . . . who was waiting for him to clarify his doubts about Grant's innocence. Which shade of guilt, in other words—unwitting accomplice, willing conspirator, cold-blooded assassin? "I think it's possible, Natalie, *more* than possible that Grant intended to kill her, planned to kill her and did kill her."

There wasn't the slightest doubt—of him, of his sanity—in her thoughtful green eyes. But she wanted to comprehend, to the extent such an aberration could be comprehended, the reason for Grant's crime. If there was a crime. "Why, James?"

"Why did Grant kill Paris? Or what makes me think he did?"

"Either. Both."

"The why is easier. He believed he could do it and get away with it."

"He was wrong."

"I'm not so sure."

"He's in jail."

"Where, all along, he expected to be. Wanted to be."

"To get the show on the road."

"Yes. His show. From the beginning he maintained that once he saw the evidence that was used to frame him, he'd be able to point the detectives in the direction of the real killer. There was a confidence in the way he said it. But it was a confidence I shared."

"You believed in his innocence."

"And in a system that ultimately sets an innocent man free. But now I think it hasn't been Grant's innocence that made him so certain—it's the arrogance of his guilt. He believes, perhaps even knows, that he's committed the perfect murder. He's loving every minute of it, savoring the prospective triumph. He particularly likes toying with me. I suspect he wants me to know what he's done—and that there's not a damned thing I can do about it."

"But you do know, and you'll never let him get away with it."

"I'll never want to let him get away with it. But I have no proof, Natalie. None. And I can assure you that the evidence Grant has planted against whoever it is he's decided to frame will be very incriminating indeed."

"He'll have made a mistake. Psychopaths always do."

"Grant may not be a psychopath."

"He'd have to be if—"

"He really did what I think he did? It is just what I think, Natalie. I don't *know*. I can't know without proof."

"But what about Grant's arrogance, his toying with you, his wanting you to know?"

"It could all be a game."

"A *game?*"

"Or a test. To see if Grant can trick me into making a groundless accusation."

"For what purpose?"

"No purpose. Just another of Grant's mind games—for want of a better term."

"Another."

"One of psychology-major Grant Monroe's favorite college pastimes, right up there with plotting perfect murders. The games were harmless, and played primarily with his professors, never with me. Our friendship wouldn't have survived, as I'm sure he knew. And our friendship was important to him then. Far more important to him than to me."

"I wonder how important your friendship is to him now."

James smiled. "Ever since he torpedoed it by falling for Christine?" The smile disappeared. "Either it's not important at all, or more important than ever. That's why this could be a test. Do I really believe he's capable of murder?"

"Which, whether or not he killed Paris, you do."

"Yes. I do."

"So he is a psychopath."

"Or he may be something worse. More evil. Someone for whom killing is no more than the ultimate intellectual challenge—the perfect game. And even if he is a psychopath, he's spent his adult life studying the mistakes other killers typically make."

"He'll have made a mistake, too, and you'll have your proof."

"Assuming he killed Paris."

"Assuming he killed Paris." And assuming he had made a fatal mistake, and James's accusations were believed, and Grant was convicted. That was the path of least torment. A swift and unambiguous journey from crime to justice. But what if Grant, though fully capable of such a slaughter, had not, in fact, killed Paris? Or had, but so flawlessly that even James couldn't find the mistake? Or had, and was set free on a technicality? Or, or, or. . . . I know what's bothering me, James had said. I just don't have the answer. James might never have the answer. But he'd keep searching, a path of unrelenting torment, but the only path a man of honor could take. A noble path, but ultimately, Natalie feared, a hopeless one. Natalie looked down at the Pandora's box that lay between them. "Maybe he's already made a mistake. Maybe the proof's right here."

"Grant would never make that kind of mistake. He knows that if he gave me anything that might be evidence of a crime I'd immediately turn it over to the police. He wants me to wonder, though, to worry until I finally make the decision to see what's inside."

"Which, when you do, will prove that you didn't believe what he told you about the contents."

"That's right."

"The envelope could contain exactly what he said it did, photos from unsolved cases at the FBI."

"Yes. It could. Or it could contain photographs taken by Grant himself—sexually explicit portraits of his lovers, including, I suppose, Christine."

"That's something Grant does?"

"He used to. In college. Does that strike you as strange?"

"Not in college." Or high school, Natalie thought, remembering, regretting. All the girls in her crowd had posed nude for their boyfriends. Modeled for them, they'd told themselves. It hadn't seemed a big deal at the time, the only risk being if an adult happened upon the risqué photos. The privacy afforded by digital photography, not to mention the ease of creating and disseminating pornography, hadn't existed then. "Did Grant take Polaroids? Or did he develop the film himself?"

"Polaroids. I never saw them, by the way. Never

wanted to. Not Grant's or any of the other nude photos of girlfriends that floated around the dorm."

"That was gentlemanly of you."

"I'm not sure the girls in the photos would have cared. But looking at them would've felt . . . voyeuristic."

"You think Grant may still be taking such photos?"

"I don't know. It's not something he'd have mentioned to me either way. But if so, and in the spirit of a test, that's what could be in the envelope. Natalie?" When she didn't look up, James reached across the coffee table, touched her chin and gently lifted it. Then he took his hand away. "I'm sorry. I shouldn't have burdened you with this."

"Yes, you should have. I was just letting myself get a little mired in a swamp of what-ifs—and what-if-nevers."

"I believe I'm familiar with that swamp."

"I'm sure you are. Will you promise me something?"

She expected a frown. Hesitation. Perhaps a disclaimer or two. *We'll see. That depends.*

But James neither frowned nor hesitated. "Anything."

"Oh!"

"That surprises you?"

"I guess I've never gotten an unconditional promise before."

"I trust you not to ask me to promise anything I can't deliver."

"Oh." *Oh.* "Well, this is definitely something you can deliver. I'd like you to promise that whenever you wander back into that swamp, you'll take me with you. Or, if that's not possible at the time, you'll tell me all about it when you can."

Now he hesitated. And frowned. "It's a very deep and murky swamp."

"I know."

"Will you make me the same promise?" he asked.

"Yes."

"Then you have my word."

"Thank you."

"Natalie? Thank *you*."

"Talking has helped?"

"No. Talking to you has helped. Now it's your turn to talk to me."

"About what?"

"Whatever's worrying you and has nothing to do with Grant or Christine."

"What makes you think there's anything?"

"I heard it in your voice last night, when I awakened you."

"I don't have any worries, James." *None that fit the criteria of the only kind of worry you want to hear—one that has nothing to do with Grant or Christine.*

"You're sure?"

"Positive." *My only worry, you see, has everything to do with Grant and Christine. It was Christine, after all, who told me you hadn't wanted children until you fell in love with her. And now I'm pregnant, James, with your baby. And the way you've been looking at me, the way you're looking at me even now, with desire—and more—makes me wonder if I should simply tell you. Because I see such tenderness on your face and maybe, maybe, a hint of love. But how would I know? I've never been loved. And now there's this new worry. Yes, I've wan-*

dered back to the swamp. Alone. A promise broken already? No, because it's one of those worries you don't want to hear. It has everything to do with Grant. And Christine. Whom you don't love anymore. But you might be in love with her again—who wouldn't love Christine?—if Grant was convicted of murder and Christine was free.

"Natalie?" His voice was harsh. Startling.

"Yes?"

And commanding. "Tell me what you were thinking about. The truth."

The truth. She could do that. "I was thinking about the last time you were here." *And the precious life we created.*

"Not a pleasurable memory, I guess."

"A *very* pleasurable memory."

"But?"

"Well, I suppose I was just thinking it was too bad it couldn't happen again."

"Why's that?" The startling harshness was gone. But in its place, and also startling, was the fierceness of desire . . . and the gentleness of—maybe, maybe—love. "No wait, let me guess. I look too awful."

Natalie cast an appraising glance at the sexiest man she'd ever seen. Oh, he was pale and gaunt. But so vital. So alive. And wanting her so much.

"Not too awful," she murmured. "But I wonder if we should grab the chocolates on the way to the bedroom. You know, just in case."

"That in my weakened condition I need extra sustenance?" Amusement sparked a new fire in his gleaming blue eyes. He rose and extended his hand. "Come with me, Natalie."

James led her to the bedroom, not stopping for chocolates, and proceeded to show her that she was all the sustenance he could possibly need.

12

Operating Room Seven
Queen Anne Medical Center
New Year's Eve, 10:38 p.m.

"Okay, Kathleen." The anesthesiologist nodded as he spoke. "She's under."

"Okay." Taking a deep breath, Kathleen made the careful incision through Georgia Blaine's massively distended abdomen and into her pregnant womb.

Delivery by C-section went quickly, even when there were seven babies waiting to be born. And Kathleen's weren't the only gloved hands that would be lifting the tiny bodies from the ebbing sea of amniotic fluid to the sterile blue towels awaiting them. Once safely in the towel and freed from the umbilical tether, each of Georgia's babies would be taken to his or her preassigned team for clinical assessment and immediate intensive care, followed by transport via incubator to the Neonatal ICU.

Only one of Kathleen's partners—Stephanie—assisted in the actual delivery, but all of them were there, witnessing the near silent drama of seven new lives, seven brothers and sisters, entering the world virtually at once.

The obstetricians' spoken words were simple and few. Baby One—a girl. Baby Two—girl. Baby Three and Baby Four—twin boys, one placenta. Baby Five—a boy. Baby Six and Baby Seven—twin girls, two placentas.

And maybe Stephanie's thoughts, like Kathleen's, were simple as well.

A simple wish, a silent prayer.

Be happy, little one. And may you live your dreams.

It was the wish, the prayer, Kathleen made for every baby she'd ever delivered, always at that breathtaking moment when she first held the newborn infant, adrift from its mother. She provided a comfortable place, she hoped. And a comforting one. A warm and soothing welcome to the world.

The Blaine septuplets were delivered in under seven minutes. All seven had impressive Apgar scores at both one and five minutes, and all weighed in at between two-pounds-thirteen and two-pounds-fifteen ounces. The remarkable uniformity of size was greeted with relief. No baby had been deprived of nutrition in utero. That, and the Apgars, and a gestational age almost a month beyond what any previous septuplet pregnancy had achieved, made for cautious celebration in the recovery room.

"They're beautiful, Georgia," Kathleen said to the groggy new mom. And the beaming new dad. "They look very good. Small but strong. And well nourished."

"Thank you. Thank you so much."

"Don't thank me. It was a privilege to go along for the ride."

"We should name them all Kathleen," Georgia murmured.

"Don't you dare. Your sons would have major issues with that, and each of your daughters deserves her very own name."

Georgia, groggy and drifting, floated on a new smile to another thought. "Three sons. Four daughters. Thomas! We have seven children!"

"I know, my love. I can hardly believe it."

Kathleen excused herself after reintroducing Georgia and Thomas to Stephanie, who'd been involved in Georgia's care before Kathleen arrived. The Blaines remembered Stephanie, of course, and liked her, and greeted the news that she'd be following Georgia postpartum with joyful smiles.

They thanked Kathleen again, profusely, then urged her to go home and celebrate the new year.

As she was leaving the recovery room and glanced at the clock, Kathleen realized that she'd celebrate the new year not in her home, but with the man who was her home.

She even had a few minutes to swing by her on-call room, take a shower and change into a freshly laundered pair of scrubs and a newly starched white coat. Then she'd watch the fireworks with Ian, and they'd talk, in the darkness, about babies, and when eventually they slept it would be in separate rooms—but, for the first time, both would go to sleep under the same roof.

The first time of so many times. A lifetime.

Two months earlier, it had been James's pager that sounded shortly before midnight. Tonight it was Natalie's phone.

And now as then, the late-night call wasn't viewed with alarm.

It would be one of her across-the-hall neighbors, updating her not on Ian Collier—who was fine—but on the septuplets that were to be delivered by Natalie's friend, who was also Ian's friend, Kathleen . . . and about whom the hospital was abuzz. What was the austere obstetrician's relationship with the stunning CEO? Yes, Kathleen had been a Rain Mountain Scholar. That was known. But, quite obviously, there was more.

Quite obviously . . . yet not obvious at all. Kathleen had awakened Ian, saved Ian, with her voice, not her touch, and no one had seen them touch throughout the day.

The critical-care nurses deduced, correctly, that Natalie could shed light on the perplexing matter. Despite direct questioning, however, Natalie had confirmed only what was already apparent. Kathleen Cahill and Ian Collier were friends.

But hope sprang eternal, and the possibility that Natalie might eventually reveal an intriguing tidbit gave rise to the frequent updates Natalie had been most grateful to receive.

"The septuplets," Natalie predicted as she reached for the nightstand phone.

It wasn't a long reach. Only her arm had to leave James's gentle embrace. They'd been talking after loving—between loving—and had just decided to spend tomorrow afternoon, before the wedding, watching both *Dial M for Murder* and its contemporary remake.

"Hello!" Natalie greeted her caller, who indeed was

Trish, one of the critical-care nurses from across the hall.

But this update was unexpected, unwanted.

And so horrifying that the warm, soft body in James's embrace became instantly taut, astonishingly cold. Natalie sat up abruptly.

James sat up, too, and listened with dread to her lovely voice transformed by despair.

"What? *No!* I don't understand. He was *fine.* . . . But how could . . . I—oh, no. *Kathleen* . . . She's not? She doesn't *know?* . . . Yes. Okay. Thank you for telling me."

Fumbling, Natalie replaced the receiver. Her hands were trembling. Shivering. *She* was shivering. In his arms. "Oh, James."

"It's Ian."

She nodded. "He's dead. I don't know why. *They* don't know why. He just . . . arrested, Trish said. They've been trying to resuscitate him. They're still trying, but it's hopeless."

"What about Kathleen?"

"She's not there. She doesn't know. She was in the operating room, delivering the babies, when the code blue began. She wouldn't have heard, and no one called the OR to tell her. They decided not to, I guess. But now no one knows where she is. The trauma chief is looking for her, to tell her in person. She's going to be devastated, James. She was so happy. She loved Ian so much."

James felt her silent sobs, her flowing tears. He felt them start, and he felt them stop.

Natalie straightened. "You have to go to her, to help her, don't you? That's what Ian would want you to do."

"Yes. It is what he'd want, and I do have to go. But

come with me, Natalie. Kathleen's going to need a friend."

"Two friends," she said. "You and me."

13

Queen Anne Medical Center
New Year's Eve, 11:49 p.m.

Foggy. Kathleen smiled at the mental self-portrait, for in her twenty-fourth hour of wakefulness, especially following a steaming-hot shower, foggy was apt indeed.

And since she had nothing but lovely things to do between now and sleep, no patient-care responsibilities—no cares at all—she surrendered happily to the fogginess of her tired brain. Her thoughts floated to a lovely but possibly tricky idea: convincing Rob Traynor that his patient could be discharged directly from ICU-telemetry to home, tomorrow, for his wedding.

Kathleen believed she could convince the trauma chief. Ian wouldn't be without medical expertise standing right beside him as he—and she—exchanged their vows. But if Dr. Traynor would like to attend the ceremony, and dine with the wedding party at Canlis afterward, both bride and groom would be delighted to have him.

Maybe an invitation to a wedding was the way to broach the subject of Ian's discharge. We're having a wedding, Rob, and we'd love it if you could come. Bring a guest if you like. Oh, and could you make sure the groom gets there, too?

That would be her approach, Kathleen decided as she left the on-call room. And it would work.

The thought came with a smile, to her lips, to her heart, to her soul.

And to the body, low on sleep but afloat on happiness, that insisted on a two-steps-at-a-time dash up to the Surgical ICU.

James and Natalie had made their way through the crowd that had gathered between Natalie's apartment and the medical center to watch the Space Needle light show that was only minutes away. It was a festive crowd, eager with anticipation, thrilled with a midnight clear and oblivious to the sadness that would greet them when they turned on their radios during the car ride home.

James and Natalie knew that sadness. It weighted them but didn't slow them as they climbed the hill, entered the hospital and followed the signs to the Surgical ICU.

"May I help you?" the receptionist asked. Her polite query was automatic. Her distraught expression belied the fact that this night was anything but routine.

"I'm Natalie Davis. Trish called me about Ian Collier. She knows I'm a friend of Kathleen's. And this is Ian's attorney, James Gannon."

The receptionist nodded and pointed to a corridor off to the right. At the end of it, outside a corner room with its door shut, stood a worried sentry. Dr. Rob Traynor. Natalie recognized him from the press conference. Such happy news, such a short time ago.

James recognized Rob, and vice versa, from a vehicular homicide case that James had prosecuted. The trauma chief had been an expert witness for the state.

James introduced Natalie, explained their respective relationships to Ian, to Kathleen, to Trish—who, with several other nurses, were on the other side of the tightly shut door.

The room was a bloodied battlefield following the code, and Ian himself the mortally wounded hero. The nurses were preparing both for viewing by Kathleen.

"Where is she?" Natalie asked.

"I don't know. The best guess is she stopped by her on-call room after delivering the septuplets and will be showing up here any minute now. I tried to track her down but missed her, and decided just to wait for her here."

"So she still hasn't heard?"

"Not as far as I know."

"What happened?" James asked.

"To Ian? He had a cardiac arrest. That we know. We also know that it was detected as it happened. He was being monitored at the time. But despite virtually immediate resuscitative efforts we couldn't bring him back. Whatever caused him to arrest was both catastrophic and irreversible. A pulmonary embolus. A massive MI. A cerebral bleed."

There was nothing more to say.

They became three worried sentries then, keeping watch on the shiny linoleum corridor down which Kathleen Cahill would walk.

Like a bride walking down the aisle to her groom.

For one foggy moment, as Kathleen rounded the corner and saw the trio awaiting her arrival at the end of the corridor, she felt like that bride. Her witness, Natalie, was here. As was James, Ian's witness, whom she'd never met but recognized from an article Ian had sent her. And Rob, whom she hadn't yet invited but was planning to.

The judge and her husband were probably in Ian's room discussing the vows that would soon be exchanged—for in his eagerness to begin their life together, Ian had changed the time of their wedding to the stroke of midnight, when fireworks would illuminate the new-year sky.

The fog evaporated with piercing sharpness, a blinding ray of sunlight stabbing through a fleecy cloud.

Kathleen wished for true blindness—that she wouldn't see, would never see, the expressions on the faces that watched her.

"No," she whispered, dreading, knowing.

"He was asleep at the time. And he never awakened, Kathleen. Never knew."

"But . . ."

"We don't know what happened. Why it happened."

"I'm so sorry, Kathleen," Natalie murmured. "We're so sorry. This is James."

Kathleen nodded, vaguely. "I have to see Ian."

"Of course," James said.

And Rob added, "The nurses are still with him. I'll see if they're ready for you."

"We're here to help, Kathleen. In any way we can. We hope you'll let us."

Natalie wasn't certain that her quiet offer had been heard. Rob opened the door only narrowly as he passed through, then closed it again once he was inside. But the door was where Kathleen's attention was focused.

The door—and what lay beyond—and surely the screams inside her were so loud she was deaf to all other sounds.

Not completely deaf, Natalie realized as Kathleen slowly turned toward her. Not deaf at all. There was simply a delay between the words being spoken and Kathleen's response—as if, like a signal bouncing off a satellite, the words had traveled first to a faraway place.

"Thank you." Kathleen's polite reply was bleak.

Then Kathleen was faraway again, her gaze returning to the door, a stare that didn't blink, didn't move, until the door opened and Rob, Trish and two other nurses emerged from the room.

Rob met the emotionless stare. "You can go in now."

Without a word, she did.

It was nice of the nurses to have swabbed the blood from the floor and to have gathered up discarded needle caps, medication vials, IV tubing, alcohol wipes. Nice, but unnecessary.

Kathleen never saw the mopped-up battlefield.

Nor did it occur to her that the nurses' kindness had extended to swabbing blood from Ian's face, a gentle washing, and draping him with an unstained bedspread, and placing his head, resting comfortably, on a freshly plumped pillow, leaving illuminated only a fluorescent light above the sink.

Ian could have been sleeping. Dreaming. In the dim light, his lips weren't blue, and one could imagine, in the shadows, the faintest flicker of his lashes as his dozing eyes watched the race of dreams.

Kathleen might have thought he was sleeping if she didn't touch him, which she wouldn't, never had—but now did.

He was cold. Too cold, the physician knew, to be alive.

Too dead, the woman knew, to feel her touch—too late.

But it wasn't too late to whisper to the man who knew her voice so well.

Eventually, soon, Ian Collier would take up permanent residence in her heart. She'd keep him close, keep him alive, deep inside.

But Ian was still in this room. Floating nearby.

"I know you can hear me. You can, can't you? *Please hear me.* You have a son, Ian. *Another* son. Our baby's a little boy. I know it. I *feel* it. We're going to raise him together. I can't do it without you. I *won't* . . ."

14

"**S**he's not going to come out on her own," Natalie said to Rob and James as if she and Kathleen were the closest of friends and she knew the other woman's heart as well as her own.

Natalie was speaking *her* heart, of course. If the man she loved had just died, she'd want to stay with him, whispering to him, forever. Till death us do part wasn't enough. Death wasn't.

At some point, a human being would have to intervene.

That point, Natalie thought, was fast approaching. Kathleen had been with Ian for over an hour. The orderlies had arrived to transport him to the hospital's basement-level morgue.

Not that the orderlies were in any rush.

No one was.

Except, apparently, Natalie. Why? Because Kathleen *would* stay with Ian until someone intervened—and at some fast-approaching point Kathleen's vigil would do her far more harm than good.

"I think I should go in and get her," Natalie said. Then, not waiting for the men to concur, she added, "I'm going to."

Natalie entered the shadowy room. It was quite dark now. The city lights, aglow until the new year had well and truly arrived, had since been doused.

Natalie crossed to the bed where Ian lay and where Kathleen, leaning close, spoke to him softly.

Natalie couldn't hear Kathleen's words. She didn't want to, didn't try.

"Kathleen?"

A delay preceded Kathleen's reply. "Natalie?"

"Yes. It's me. I wonder if maybe it's time . . ." *to let the orderlies take Ian away.* Natalie wasn't going to speak the words. Nor did she have to. "Don't you think?"

Natalie heard Kathleen's shuddering breath. "I guess so. Yes."

"Okay. I'll wait for you over here, in the doorway."

Natalie saw Kathleen's answering nod. Barely. Her eyes hadn't yet adjusted to the darkness. Her vision didn't have a chance to adjust. Didn't have time. After a final whisper, Kathleen rose and walked, a regal shadow, a wounded queen, toward the door . . . and into the dim—but too bright—corridor beyond.

Rob and James stood in the glare.

When she reached them, Rob spoke. "There's something I need to tell you, Kathleen."

Something worse? Something more? "What?"

"Why don't we go into the staff lounge? We'll have it all to ourselves, and I'll explain."

"If what you want to tell me is that Ian died because of a terrible mistake, that he was given the wrong medication or—if that's what it is, I don't want to hear it." *I can't hear it.*

"That's not it, Kathleen. Just the opposite."

"The opposite?"

"Come with me. Please."

Kathleen acceded to Dr. Traynor's request. And she didn't object to his suggestion that James and Natalie join them.

As promised, they had the lounge to themselves.

"Ian was dying," Rob began. "At most, he had a few weeks to live."

"Dying? No!"

"He had cancer. Widely disseminated, very aggressive—"

"You're wrong. Ian would have told me."

"Ian didn't know. His last exam, a routine physical, was ten months ago. Even in retrospect, there wasn't any indication of a tumor at that time. And he's been relatively symptom-free, I gather, despite what we now know was advanced disease."

"Relatively? You mean he was having symptoms?" *Oh, Ian, why didn't you tell me?*

"He may have had one symptom, experienced once. He described feeling breathless at Crystal. He attributed his shortness of breath to the altitude, and said it got better, that he acclimated, as he skied."

"So even that may not have been a symptom," James said.

"That's right. In which case—and remarkably—he may have been entirely symptom-free . . . despite the presence of end-stage cancer."

"I can't believe he had end-stage cancer."

"But he did, Kathleen. There's really no doubt."

"How do you know?" James asked.

"The chest X ray was suggestive, and lab results were consistent with metastatic disease. But the diagnosis, which was definitive, was made by examination of tissue and bone fragments obtained at surgery." Rob didn't expand on his answer. It wasn't necessary to say that Ian Collier's ribs were so filled with tumor it was no wonder they'd shattered. And splintered. Also unnecessary would have been his amazement that Ian's paper-thin bones, eroded from within, hadn't fractured long before the accident at Crystal and with no more trauma than a too-deep breath or a hearty embrace. Rob also didn't elaborate on the tissue-type, a poorly differentiated adenocarcinoma, or the fact that the primary was unknown. But he reiterated the seriousness—and lethality—of Ian's illness. "He had known metastases to bone and radiographic spread throughout his lungs."

"He also had lesions in his brain." Dr. Kathleen

Cahill's voice was calm and clear. "That's why he didn't see Corey on the ski slope . . . or me, standing in the doorway, while he was on the phone."

"Ian told you he didn't see Corey?"

"Yes. He didn't see Corey, *never* saw him, yet he had a clear memory of everything else about the run. He must have had visual field defect." Kathleen's eyes, calm and clear, focused on Rob. "Did you tell Ian about the cancer?"

"No."

Kathleen nodded, and stood. "I have to go."

"Go where?" Natalie asked, standing, too. They all did.

I don't *know!* I have no place to go, nowhere to be . . . except with Ian. *In the morgue.* She could stay with him all night, talking to him about happiness, and babies, and it would be all right, not too crazy, and she'd be stronger in the morning. Strong enough to deal with . . . every-thing. No, you *won't* be. You'll never be. Not if you hide in the morgue tonight, denying the truth of Ian's death just like you denied the reality of your mother's disap-pearance until it was far too late for the police to find her killer.

You have to face everything . . . now. You have to be strong. *Now.*

"Ian's office. He'd made funeral arrangements. The information's there." She turned to James. "I'll need your help. Ian told me you'd have power of attorney in the event of his death."

"I'd like to help, Kathleen. In any way I can. Begin-ning, if you like, by getting the file."

"There's a safe-deposit key, too."

"Okay. Where?"

"In the same folder, labeled 'Miscellaneous,' in the lowest file-cabinet drawer."

"All right. I'll get the entire folder. But let me take you home first. Give me five minutes to get my car and I'll meet you at the main entrance."

"I'm staying here tonight."

"Here?"

"Yes."

"But—"

"I have to go."

Kathleen was across the lounge and out the door before either man could stride ahead of her to open it. As Kathleen made her swift escape, James looked at Natalie, the only one of the three who hadn't moved.

"Do you think you should go with her?"

"No. I think she really wants to be alone. And I think she really wants to be here, in the hospital, as long as Ian is."

"This has to be a stunning blow for her," Rob said. "Yet she seemed so calm."

"Calm?" Natalie moved then, a palms-up gesture of disbelief.

"You have to admit," James added, "she expressed very little emotion."

"She didn't dare. She was barely functioning as it was, and if she'd let her emotions out . . . Couldn't you see how hard she was fighting to maintain what little control she still had?"

"No."

"Not really. Tell us," James said, "what you saw."

"What I saw—and what I know is true—is a lovely, emotional, compassionate woman who just lost the man with whom she planned to spend the rest of her life. Now she's the one who's lost. Devastated beyond words. She's afraid of breaking apart. That's why she had to get away from us. The more we reached out to her, the more precarious her control."

"And it would embarrass her to lose control?"

"Probably. But I don't think that's what's making her fight so hard not to. She's afraid of what will happen if she does break apart."

"Which is what?"

What happened to me when my bones broke apart and my baby died. It had been a shattering of self into knife-sharp splinters and particles of dust. The particles had blown away, lost forever in the emotional storm. And the self reassembled from the remaining splinters? Never the same, never again whole—

"Natalie?"

The soft worry in James's voice, and the tenderness she saw in his dark blue eyes amended from anguished to hopeful her unfinished thought. *Never the same, never again whole, unless by some miracle you're given a second chance.*

"She's afraid," Natalie told him. "Afraid that if she breaks apart, she'll be broken forever."

"So what do we do for her?"

"Be there if she'll let us. When she'll let us. We may have to be a little obstinate, to push back gently when she tries to push us away."

"But we shouldn't do that now?"

223

"I don't think so. She looks so exhausted, and is hanging on by such a delicate thread. She needs to be alone. To rest if she can, to sleep if it's possible."

"Sleep may be possible," Rob said. "Given the events of the past twenty-four hours, both with Ian and the septuplets, no matter how much adrenaline her body normally stores, it's got to be depleted by now. She may have no choice but to sleep. Even she may not have the energy to fight what her body so desperately needs."

"Good," Natalie said. "Now we just have to figure out how to know when she wakes up, so we can be here for her when she does. Where will she be sleeping?"

"Her on-call room, I imagine, in L & D."

"So if Trish asked one of the L & D nurses to let us—" Natalie, facing the men, also faced the door. So she saw at once what they did not. And smiled. "Kathleen. Hi."

As they turned, both men saw the truth of what Natalie had told them.

"I'll need the phone number of the funeral home."

"Tomorrow," Rob said. "Not tonight. In fact, because of the holiday, it may be mid to late afternoon before the paperwork at this end gets processed." *And the body can be released.*

"Paperwork," Kathleen echoed. Dr. Kathleen Cahill had never been called upon to fill out such paperwork for her patients. Not since specializing in OB. But as a medical student, and as an intern rotating on medicine and surgery, she'd learned about the paperwork that accompanied death, beginning with the first signature: the consent for the postmortem examination. Kathleen looked at the man who had the legal right to sign that

224

form. "No autopsy, James. *Please.*"

Emotion trembled in her plea, but her pale blue eyes grew stark and cold—as cold, as stark, as Kathleen herself appeared to be. It was an illusion, James now knew. A fragile veneer of the thinnest ice. And beneath that veneer . . . fearsome emotions struggled to be free, and Kathleen fought desperately to keep them contained.

"No autopsy," James concurred softly, without so much as a glance at Rob. Former prosecutor James Gannon knew what constituted a coroner's case, when a postmortem exam was mandated by law. Ian's death hadn't been the result of foul play, nor had he died within twenty-four hours of admission, nor had he failed to regain consciousness.

"Thank you," Kathleen whispered, wanting to flee but needing to do more, say more, for Ian. She looked from the attorney who could have chosen to sign the consent for autopsy to the surgeon who would fill out the death certificate—a document that would be a matter of public record. "I'm worried about Corey, and I know Ian would be, too. It was very important to Ian that Corey not blame himself for the accident, and it would be awful, Ian would hate it, if Corey felt responsible for Ian's death. He's not responsible, of course, whether Ian's death was related to the accident or not . . . especially since it probably wasn't."

"I agree, Kathleen." Rob's voice was gentle. "About Corey and the probable cause of death. I'll talk to him myself. His father and I have already spoken several times."

"Thank you," she whispered again. "There must be

something I should do."

"There is," Natalie said. "Sleep."

"I meant something for Ian."

"So did I." This was a time to push, Natalie thought. And she did. "You need to sleep, Kathleen, to be as rested as possible for the days ahead. You heard what Rob said, that there's really nothing to do between now and mid-afternoon, so why don't we all plan to meet at three?"

"If there *is* something for me to do . . ."

"We'll find you," James promised. "But if not, let's meet as Natalie suggested. At three."

"In my office," Rob said.

Kathleen managed a nod.

Then fled.

15

Sarah's Orchard
Wednesday, January 1, 7 a.m.

"He died, Holly." Sam spoke to brown eyes that seemed to understand the sadness of the words—or maybe the baby creature heard the sadness in the voice that had become such a gentle haven in her world. "He wasn't supposed to, but he did. And I need to go to Seattle. Don't ask me why. I honestly don't know. We'll both go, okay? It's a bit of a drive, but we'll stop along the way. You're perfectly comfortable in your crate, aren't you? No, don't give me that, I know you are."

So comfortable, in fact, atop her Rain Mountain bed,

that when Sam had placed her there at midnight, she'd sighed with pure contentment as she'd sunk into its familiar softness. And three hours later, after he'd awakened her for a quick trip outside, she'd chosen to trot right back to her very own ocean-blue room.

That was what the puppy books said a crate would be if used correctly—a private sanctuary, a personal cave. Like a child's room. Sam, of course, didn't relate to a child's room as a place of wonder and secrets and treasures and dreams. Yes, his own boyhood room in the Hargrove mansion had been a sanctuary for him. But he'd hidden in that haven, alone and lonely, wondering what was wrong with him, dreaming only of the puppy he'd never be permitted to have, and imagining the secrets he might have shared with his baby brother if only his mother and stepfather hadn't decided he was a danger to their Tyler.

Sam had been grateful for his boyhood room. But he'd never trotted happily to it, nor sunk contentedly into its single bed, and as soon as he was old enough, he'd left it, left all of them, like his now-dead father had left him—without a backward glance.

Sam Collier had his puppy now, and he was grateful she liked her crate, and he was even glad he'd followed the advice of the puppy books and encouraged her to sleep in her own little room on her second night home, and not as she'd done on the first night, cuddled on top of him.

Sam had missed having the warm small body snuggled close. But Holly's comfort with her crate would make today's ten-hour journey easier for them both. And easier, too, once they reached Seattle. There'd be a few hours, several days from now, when she'd need to remain in the dog-friendly motel room he'd find while he attended the memorial for Ian Collier.

By six in the morning, when Sam had learned online of Ian Collier's death, the promise of some kind of gathering to remember him had already been set in stone. People wanted to say goodbye—including, Sam deduced with a little reading between the lines, a number of high-profile Seattleites, elected and otherwise, who wanted to give eulogies at what would undoubtedly be a locally televised farewell.

As for more tangible remembrances, Rain Mountain "spokesman" James Gannon suggested donations to any of Ian's favorite causes: Rain Mountain Scholarship Program, Victims of Violent Crimes, Make A Wish Foundation and Fred Hutchinson Cancer Institute.

"It makes him sound like a prince of a guy, doesn't it, Holly?" Sam's question was bewildered, not bitter, a mellowing he attributed to a combination of the puppy herself, the articles he'd read following the press conference last night, and the emotions that had both flooded him and drained him as he did.

And now, as he prepared to complete the journey he'd started twenty years ago, he felt both a restlessness to go and a certainty that he must.

It was time to return to Seattle.

To journey home.

To his dead father . . . and something else.

Kathleen got a few hours' sleep. As Rob Traynor had

predicted, her energy was so depleted, her exhaustion so extreme, that she eventually succumbed. Her body rested, a little, during her fitful sleep. Her brain did not.

She couldn't remember the dreams that haunted her. But she awakened gasping, as if struggling to escape the ravenous mouths of demons, only to realize, as she awakened, that there'd be no escape.

The demons didn't lurk in the netherworld of dreams. They were right here, devouring every atom of oxygen she needed to breathe, digging their talons into her womb, as if seeking sustenance there—and shredding any tiny new life to pieces in the process.

There'd be no baby.

There was no Ian.

No!

"Yes," she told herself sternly. "And you have to deal with it."

And how would she accomplish that impossible feat? Directly. Unwaveringly. Face-to-face.

Beginning now.

She stripped the sheets from her bed, made a separate pile of scrubs and coats to be laundered, and placed the bundles, which she would take to their various bins, in the center of the room. Then she retrieved from the closet the dress she'd planned to wear today—the same dress, plus nylons and heels, she'd worn into the hospital twenty-two days ago. She'd purchased the dress in New York, part of the wardrobe of stylish clothes she'd wear in her new life with Ian.

And now? She stuffed the dress, heels and nylons, and a tailored jacket into her overnight bag and donned her familiar armor of crisp white coat, freshly laundered scrubs and running shoes.

Flimsy armor, as it turned out. And unnecessary. The physician wasn't needed today. Indeed, her only responsibility was to the patient who had died—and who, before his death, had taken care of the most tormenting responsibilities himself.

Even the phone call to the funeral home wasn't—legally—hers to make.

So what would Dr. Kathleen Cahill do on this rainy day? Attend the three-o'clock meeting, collect her overnight bag, and go home . . . to face directly, unwaveringly, the ghosts of a life that would never be.

Natalie slept well, alone, yet not alone. Her baby slept within, and the memory of her baby's father caressed her, as James had caressed her, when they'd left the medical center and he'd walked her home.

They'd made the walk in silence but touching, her hand entwined with his, where he wanted it to be—and where, Natalie felt, he needed it to be. He'd come into her apartment just long enough to scan the cozy nest with his solemn blue eyes—searching, it seemed, for reassurance that it was safe to leave her, that no evil would leap from the shadows to stop her heart, to steal her away.

Natalie didn't know when James had shifted his pager from ring to vibrate. About the same time, she imagined, that Dr. Rob Traynor had made a similar switch, and for the same thoughtful reason. Kathleen hadn't needed to hear the insistent *beep-beep-beep,* the signal that Ian's many friends, media included, were calling to express their shock, their sadness, their disbelief.

The pagers would have rung incessantly, Natalie realized when James told her his new-message indicator read sixty-three. And counting. Even as he checked, the pager vibrated in his hand.

Natalie offered to help James return the calls. Or feed him Godiva chocolates as he dialed. Or she could get the folder from the file cabinet in Ian's office while he patiently responded to each message, even as new ones accumulated.

James declined Natalie's offers with a weary smile. As gracious and as tempting as her propositions were, this was something he needed to handle on his own, from his condo, while she slept.

James kissed her good-night, a caress that warmed her long after he was gone. It was two in the afternoon before she heard from him again.

He'd pick her up at two forty-five, he said. They'd drive, not walk, to the medical center. The Emerald City was in the midst of a rainstorm that gave no sign of relenting.

The downpour at two forty-five was so torrential James had to keep his eyes on the road and both hands on the wheel.

But his handsome profile told the tale.

"You didn't sleep," Natalie said.

"No."

"I should have been with you, helping you."

"You're helping me with what matters most—Kathleen."

"I haven't done anything yet. She hasn't let me. May never let me."

"I think she will. But even if she doesn't, you've helped me understand her."

"I just pointed out the obvious."

"Because I'd missed the obvious."

"Yes, but it's not your fault. I mean, you can't really help it that you're so quintessentially male."

A smile curved his haggard cheek. "That problem again."

"That problem, with which I have no problem . . . at all."

Only Natalie, James and Kathleen met in Rob's office. The trauma chief was scrubbed in on an emergency surgery. But Rob had called James, told him the requisite release papers were in Admitting. James had signed the documents on his way up.

After explaining Rob's absence, James said, "The folder was exactly where you said it would be and contained everything you said it would."

"Are there additional decisions to make?"

"Regarding the funeral arrangements, no. None."

"But other decisions about other things?"

"There will be some. Beginning tomorrow, I think. Not today."

"Okay. I have thought of something I can do. Would like to do." It had come to her as a gift. From Ian. As if he'd known they wouldn't have forty years to discuss the issues he'd insisted on discussing yesterday afternoon. . . . As if he'd known that very soon she'd need a mission to cling to while she confronted her grief. An important mission—for him. "I'll be responsible for finding Sam."

"Who's Sam?"

"Sam Worthing Hargrove. The beneficiary of Ian's will. I guess you haven't looked at it yet?"

"No. It's in Ian's safe-deposit box. But I'm afraid I didn't make an effort to see if I could get someone from the bank to let me in today."

"Oh," Kathleen murmured. "Today's a holiday, isn't it? I . . . forgot. Of course you didn't try to get someone to let you in. It's not necessary."

"I'll get the will tomorrow," James said. "But tell me about Sam."

"Ian lived with Sam's mother, Vanessa Worthing, for the first four years of Sam's life. There was a gardener's cottage on the Worthing estate in those days. Ian lost contact with Sam after Vanessa took him away. Her husband, Mason Hargrove, became Sam's father. But Sam remained very important to Ian, and when Ian created Rain Mountain, and finally had a reason to write a will, he left everything to Sam."

"That would've been over twenty years ago."

"Yes. And Ian's revised his will at least once, ten years ago. I don't know what the revision was, but I do know that Sam remained—remains—Ian's primary beneficiary. That means he'll need to be found, and told. You'll be the one to tell him about the will, of course. But I'd like to be the one who finds him." *And tells him about Ian—his life, not his death—and the great love he had, a love that never died, for the little boy who wasn't his.* "Is that okay?"

"Certainly." Kathleen's search for Ian's heir was okay, but if Ian hadn't revised his will for ten years, where did that leave the woman he'd planned to marry? Where she wanted to be, James decided. Making certain Ian's dying wishes were fulfilled. Still . . . "Ian mentioned to me that he was planning to revise his will."

"He told me that, too. But he had very mixed feelings about removing Sam. And now, since he didn't, it will give me, all of us, a chance to let Sam know how much he mattered to Ian—and what a wonderful man Ian was." Kathleen drew a ragged breath, then straightened. "I guess it's time to call the funeral home."

"Why don't I do that?"

Kathleen nodded. "Thank you."

James rose from the table and went into the outer office to make the call.

Natalie guessed he'd speak so softly that Kathleen couldn't possibly overhear, but she began to talk, adding an extra cushion of sound just in case.

"This is so difficult."

"It is. I thought I'd be better today . . . be able to handle what happened."

"You are handling it."

"Not the way I should be."

"There aren't 'shoulds' when it comes to a loss like this."

"I suppose not." Kathleen shook her head. "I keep trying to make it all right for Ian. Trying to convince myself that this was the best thing for him."

"To have died peacefully without knowing about the

cancer that would've taken his life in a matter of weeks. I've been trying to convince myself of that, too. I can even convince myself it's true. It doesn't really make it better, though, or the loss any less. The loss for you, especially."

"The loss for Ian." That loss, his loss, tormented Kathleen the most—the happiness he would miss, the joy he could have known, the forty years or so of . . . but Ian Collier wouldn't have had forty years. Or even forty days.

"Kathleen?" Natalie pushed very gently. "Where are you?"

"All sorts of places I don't want to be. Do you know what decisions James wants to discuss with me tomorrow?"

"I imagine he wants your input on the memorial."

"The memorial?"

"James has heard from so many of Ian's friends who've been wondering about a gathering of some kind, a way of celebrating Ian's life and saying goodbye, that he's already implied to the media there will be such an event. But that can be undone, Kathleen, if you disagree."

"I don't disagree. It's just that I should—yes, should—have thought of it myself."

"You have other things to think about. You."

"I can think about me later. Right now I need to look into possible venues for the memorial—"

"No, you don't. And neither does James. He's delegated that to a few of Ian's friends, all of whom want and need something to do. Once James gets the information, he'll present the various choices to you."

"Ian liked him so much."

"James?"

"Yes."

"It was mutual."

"James is being so kind to me."

"That's who he is."

"Well, I'm very grateful for his help. And yours." Kathleen tilted her head. "I think James would be thrilled about your news, Natalie. As thrilled as you are."

"Oh!" Natalie's surprise wasn't at Kathleen's words but at her sudden shift from her own loss to Natalie's joy. Kathleen wanted the new and happy topic. Obviously. And despite her grief, she'd been aware of other emotions, too—the emotions of others. Aware, and caring, and willing to listen, if Natalie was willing to talk. She was. "I don't know, Kathleen. Maybe he would be. But we really don't know each other very well. By which I mean *he* really doesn't know *me*—about me and my disreputable past."

"He wouldn't care!"

"I made the mistake of believing that once before."

"But not with James."

"No. Not yet. But this isn't the time to tell him."

And this wasn't the time, either, to discuss the issue further.

James had reappeared.

"The funeral director was expecting my call. He knew Ian personally, and will care for him personally."

"When will he be here?"

"No later than five."

"Natalie said you'd like to discuss the memorial with me."

"I would. Tomorrow. I hope to have a list of possibilities by then."

"And I hope to be quite a bit more . . . helpful by then. Who knows, maybe I'll even have found Sam."

"You're doing fine, Kathleen. And you'll find Sam when you find him. I'll look at the will tomorrow, but there's really no rush with that. The memorial's another matter."

"I'll be at the house." Ian's house, without Ian. "Just come over whenever."

"Okay. Now," James said gently, "why don't the three of us find a quiet place to have an early dinner?"

"Oh, thank you, James. But no. I'm going to stay here a little longer." *Until Ian's friend, the funeral director, ever so carefully takes him away.* "I want to visit Georgia and the septuplets, and . . . you go. The two of you."

"We'll wait for you, Kathleen," Natalie said. "Or come back later and pick you up."

"No. Really."

"The rain is torrential."

I don't care! "I'll take a cab if it's raining, and make the driver happy with an enormous tip. Or get a ride with someone on staff."

She wouldn't, Natalie knew. And James knew. But both recognized this as one of those times when it was best not to push.

16

The Worthing Estate, Seattle
New Year's Day, 6 p.m.

Sam slowed to a stop at the gated entrance. In the distance, a single light glowed through the pouring rain.

One light, a porch light, and nothing else.

No one home.

Abandoned by Ian Collier in death, as Sam had been abandoned by Ian in life, the mansion stood dark, empty.

Forsaken.

But maybe there were memories in the shrouded house, or hidden in shadows along the white-brick driveway. Memories that had been linked long ago to the emotions that had guided Sam for decades. Those same emotions had guided him to the home that had been the Worthing family residence during the first four years of Sam's life. Or so he'd learned from the article entitled "Ian Collier Purchases Historic Queen Anne Estate."

Sam knew he'd lived in Seattle during those four forgotten years. But he'd had no idea where. This had been his grandparents' home at the time, however, and it was likely he'd visited here, that his mother had brought him here, taunting them with Sam Collier—the murderer's grandson—as Vanessa Worthing Hargrove had continued to taunt them with his unsavory pedigree throughout his boyhood in Greenwich.

Maybe this was the something else that had compelled his journey to Seattle. Maybe memories and emotions were to be reunited at last.

Sam set the parking brake, opened Holly's crate and immediately had a wiggling, wide-awake puppy in his arms.

"Time to stretch our legs," he said. Tucking her inside his jacket, he stepped into the rain. "I'm carrying you, though, until we find a dry place to put you down."

There'd be dry places on the property. Clusters of rhododendrons, their leaves overlapped, would create rain-free cover for small creatures seeking refuge from the storm.

Small creatures—including small boys? Was that why he knew, as he seemed to know, the plantings they would find?

Maybe. Or maybe he just remembered learning that rhododendrons flourished in Seattle, and presumed— logically, not emotionally—there'd be gardens of them on one of the city's grand estates.

There were. The driest of which would be in the lee of the mansion itself. The massive structure loomed ahead, ghostly white in the darkness, its single light illumi- nating only a fraction of its form. It felt a little haunted, this shadowy ghost of a place where his mother's family had lived . . . and hauntingly familiar?

Not really, Sam acknowledged even as emotion offered a hopeful—and painful—explanation. The house wouldn't be familiar on a night like this. A beloved little boy would never have been out on a night like this. And for that beloved little boy, the lights inside would have been shimmering gold.

The thought—memory?—flogged his heart. He hadn't

ever been a beloved little boy . . . had he?

"Oh, Holly," he whispered. "I don't know."

She squirmed in his arms; it was time to put her down.

There was a perfect canopy of rhododendrons to the left of the mansion's covered porch. Sam set her onto a dry patch beneath the leaves. Holly studied a fallen leaf for a while, then looked up to assure herself that Sam hadn't moved, and trotted deeper into the dry terrain she wanted to explore.

She wouldn't go far. She stayed close, kept him well within sight and scent. Sam made it easy for her, not leaving the spot where he'd set her down. It was a soggy spot, and a dark one, beyond the reach of the porch light.

Sam saw, from the darkness, a second ghost, a new one.

A familiar one, he realized, as the bright white apparition neared.

Her physician's coat would have flapped in the gusting wind had it not been so weighted with rain. She seemed weighted, too, her dark head bent, her shoulders slumped, trudging toward the mansion with dread.

And determination. Sam watched her bearing change. It was a willful transformation, as if she'd given herself a stern mental shake. It took time to lift her head against the immense force that had pressed it down, and longer still for her slender frame to straighten against the battering wind.

But she did it.

She could hold her own against the rainstorm, and against the greater turbulence that stormed within. She was proving that even as he watched. She was strong. In control. But she could shatter, he thought, the way a perfect diamond would splinter into dust if struck just so.

A stranger stepping out of the shadows might be, for her, such a startling blow.

Sam retreated deeper into darkness.

She had a key to the mansion, or knew where one was hidden. He'd wait until she'd let herself in and had turned on the lights, and she'd be startled, but not shattered, by the doorbell's chime.

Maybe she'd welcome the sound with relief—and gladness that someone else had journeyed to Ian Collier's home on this stormy night.

Sam would wait.

But Holly would not.

Instinct wouldn't permit it. There was, apparently, territory to defend.

She charged from her rhododendron shelter onto the driveway, a splashing advance accompanied by the most ferocious bark she could muster.

It was her first bark, a baby one, and not ferocious at all.

But startling to Kathleen nonetheless.

Startling, not shattering. As she set her overnight bag onto the rain-soaked driveway and bent toward the tiny trembling body hunkered a full six feet away, Sam saw on her face the ghost of a smile.

"Hello there." At the sound of her voice, the barking stopped. "Who are you?"

Kathleen pondered her own question with a frown. This puppy was far too young to be on her own. And yet—Kathleen looked from the vacant front porch to the empty driveway to the pitch-black darkness of the grounds—here she was. Alone. Her golden-red coat was dry, though becoming less so, and she was obviously well nourished.

Was she a gift from Ian? A surprise to be delivered on this, their wedding night, the first of many babies they would have?

Ian might well have planned such a lovely surprise, and canceled the postnuptial dinner at Canlis in favor of dining at home with the puppy. Perhaps whoever had brought the dog had no idea that Ian Collier had died.

But anyone who cared about puppies—and this was a cared-for puppy—would never leave it alone and at large on the property. As inconceivable as that was, it was more rational than the possibility that this lovely little creature was heaven-sent.

"Ian chose you for me," Kathleen whispered. Before his death, she told herself, not after. She sank to her knees on the puddle driveway and spoke to uncertain brown eyes. "Didn't he? He knew I'd need a friend. And I do. I *do*."

Kathleen struggled for control, which didn't want to come. What control she had was as exhausted as she. But if she allowed herself to sob, to rage, the emotions she'd fought so hard to keep in check would shatter. "I can't give in. Not yet. There's too much to do. It's going to be easier with you here. So much easier. We can admire all the wonderful furniture Ian bought. I haven't seen it. It was delivered just last week. It *will* be wonderful. Ian's taste is impeccable. But he'd been worrying about what he'd chosen. Oh, I wish he hadn't worried . . . had never worried."

Kathleen inhaled a gulp of frigid air. "I need to talk about him. I really do. So, if you don't mind, I'll talk about him to you. He would've loved you, you know. He would've thought you were the cutest little thing. Which you are. If only he could've watched you grow." She faltered. "Ian bought a supply of groceries, too. I wonder if he included puppy food. I'll bet he did. We can hide out here and become friends, and . . . does that appeal to you?"

Kathleen believed it did appeal to the puppy, that she'd seen a hopeful sway of the tail. But it must have been the wind, she realized, as she extended her hand closer to the pup and the response was one of cowering fear.

"Oh, don't be afraid of me," she implored. "*Please* don't be afraid."

Sam heard the quiet plea. The desperate plea. It sounded like, felt like, the echoes of his own long-ago despair. *Hold me. Love me. Please.*

"She's not afraid of you."

Kathleen looked toward the voice as the puppy ran toward the blackness from which it had come. Still on her knees, and drowning in a rainfall as punishing as the torrent in which her mother had been murdered, Kathleen felt her mother's fear, her mother's terror, as she awaited her fate. And Kathleen wondered, as she waited for the stranger to emerge from the darkness, if at some point Mary Alice Cahill had surrendered to the inevitability of her impending death and had even welcomed, with glorious calm, the escape from pain and reunion with her husband.

No killer's DNA had been found beneath the gnawed

fingernails. But maybe it hadn't been the shortness of the nails that had precluded the retrieval of the genetic fingerprint of a murderer.

Maybe, just maybe, Mary Alice Cahill hadn't even put up a fight—not for herself, not for her daughter.

And that forsaken daughter? And now abandoned bride?

She would fight. She had no choice. She had purpose, a mission for Ian. She alone knew of his love for a little boy named Sam. She had to find Sam, tell Sam.

Sam Worthing Hargrove's heart was another heart in which Ian Collier must be, would be, kept alive.

Kathleen rose from her knees, faced the darkness from which the stranger would emerge, and tried to reassure herself with simple logic. The deep—and hauntingly emotional—male voice didn't belong to a killer but to whoever Ian had asked to come to the estate, an hour before the wedding that would never be, to deliver the puppy. Far from lurking in shadows, lying in wait, he'd undoubtedly been exploring the perimeter of the mansion in search of some room filled with light.

He was approaching her, moving from the blackness of shadows to rain-blurred gold, the puppy at home in the crook of a powerful arm, so safe there that she was curious now and unafraid.

The porch light illuminated the puppy first.

Then him. The black-haired, green-eyed stranger.

"Who are you?"

"My name is Sam Collier. I'm Ian's—" *son*.

That was all Sam would have said. He wouldn't have qualified the relationship in the way it had always been qualified, as an untended wound in a lonely boy's heart. Ian's forsaken son. Ian's unwanted son. But Sam didn't even speak the word son. Didn't have to. She knew.

And her expression made him wonder, for the second time on this stormy night, if the appropriate adjective should have been beloved.

"You know who I am."

"Of course," she whispered. "I'm Kathleen."

"I know. I saw you during yesterday's press conference."

"You were here? In Seattle?"

"No. I watched it online."

"I was going to search for you, beginning tonight. But now you're found."

"Yes." His voice was soft. Hauntingly emotional. Again. "Why?"

"Why was I going to search for you? *Oh.* You don't know about Ian."

"I know that he died."

"That's why you're here."

"Yes. But you're right. I don't know about Ian. I was hoping you'd tell me."

Kathleen nodded. Then frowned. "My search would have been for Sam Worthing Hargrove."

"He doesn't exist."

"You kept Ian's name."

I was never offered a choice. That was the truth. But because of the way she said it, as if by keeping Ian Collier's name he'd given his father an extraordinary gift, he lied. "I did. Kathleen?"

"Yes?"

"It's raining." He didn't care, and wouldn't have cared even if he'd been as drenched as she. Kathleen didn't seem to care, either. But her lips were blue. "I overheard you say something to Holly about going inside."

"Holly." *Oh, Ian, he remembers so much about you. You did matter to him. You still do.* "That's your puppy's name?"

"That is her name, but she's her own puppy, not mine."

"Who's chosen to be with you."

"Only because she met me before meeting you. Holly's not afraid of you, Kathleen. She's just a little cranky. It's been a long day." Sam wanted to take Kathleen's hand, the one she'd offered to Holly. He picked up her sodden overnight bag instead. "I take it you know how to get in."

"I have a key."

It was in her white-coat pocket and retrievable only after her trembling fingers had burrowed through the two layers of fabric that in their wetness had become one. Then the key trembled.

"Let me," Sam said.

"Thank you."

The door was easy to open, willingly unlocked. The house itself was not so receptive to intruders. Its alarm gave fair warning, however, on the off chance that whoever had breached its security knew how to disarm the system before sirens responded.

"Do you know the code?" Sam asked as he moved toward the source of the signal.

Kathleen knew what Ian had planned it to be. "Today's date."

"Month, day, year, four digits?"

"Yes. Then press Enter."

Sam punched the appropriate keys. The warning stopped.

"Good," Kathleen said. "The alarm would've been distressing for Holly."

And, Sam thought, for you. He discovered a light switch near the entrance and with a single flip turned on an array of lights, a selection that provided illumination in the foyer where they stood as well as all directions beyond.

"We need to get you warm and dry," he said.

"You, too. Both of you."

"We're fine, Kathleen. A little damp, but not the least bit cold." She was becoming dangerously chilled, and unaware, it seemed, of the peril to herself.

"Kitchen towels should work nicely for Holly," she persisted. "The kitchen's down this hallway to the left. I'll get bath towels from upstairs and meet you there."

It was a sensible plan. But its implementation was another thing.

Kathleen looked at the staircase but didn't move, and as her gaze became a stare, he saw the sadness on her ashen face.

Sadness, and dread. She didn't want to make the ascent, Sam realized. Because of what awaited her there. His father's bedroom.

And hers.

"You live here."

"I was going to. Beginning today. Both of us were."

"You were lovers." The emotion that swept through

him, a furious wanting, was one he'd never known. But Sam could identify it without difficulty. *Jealousy.* Of his father. Condemning the intolerable emotion to death, he found gentleness for the desperately sad woman before him. "You and Ian were in love."

"I loved Ian," Kathleen said. "And he loved me. But we were friends, not lovers."

Despite Sam's condemnation, the furious wanting hadn't died. It pierced deeper, in fact, became sharper. His father had been this lovely woman's friend. She'd trusted Ian Collier, loved Ian Collier, treasured their friendship far more—the softness of her voice conveyed—than she'd ever valued passion.

Because, Sam thought, she knew what he knew. Sexual intimacy was easy, trivial, compared to intimacy of the heart. There was a difference between Kathleen and Sam, though. They'd both had lovers. But only one of them had ever found a friend.

And lost a friend.

Kathleen had told Holly in the rain that Ian had furnished the home he and Kathleen would share, making choices he hoped she'd like, and worrying even though he needn't have. Whatever Ian had selected, she'd said, would be wonderful—including the furnishings for the room that would be hers.

She was shivering from her loss, from the cold. And from the dreadful sadness of seeing what the man she had loved, trusted, treasured, had chosen for her.

She'd known how difficult that would be. But easier, she'd confessed to Holly, now that she didn't have to do it alone.

Sam touched her cheek, felt its iciness . . . but had her attention. "Your bedroom's upstairs?"

"Yes."

"Okay," Sam said quietly, "let's go."

17

"To my bedroom?"

"You were planning to show it to Holly." Sam looked from wondering blue eyes to alert brown ones. Holly knew her name. Loved the way it sounded when he spoke it. And she was deliciously content to view this brand-new world from right where she was, in the warm, strong curve of his arm. "It turns out we're a package deal. So, shall we?"

Kathleen led the way, but Sam's voice guided her every footfall. This wasn't the time, he explained, for a grand tour of the mansion's second floor. They'd do that later, when everyone was warm and dry.

"Only two of the upstairs rooms are furnished," Kathleen replied as they neared the top of the staircase. "Mine and Ian's—yours."

"Mine?"

Kathleen stopped her ascent. "You're planning to stay here, aren't you?"

That had become his plan, of course. He wouldn't leave her alone with her sadness.

"I'd like to stay here, Kathleen."

A step behind her, Sam had stopped, too. And in an inadvertent moment he caught an up-close glimpse of her back. Her white coat was no longer white. The rain-soaked fabric had become transparent, as had the pale pink scrub shirt worn beneath. Her sharp bones, her quivering flesh, were fully revealed.

Sam had known this since the foyer; he'd seen what the rain had done. But Kathleen hadn't known. Her thoughts had been elsewhere, and Sam had kept his gaze elsewhere, as well, respecting her modesty.

He continued to do so now, focusing on the crystal chandelier that illuminated their journey to the second floor. "I'd like to stay here very much. But I wonder if I should find another bedroom—one other than his."

"I'm not sure there are others." She turned, oblivious to her near-nakedness and the modesty so fiercely guarded by him. What Kathleen saw, in his black-lashed eyes, was gentle concern. "Well, none that are furnished."

"The living room is furnished." Sam knew. When he'd averted his gaze as she'd led him across the foyer, he'd noticed. "I'm happy sleeping on a couch."

"No. I mean, whatever you prefer. But—"

"But?" he echoed softly. *But you'd feel safer, less lonely, if I was sleeping closer by?* Sam clamped down on the ridiculous thought as mercilessly as he'd moved to quash the jealousy of Ian he'd felt. He was unprepared, however, for the reply that came.

"Ian would want you to stay in his bedroom. It would mean so much to him, *so much,* to know you were here. I have to believe he does know." Kathleen saw the gentleness vanish, and in its place longing, maybe, and pain. "Sam?"

"I'll stay in his room." Sam managed a smile. "Onward."

"Okay." She climbed the final step, and he did, too, but once again she stopped. "His room is this way."

"I'll find it. Let's find yours."

Kathleen's room, in the opposite direction, was a discreet yet companionable distance away. She'd chosen its color palette, lavender and cream, and even empty, as it had been the only time she'd seen it, the bedroom was perfect. Which she'd told Ian. Often.

She'd hung stylish never-worn dresses in its louvered closets on that early December visit with Ian, and put well-worn jeans and turtlenecks in its built-in drawers, and looked forward to reassuring Ian in person, not simply in advance, that the furniture he'd found for her would be perfect, too.

It was. The four-poster bed, the mirrored vanity, the cushioned chair, the chaise longue. And drapes, in lace and lavender, sewn from the same fabric as the billowy comforter on her bed.

And at the head of the bed, nestled among the shams, a square pillow. Welcome Home, the embroidered script read in threads of cream. And in lavender, Kathleen.

Tears spilled at last—and far too soon.

Kathleen wiped them away.

"I can't cry. I *can't.*"

"Of course you can," Sam said. "How can you not cry when you've lost such a friend?"

Kathleen closed her eyes and became very still. And very taut. It was a bravura performance of concentration and will. When she looked at him again, the tears were gone. "Like this."

"To what end, Kathleen? To prove how strong you are?"

"I'm only as strong as I have to be."

"Which means refusing to cry?"

"I *can't* cry."

"You can. You just don't want to. Why?" Sam's voice was a little harsh.

Holly's sudden squeak said as much—and more. She needed reassurance. She got it, at once, from both of them. Sam laid a soothing hand on her back as, without a thought, Kathleen reached to touch the worried face.

Kathleen had forgotten Holly's earlier fear of her. And, safe in Sam's embrace, the puppy had apparently forgotten it, too. She greeted Kathleen's fingers with an interested pink tongue.

"Licking is kissing," Sam said. "She'd like to take you up on your offer to become friends."

"Done," Kathleen whispered as her just-kissed fingers caressed baby-soft fur.

"I'd like to be your friend, too, Kathleen. I'm sorry I pushed."

"You had every right to push, Sam. You were defending Ian, wondering how I couldn't—didn't want to—cry at such a loss. I do want to cry. It's all I want to do. But I'm not sure what would happen if I did."

"You'd cry, and then you'd stop crying."

Kathleen stroked a floppy, silky ear. "You think I'd stop?"

"I know you would."

"Spoken like a true friend."

"I hope so." Sam gazed at the shivering fingers, snow-white against Holly's golden-red fur. And journeying, perhaps, toward the warmth of his. It would be so easy to warm her icy hands in his, and heat her quivering body with his own. Easy and trivial, that physical intimacy. Sam wanted so much more. "Kathleen?"

His tone, more hoarse than harsh, startled her from a lunatic thought. If Sam Collier held her as she cried then maybe, just maybe, the tears could flow and the emotions could take flight, but she, she, wouldn't break apart.

Startled though she was, when she looked from Holly to him, the crazy thought didn't budge. "Yes?"

"Hot shower. Dry clothes. After which, if you're not too tired, you could talk to Holly—and me—about Ian."

"Tell me."

"Tell you what, James?"

"Whatever it is you've been thinking about telling me since we left Rob's office." James glanced over her naked shoulder to the clock on her nightstand. "Almost four hours ago."

"That I've been looking forward to this." *Being in bed with you, being touched by you, being consumed by you.* It wasn't a lie. The thought was ever-present. "Haven't you?"

"Always. But that isn't a worrisome thought, and the one you're not telling me is. And—" James kissed her temple "—I don't want you to be worried, much less distracted, when and if we make love."

"If?"

The desire in his eyes told her how impatient he was.

Their dark blue solemnity told her he was going to wait. "You actually started thinking about whatever it is a few minutes before we left Rob's office, sometime between when I left to call the funeral home and when I returned. At first I thought it was something Kathleen had said to you, in confidence, about Ian. At some point during dinner I decided that was wrong. I can tell you the exact point, if you like—when you checked my messages and found the one from Christine."

It wasn't as if Natalie had taken his pager without his knowledge, or had been intending to inspect his messages. She was in the market for a better text-messaging service, and the only reason she'd broached the topic, after they'd placed their orders but their dinners had yet to arrive, was to prevent herself from telling James exactly what he was demanding she tell him now.

James, quite happy with his paging service, had handed her his pager and told her how to access the messages that had accumulated since he'd checked before their meeting with Kathleen. With James's blessing, she read aloud, by candlelight, the eleven that had come in. The last of which was Christine's. *I just heard about Ian. I'm so sorry, James! I know how devastating this must be. I'll be there if you need me. I want to be. All my love, Christine.*

Christine's message wasn't terribly different from two others Natalie read aloud—from an Erin and a Tania—and James's reaction to all three was the same: a faint dip of the head, an acknowledgment of the condolence offered by a friend.

Natalie had believed her reaction to Christine's message was similarly bland—just as she'd deluded herself into imagining James hadn't picked up on her troubling thoughts.

"Here I was counting on your being the quintessential male."

"I will be," James promised, "if—no, when—we make love. But since misreading Kathleen so miserably the night of Ian's death, I've been working on improving my mind-reading skills. How am I doing?"

Natalie's sigh was eloquent. *Too* well.

"So tell me what's worrying you about Christine."

"It's not really Christine, but the authenticity, I suppose, of who she is—compared to me. Do you know what I mean?"

"I haven't got a clue."

"You probably—well, might—think I'm well educated and have a firsthand familiarity with the sort of homes I show, as so many high-end agents do. But I'm not, and I don't. I'm actually a bit of an imposter. I come from a blue-collar background, James. *Grimy* blue."

"And you think that might matter to me?"

"It would be understandable if it did."

"Not understandable to me."

"Still," she said, "I feel it's something you should know. I didn't want to mislead you into thinking I'm someone I'm not."

"You're not talking about who you are, merely where you came from. I don't believe I've been misled about who you are. Do you?"

He seemed so certain of who she was, her true self,

and it sounded to Natalie, to her heart, as if he liked that Natalie very much. In fact, to her heart, it sounded like love.

"No, I don't believe you've been misled." *I hope not.*

"For the record, I now know where you came from. And, for the record, it doesn't matter." He smiled. "Okay?"

"Okay." She smiled, too, but it wavered.

"There's more, isn't there?"

"I was a pretty wild teenager. Pretty—very . . . promiscuous."

Her modest background didn't matter to the man with the impeccable pedigree. Neither did her mediocre scholastic achievements make any difference to the editor of *Stanford Law Review.*

But his blue eyes darkened at the revelation that the woman he desired as no other had satisfied the lust of countless grimy-collared teens. Natalie couldn't tell if it was the age at which she'd given herself to anyone who wanted her, or the age of the men—boys—who'd had her, or if it was simply her wantonness that James found so distasteful.

The reason was of no consequence to her breaking heart.

Natalie steeled herself against the words James might speak—and shivered at the memory of ones hurled at her before.

I'm not a *tramp.* How can you call me that?

Because you are a tramp. A *slut.* What do you think they call a girl who gives it away? If you'd rather be a *whore,* I'll be glad to oblige.

James wouldn't throw money at her. He didn't know about the baby.

And if he did?

"I'm *sorry*." The apology, a whisper of despair, was to James, and to the baby girl who'd never know him, and to the baby girl she'd lost, and maybe even to the teenager Natalie had been—the girl who hadn't known that in giving herself away she was throwing away her dreams.

"What do you have?"

"Have?"

"Is it HIV?"

Natalie heard his anger. Saw it. "What? No. I don't have HIV."

"You don't?"

"No! I don't have HIV or any STD. I've *never* had any."

"Then why did you tell me about being a promiscuous teen?"

"For the same reason I told you about my less-than-genteel roots. So you'd know the truth and wouldn't feel misled. I'd have told you if I had HIV, James. I'm sorry you believed I was capable of intentionally putting you at such risk."

"I didn't believe that."

"Yes. You did." And it was far worse than any contempt he might have felt at her behavior as a teen. "I saw your anger. And your relief."

And now, astonishingly, she was seeing the glitter of desire set free at last.

"Here's the interesting thing, Natalie. I didn't even

think about what it might mean for me. My only thought, and the anger you saw, was what it could mean for you. I wasn't in the mood, you see, to watch you die." James said it lightly, but the huskiness of his voice betrayed the fear he'd felt beneath the fury.

The fear of losing her. "James . . ."

He kissed a trail from the corner of an eye to the tip of her nose to one side of her mouth. "Anything else you'd like to tell me?"

Just one thing. She could tell him about their baby. It felt safe enough to tell him. *She* felt safe.

But she'd made a decision, a promise to herself—and to her baby girl . . . her baby girls—the daughter inside her now and the daughter who had died. It was more than a promise. It was a belief. Or maybe a superstition. And she readily acknowledged that her promise-belief-superstition was very likely fueled by the abundance of hormones coursing through her veins.

It didn't matter. Because whatever it was, and despite how irrational it might be, she believed with all her being that she must wait until after January 6 before sharing her joyous news with James . . . that she must navigate the treacherous emotional waters of that anniversary on her own.

"Natalie?"

She felt his smile against her cheek, and her smiling lips found his. "Nothing else at the moment."

"So I can regress to being a quintessential male?"

"Please do."

18

Tummy full and surrounded by familiar treasures—
Sam, fox, crate—Holly had just settled onto her yellow
blanket on the kitchen floor when Kathleen appeared.
Promptly abandoning what would have been a languid
postprandial chew, she darted toward Kathleen, barking
all the way.

Kathleen, warm and dry in jeans and turtleneck,
greeted the assault with affection.

"Have you forgotten me already, Holly Collier?" she
teased as she sat an arm's length from where the gal-
loping pup had come to a skidding halt. Kathleen
extended her hand to the apprehensive yet interested
face. "I'm not nearly as soggy, and the hospital scents
have been washed away, but we're friends. Remember?"

"She remembers," Sam said as he knelt beside Holly.

His presence evoked memory or courage, or both—
for, with Sam at her side, Holly's tail began to wag and,
although her paws stayed put, the rest of her tiny body
followed her nose toward Kathleen's hand. When she
was within licking distance, she did.

"What *nice* kisses." Kathleen's praise unstuck Holly's
lagging paws. "Are you thinking about climbing on my
lap? You'd be welcome to."

Holly was obviously tempted but wary, and when Sam
moved away, she scampered after him. His destination
wasn't far, the yellow blanket, and after grabbing the
chew stick he—and Holly—returned to Kathleen. She
took the tantalizing rawhide treat, placed it on a denim

knee, and in moments had a warm, contented puppy devouring it.

Only after Holly was happily situated on Kathleen did Sam join her on the floor. Both gazed at the puppy, marveling at her bliss as they listened to a duet of chewing and rainfall.

"This is . . ." Kathleen's attempt to find the right word came up empty.

"Some combination of soothing, peaceful and addictive?"

Kathleen nodded. "I could definitely become addicted to having this lovely little creature on my lap."

"Holly clearly feels the same way. I think you're rapidly becoming her favorite toy."

"I doubt that. I can't imagine anything better than being held by you." Kathleen was talking about Holly. But as she heard the echoes of her words, she wondered, worried, if Sam was wondering—and worrying—that she was really talking about herself. Maybe she was. But it was an unintentional confession. Surely he could see that making provocative remarks wasn't her style. She *had* no style. Kathleen had no idea what Sam was seeing at the moment. Her own gaze remained fixed on the same glossy patch of fur she'd been studying since their conversation began. "I mean . . ."

"Holly likes being held. But she gets restless. She has other fun things to do."

His voice was pleasant. Unworried. Kathleen met smiling green eyes. "Like chewing," she murmured.

"Chewing's very big."

"What else?"

"Running. Sprinting, actually. She goes fast but not far. She likes to keep me within sight."

"And vice versa."

"And vice versa," Sam affirmed.

He was watching Kathleen now, with a vigilance that made her feel utterly safe—and in great peril. It felt as if Sam was searching for something and believed she held the answer. Worse: as if she *was* the answer. And worse yet: as if he *did* and *didn't* want her to be.

Kathleen looked to the countertop, where a Christmas tote adorned with pastel reindeer sat beside a sailor's duffel bag, then to the floor that had already become Holly's home. Her dishes were there, and her yellow blanket and her bushy-tailed fox, and beneath the built-in computer desk, where the chair had been, her sea-blue crate. And inside the crate . . . "Is that a Rain Mountain parka?"

"I was wearing it when I got her and—I'm sorry," Sam whispered as tears flooded her eyes. "It was the only way to get her home. I'll take it out. The blanket should be fine."

"No." The strangled word was all she could manage. Kathleen also shook her head, a gesture that splattered a tear or two onto Holly's soft fur. Holly stopped chewing and looked up. "I'm a mess, aren't I?"

Kathleen's question, posed to Holly, was answered by Sam. "Not at all."

"Well." She made an ineffectual swipe. "I'm not sure I could stop these if I tried."

"Don't try."

"I hate to drench Holly."

"Holly will be fine. How about you?"

"Also fine." The conviction of her words, like the words themselves, became uncertain as another wave of emotion crested in her heart and made its way to her eyes. "Will be."

Or not. This was what she'd feared, the tears that would come without warning and stop only when there was nothing left. What she'd feared, and yet, even as the tears spilled, Kathleen didn't feel herself being washed away.

Washed, yes, but not away. Washed . . . clean. And filled, not emptied.

But maybe this feeling of life and not death was part of the treachery of tears, an illusion that made the hapless weeper gladly comply. Or maybe it was a different illusion entirely—the delusion that while she wept she was being protected by this man, held by him even though they didn't touch.

A suddenly on-the-move Holly focused Kathleen's thoughts. The smart little thing was not about to stay where she was.

"She needs to go outside," Sam said, scooping Holly up. "She doesn't entirely understand why she gets restless like this, but she's already learning that if we go outside whenever she does, all is right with her world by the time we return. We'll be back, Kathleen. Soon. Don't leave."

Don't *you* leave! Kathleen, who couldn't stop her tears, was somehow able to prevent the frantic plea from becoming a spoken one. And after Sam and Holly disappeared through the back door, she stood. Without swaying.

Her plan had been to watch them from the window, her vision doubly blurred by tears and rain. But as she stood, without swaying, she was cocooned by a sense of calm. More treachery, perhaps—except that the tears were growing calmer, too. Receding.

And gone by the time Sam and Holly returned.

"You're still here." Sam's relief was unconcealed. "And the tears have stopped."

"I am, and they have." And, she thought, the reverse was also true. The tears have stopped . . . and I'm still here. "And all is right with Holly's world?"

"It is. So much so that she's about to crash."

Kathleen smiled at the sleepy-faced droopy-limbed puppy draped over Sam's arm. "She *is* crashing. Fast. Time for the Rain Mountain parka?"

"If it's really okay."

"It's really okay."

Sam settled Holly in her crate, on her parka, a transfer accompanied by soft words and gentle patting, both of which ended only when, with a sigh, she fell asleep.

Sam retreated quietly and watchfully. Holly didn't stir.

"She's probably down for the count," he whispered to Kathleen. "But maybe we should leave her alone."

Kathleen nodded, and Sam flicked off the kitchen lights. Moments later they were in the foyer, still whispering.

"How long is the count?"

"Three hours. I've just cut you off from all sustenance, haven't I?"

"I don't need anything to eat. Or drink, despite my little . . . cloudburst. Which, if it's all right with you,

I'd like to explain."

"I was hoping you would." Sam did a quick inventory of where they were—the foyer's bright chandelier, its hard marble floors—and where else they could be. The options were limited. Her bedroom was the only room decorated by Ian that she'd so far seen and now wasn't the time to tour the others. "Why don't we get rid of some of these lights and find a comfortable place on the stairs?"

19

The comfortable place was the carpeted landing halfway up. It was spacious as well. They sat across from each other, she against the wall, he against the banister, their faces illuminated only by the porch light below.

"Your cloudburst," Sam prompted gently.

"It suddenly hit me how much Ian would've liked being in the kitchen at that moment—and that he should have been there."

"Tell me what he would've liked."

"Everything. Beginning, of course, with you."

Sam had been steeling himself to hear loving things about the man Kathleen had loved. And for that woman, who needed to talk, Sam had vowed to listen without protest. He'd suspend disbelief, he'd decided, as Kathleen shared the fiction—which she so clearly believed— about her friend.

And when the loving things Kathleen shared were lies about Ian *and him?* Sam would listen to that, too, without protest, for Kathleen—and maybe, just maybe, for himself.

"He'd have liked having me here?"

"He would've been elated, Sam. And very moved. Especially since you arrived with a cocker spaniel puppy named Holly who sleeps on a Rain Mountain parka and whose luggage—I'm assuming it's hers—is a Christmas tote bag."

"It is hers," Sam murmured as he forced more steel into his resolve to remain the kind of listener he'd pledged to be—the kind who encouraged. "You said especially a cocker spaniel puppy named Holly. Why?"

"You don't remember?"

"No."

"But when you were a child, your puppy in Connecticut was named Holly."

I never had a puppy in Connecticut. Sam didn't speak, much less shout, the protest. He said softly, "No."

"Oh. Well, Holly was the name you gave the cocker spaniel puppy who would've been old enough to bring home a few days after Christmas the year you turned four. The year, the Christmas, you moved away."

"I'd already named her?"

"And chosen her. And bonded with her. She and her littermates lived about three blocks from here. You and Ian visited her at least once a day."

"What happened to her?"

"Ian wanted to take her to Connecticut. To you."

So he said. So he lied. "But he didn't."

"No. She would've been a link with a past that it was in your best interests to forget."

265

Sam was surprised at the statement of fact amid the fiction. But he concealed his surprise that Kathleen not only knew the truth of his forgotten years with Ian Collier—forgotten because of Ian Collier—but had obviously forgiven Ian's heartless indifference to his wife and son. "Did he keep her?"

"He . . . couldn't. It would've been too difficult for him. And there wasn't a problem with finding her another home. The breeder had a list of other families, other children, who were eager to have her."

"You said Ian and I visited her."

The porch light illuminated a lovely smile. "At least once a day."

"And that she was only three blocks from here. Does that mean this is where we lived?"

"On the estate, not in the mansion. There used to be a gardener's cottage."

"Where?"

"The southeast corner of the property. Near the orchard."

Sam had been expecting the revelation—some revelation—about Holly. Kathleen's use of "especially" had forewarned him.

But the discovery that his home with Ian Collier had been beside an orchard caught him off guard, a direct blow to the heart he'd believed invulnerable to assault.

Sam responded with fury to the sucker punch. He'd been abandoned by Ian Collier. But he'd clung to fantasies—and wishes—that had been born during those forgotten years . . . and when he'd been old enough to make choices for his life, he'd given himself the orchard home and the Yuletide puppy that his father never had.

The orchard. The puppy. And . . . "Tell me about Ian and Christmas."

"Are you all right, Sam?"

"Sure. How about you? Wishing you could crash, too?"

"Not yet." Kathleen wished only that she'd succeed in making Sam understand, making him feel, the depth of Ian's love. She wasn't succeeding. If anything, Sam was becoming more remote. But she wouldn't give up. She had truth, and love, on her side. "Ian dreaded Christmas after you left."

"But you seemed to imply that he'd have liked the Christmas tote."

"Because *you* brought it, Sam. It would've felt to Ian as if you were bringing back the joy of the Christmases he'd spent with you."

"Kathleen? Enough."

"Enough? Oh, I'm sorry, Sam! I wasn't thinking, wasn't realizing, how emotional this would be for you. I guess I believed, just like Ian did, that you'd forgotten all about your years with him."

"I meant," he said, "enough of the revisionist history."

"Revisionist history? Are you saying your Christmases with Ian weren't joyful?"

"I'm saying they weren't as significant to Ian as he led you to believe. *I* wasn't as significant to him."

"Not significant? You were everything—"

"He let me go, Kathleen. He wanted me to go."

"That's a *lie!* He'd have moved heaven and earth to keep you with him. He was prepared to, but . . . She told you Ian didn't want you, didn't she? Your mother?"

"Yes."

"It's a lie, Sam. She *lied*."

She was ferocious, this woman who'd been his father's friend. But Sam had known that about her. He'd seen her passion at the press conference, and her outrage. Good for you, he'd thought then. He thought it now.

Kathleen would fight to the finish for Ian. And Sam didn't want to fight with her, hadn't expected to. Yes, he'd imagined she'd defend Ian. He was so *young,* she would say. Only eighteen. The responsibility of father-hood was too much for him. He didn't handle it well, wasn't always as kind or loving as he should've been. He knew it at the time, and tried to be better, he really did, but he couldn't. He *hated* the way he treated you, Sam, and regretted it in the years to come. Can you find it in your heart to forgive him? Please?

Sam had long since decided his response. He would forgive Ian. Maybe he already had.

But it wasn't forgiveness Kathleen was fighting for.

And it was a fight, Sam suddenly knew, that he wanted her to win.

To hell with the truth.

"Okay," he said softly. "She lied."

"You have to *believe* it."

"I believe my mother's capable of doing almost any-thing to get what she wants."

"I believe that, too."

"So we're agreed."

"About your mother. But . . . what else did she say?"

"Let's not do this, Kathleen."

"We have to. You need to know how Ian felt about you. You need to know, Sam, how much you were loved."

She'd upped the stakes.

"Maybe he loved me, Kathleen. But the fact remains he let me go."

"What choice did he have? Your mother and Mason had discussed the situation with a child psychiatrist who said it would be best for you if your relationship with Ian ended just the way it did. At least that's what she told Ian."

"I'm pretty sure that's true." Someone had to prescribe all the medicine he'd received. "How did the psychiatrist say the relationship should end?"

"Without any goodbyes. That would have created a painful memory, the psychiatrist thought, at a time when the focus needed to be on creating happy ones. That's why your move to Connecticut happened just before Christmas. Your first memories in your new home would be wonderful ones, and you'd forget Ian more quickly that way. You did forget him, your mother said. Almost immediately you replaced him with Mason. Isn't that what happened?" *Oh, please, let that be what happened. Let it have been easy for Ian's little boy.* "Sam?"

"I don't know. I have no memory of the first six years of my life."

"*Six* years?"

"I required tranquilizers for two years after leaving Seattle. I was told it was because of the mental abuse I'd suffered—"

"*No.* I won't let you say it! Ian *loved* you, Sam. You were his *life.*"

"His life, Kathleen? I doubt—"

"You *were*. And when he lost you, he lost himself. He'd have died for you, Sam, and he came very close to killing himself—by racing down mountains—after you left. That's why he was so much better than all the other skiers. He didn't care what happened to him. The accident in Kitzbühel should have been fatal. Ian thought it had been. He felt himself dying."

"But he didn't die."

"No. Because . . . do you have any memory of Rain Mountain? What it means, what it meant, to Ian and you?"

"No." No memory, just an orphaned emotion. "I don't."

And you don't *want* to know, Kathleen thought as she saw torment, perhaps anger, in his dark green eyes. You wouldn't believe me if I told you it was a dream of Rain Mountain that saved Ian's life.

"Ian never married," she said. "Risk taker though he was, the possibility of losing another child was a risk he was unwilling to take—" *until . . . oh, Ian. Ian.*

"What aren't you telling me?"

Kathleen shook her head. "Nothing. I got a little off-track. Where was I?"

"You were about to tell me what it was you didn't say. Something about you and Ian that makes you terribly sad."

"Yes," she whispered. "We were going to be married. This evening. I was going to marry my best friend, my only friend, and that wonderful friend was going to marry me. I wanted to have a baby. Ian wanted it to be his. We were going to try to have a family. We'd already started trying."

"I'm sorry."

Kathleen nodded. "Me, too. And maybe it's not really all that offtrack. Because just last night, even as we were talking about our future, the children we might've had, Ian talked about you. He'd been thinking about you, remembering you, wondering about you. He never forgot you, Sam. And what he did, thirty-two years ago, he did for you. It didn't matter how hard it was for him, or the way it would affect the rest of his life. You mattered. Only you. Ian did what he believed was best for you." The truth of Sam Collier's journey from boyhood to manhood shadowed his eyes. It had been a stark journey. And a lonely one. "But it wasn't best, was it?"

"I survived, Kathleen."

More than survived, she thought. He'd become a man who made a loving home for a puppy, as he would for the children he'd have one day. "You survived. But Ian wouldn't have. It would have destroyed him to know your life wasn't a happy one." She drew a shuddering breath. "This is why he died, Sam. So he'd never have to know."

Sam had been loved by Ian Collier. And he'd loved his father in return.

Sam knew it now, believed it now—and now, at last, the longing and hope made sense. The memories still eluded him. But their emotions sang pure and true. Loved! Loved!

And when father and son were parted, the grieving little boy had done *what?* Sam didn't remember, but he knew. How can you not cry when you've lost such a friend? He'd posed the question to Kathleen as if he'd actually had a friend—ever—and had experienced the sadness of that loss. And, as if he knew about such monumental grief, he'd even told her about crying. You'd cry, and then you'd stop crying.

To the best of his knowledge, Sam Collier had never shed a tear. Wrong! How can you not cry when you've lost such a father? He must have cried and cried, and maybe the despondent four-year-old couldn't stop, would never have stopped. Two years of sedation had been required merely to stem the flow.

The boy's tears had been dammed by the medications. He'd become a silent zombie instead of a wailing one.

And the unshed tears? They'd formed a lake inside him. It wasn't as vast, that lake of tears, as the sea to which Sam Collier had chosen so often to escape. But it was vast enough. Too wide, too deep, for friendship to travel or love to cross.

The lake's surface might appear quite calm. But it was a treacherous deception. Anger churned, always, in the black depths. And, always, sadness roiled.

The most dangerous illusion came in winter. The tears at the surface turned to ice as Christmas neared.

"Sam?"

He wasn't looking at her. His sightless gaze remained where it had drifted to the shadowed wall. But her voice, both delicate and intrepid, drew him from thoughts as black as the abyss that kept him far from love. And it sounded, that fearless voice, as if she might actually be planning to make the perilous passage to him.

Didn't she know the fight was over?

"I believe you, Kathleen. I believe he loved me."

"He did. And I think you loved him, too."

She was stepping onto the icy lake. You loved him, Sam. You *can* love. This tear-filled lake isn't the obstacle you imagine it to be.

The lake's vastness didn't seem to worry her. Her legs were long, and strong. Nor was the ice the danger it should've been. She was graceful. She could glide. And if the ice shattered and she fell into the churning depths below? Even that didn't trouble her, Sam thought—so long as he was there, welcoming her, wanting her.

He did. He would. And both would drown.

Sam looked at her then, expecting her to be close. And she was, even though neither had moved. Her heart was very near, its message shining in her eyes . . . and fading as she saw the message in his.

"Yes." His voice was as harsh, as stark, as his ice-green gaze. "I loved him, Kathleen. But that was a lifetime ago."

Sam saw the hurt his harshness caused, as if she truly didn't understand that she was offering him far more— too much more—than he could offer her in return . . . and as if she truly didn't sense that he, too, was in the fight of his life. He struggled to do what he knew was best for her—oh, yes, he was his father's son—rather than what he wanted to do. Touch her, hold her, never let her go.

Touch me, hold me, love me. Emotion was singing again, singing its chorus of longing and hope, this time with an improbable refrain. It's *not* too late. It's *never* too late. Hold her! Touch her! *Love her!*

Sam smiled. "Here's what I think. Bed for you and, for me, reflecting on what you've said. I do believe what you've told me. I promise, on reflection, that won't change. But I'd like to make sense of it if I can."

"To make sense of the senseless—why your mother lied."

"That's not as hopeless as it might seem." Nothing is as hopeless as it might seem. "The key is to figure out what she wanted. The lies will have been necessary steps to achieving that goal."

"Have you heard the saying 'A mother can only be as happy as her unhappiest child'?"

"No. But in the interest of differentiating mothers like mine, whose happiness is entirely independent of her children's, from authentically loving ones, a modifier like 'true' or 'ideal' would need to be added."

" 'Unselfish, unvengeful' would also work. No offense."

"None taken. You think she lied about Ian to get revenge?"

"I don't know. Ian believed she was happy—enough—with their relationship and only left because something better, Mason Hargrove, came along. But I've always wondered if Ian was seeing their life through rose-colored glasses because of his own happiness in being with you. You, not your mother, were the center of his world."

"That wouldn't have gone over well with her. She needs to be adored. Demands it. She said Ian was cruel to her. Abusive."

"Never!"

"I believe you. She hated him, Kathleen. And she tried to make me hate him."

"To punish him for not adoring her?"

"I wouldn't put it past her. Mason wanted to send me back to Ian when I was six. He didn't want me anywhere near the baby brother they were about to bring home. She was enraged that he'd suggest returning me to the monster who hadn't loved me—or her."

"I hate her." Fresh tears flooded her eyes.

"Don't, Kathleen."

"Hate her?"

"Cry."

"Why not?"

"Because they're my tears, not yours. Mine and Ian's. And," Sam said, "they've already been spilt."

A lakeful of them. A vast and treacherous expanse in which even the most intrepid traveler would surely drown.

As she was drowning now, Sam thought. Her face was a portrait of confusion and despair.

And such loneliness, a loneliness she accepted, it seemed, as if she wasn't the sort of woman anyone would bother to save.

Or want.

"Kathleen," he whispered, reaching out to her. Touch me. Hold me. Love me.

Her confusion deepened at his touch, then surrendered to it.

She was drowning. They'd both drown—together.

Or, together, both would survive.

20

Sam stood at the kitchen window, gazing at the winter-morning darkness, when Kathleen appeared.

He saw her reflection in the glass and turned.

"Good morning."

"Good morning," she echoed to the man who'd touched her as no man ever had . . . and whose caresses she'd wanted, needed, in ways she'd never imagined she could.

She'd touched him, too, in wanted ways. Needed ways. She'd known how to touch him . . . somehow. He hadn't told her, hadn't shown her. But she'd known. She'd been quite brazen, in the darkness, and soft, too, welcoming all the desire, and all the passion, he had to give. He'd been quite fierce, in the darkness. And tender, so very tender.

It had been an illusion. The woman in bed with Sam Collier didn't exist. That sensual creature, so womanly and so free, had been a figment of emotions gone wild. A one-time figment—and a hopeless cliché. Kathleen had heard about strangers being bonded by death and affirming their aliveness by bonding—intimately, sexually—as she had done with Sam.

It was human. It happened.

But it wasn't real.

Was it? No. Even though it seemed as if Sam wanted it to be. Believed it could be. Believed *she* could be.

"Did you sleep well?" he asked.

"Yes." So well that, after falling asleep in his arms, she hadn't awakened once throughout the night. Had he been there, too? Leaving only to take Holly outside, every three hours, then returning to her bed? Kathleen didn't know. But something, someone, had kept the nightmares away. "Very well."

"But not for as long as I thought you might."

"Seven is late for me." Kathleen looked from too-intense green eyes to Sam's puppy. She was in her crate, its door wide-open, snoring. "But early for Holly?"

"She's not a morning puppy. At least not in the dead of winter. But come spring, I bet she'll be up at dawn. Kathleen?"

"Yes?"

"We'd better talk about it."

"It?"

"You know what I mean. Last night. You and me. In bed." *Loving each other.* "Remember that?"

She nodded. "Last night was . . ."

As Sam waited, with fraudulent calm, his mind taunted him with pronouncements from Kathleen he did not want to hear. A *huge* mistake was one. Or *just* what I needed, Sam, the trivial, easy intimacy of sex. You're very good, you know. I'm sure you know. Sexy and daring. Maybe the next time I find myself drowning in grief we could do it again?

Or . . . his brain shifted gears, taunting him with the way he'd describe making love with Kathleen. The way he'd already described it in his heart.

Homecoming.

"Peaceful, soothing, possibly addictive?" Sam suggested.

All of that . . . and so much more. Kathleen frowned at the thought, and amended it. But not real. "Not me."

"What wasn't you?"

"Last night. I'm not really . . . passionate."

"Could've fooled me."

"I *did* fool you."

"You pretended I was Ian."

"What? No! Ian and I weren't lovers. I told you that."

"You also told me you were planning to have his children."

"The new-fashioned way. With syringes."

"So you weren't pretending I was Ian."

"No."

"Who was I then?" *Who was it, Kathleen, that you wanted so much?*

"You." *You, you, you.*

Sam smiled, then touched her lovely face with exquisite tenderness. "And you were you, Kathleen. *You.*" The you, he thought, you want to be—and are with me—and will be with me for as long as you like. Forever, if you like. Sam wanted that forever. He hadn't the slightest doubt. He could tell her right here, right now. But even if that was what she wanted, too, as perhaps she already did, she wouldn't believe it, believe *in* it, in them . . . yet. So, as if this was just another morning in their forever, Sam said, "Why don't we have breakfast and discuss our plans for the day?"

"Doesn't the world understand it's supposed to stop

spinning?" Natalie's question came after finishing a phone call with her office. She hadn't said much during the conversation, merely transcribed the long list of messages, each on a separate slip of paper, that had accumulated since New Year's Eve. Her assistant had called her apartment at eight-thirty in the morning. "At least until after the memorial—or even our visit today with Kathleen."

"I can do that by myself."

"I know. But . . ."

"I'll be sensitive with her. I promise."

"I know that, James. I just wanted to see her, too. But I have competing offers on a property on Bainbridge Island, and it looks like one of my clients has decided to celebrate the new year by purchasing a fixer-upper on Capitol Hill, and in between handling those deals—which I really feel I have to do—I've got phone calls to return." Natalie flipped through the pieces of paper, found the one she wanted, handed it to James. "Including this one."

"Vanessa Worthing Hargrove," James read. After reading further, he added, "I wonder what, if anything, would make her world stop spinning."

"Certainly not the death of Ian Collier."

"No. Why don't I deal with this? It's an estate issue, and not an urgent one."

"Ian bought that home for Kathleen."

"I know he did."

"But if he hadn't revised his will in ten years. . . . Can you do something?"

"Like editing his will?" James's smile didn't erase his

worry—or Natalie's—about Kathleen. "No. But I'm not going to rush it into probate, either."

Natalie nodded. Sighed. "Well. I'd better get dressed . . . get going." Her words, a pep talk to her reluctant self, didn't spark any immediate action. She stayed on one of her living room love seats, a coffee table away from James, who sat on the other—as they'd sat on New Year's Eve, talking about Grant and murder and the possible grisly—or sexually explicit—contents of a certain UPS box. The box had been relegated to the floor, and the discussion itself, which had taken place a mere thirty-six hours ago, had been exiled to another lifetime. "Remember the good old days when our greatest concern was whether or not Grant was a psychopath?"

"I remember. I'd thought—and hoped—that once I was away from Boston, I'd realize I was wrong. Instead, I feel more convinced than ever that I'm not."

"What are you—we—going to do?"

"We're going to watch your movies, and I'm going to open the box, and we'll take it from there."

"But not," Natalie said, "until after Ian's memorial."

James had enough to do in the aftermath of Ian's death. And Natalie knew he wanted to give his undivided attention to those solemn tasks.

"That's what I figured. Grant's exactly where he needs to be, and the preliminary hearing isn't for another two weeks."

Sam, Kathleen and Holly were on their way to Ian's room when James arrived. It would've been the last stop on their tour of the estate.

They'd spent an hour in the dining room, sitting at the table, with Holly exploring beneath it, admiring what Ian had chosen, talking about him. And just talking.

They'd wandered to the living room after that, staying even longer there, and when it was time for Holly to go outside, they'd walked in the misting rain to the place where the gardener's cottage had been.

Vanessa's parents had had the cottage demolished within days of evicting their daughter's disreputable live-in lover.

But the orchard remained.

"I live on an apple orchard in southern Oregon."

"Southern Oregon. Where?"

"In a town called Sarah's Orchard."

"Of Apple Butter Ladies fame." Kathleen gazed at him thoughtfully. "Ian loved their apple butter. He discovered it about a year ago—and was hooked."

"What did you think?"

"Of the apple butter? I haven't tried it yet. Ian was going to send some to me in New York, but we decided . . ." *to wait.*

Sam saw the sadness, touched her cheek with his hand and her heart with his own. His hand fell away before he spoke. But his heart held her tight.

"You didn't wait when it came to the important things, Kathleen. Ian knew you trusted him to be the father of your children."

"Yes. He did."

Kathleen waited until the renewed flood of sadness reached its natural ebb. The morning had been filled with moments like this, for both Kathleen and Sam.

They'd learned to welcome such moments . . . not to rush them away.

"The Apple Butter Ladies use your apples, don't they?" she asked eventually. Then, because it wasn't quite possible for Sam to reply, she added, "I know they're not really *your* apples, they're their *own* apples, but they do just happen to live in your orchard—don't they?"

"They do."

"He knew, Sam. Ian *knew*. In some magical way. That's why he loved the apple butter. It connected him to you."

"That's pretty magical."

"Do you doubt it?"

Sam smiled at the woman with whom he'd fallen hopelessly—no, hopefully—in love. There was very little Sam Collier doubted when it came to magic. Not anymore. "Not for a second."

They'd lingered in the mist until a tired Holly plunked down in the rain-wet grass. By the time they reached the mansion she was asleep on Sam's shoulder. She roused a little as the doorbell chimed, and a little more when she heard the new male voice speaking her name—for she, too, was being introduced.

But soon, and with the sigh that heralded her surrender to sleep, she snuggled against Sam's shoulder.

James was relieved to see the Kathleen who greeted him.

Natalie would be relieved to hear about Kathleen, so much so that James felt a sudden urge to let her know. But, he realized, it had far more to do with missing

Natalie than any reassurance he might give about Kathleen.

James was in very deep with Natalie Davis—and it was exactly where he wanted to be.

The three adults and sleeping puppy settled in the living room Ian had furnished with such care. James presented what he felt was the best venue for the memorial—the Grand Ballroom at the Wind Chimes Hotel. And for the reception that would follow, he suggested the hotel's glass-enclosed atrium an escalator ride away. The tribute would take place on Monday, January 6, beginning at four, unless Kathleen—or Sam—had a problem with that.

Neither did. James moved to the speakers' list next. There was no shortage of people who wanted to eulogize Ian Collier, and who would do it well.

"There are also a great many who volunteered," James said, "only to have withdrawn the offer after failing my test."

"What test?"

"The one in which they try saying what they'd like to say aloud. The people who've withdrawn their offers got about as far as I did—halfway through the first sentence—before having to stop. Still, if there's something either of you would like to say, or would like me to say on your behalf . . ."

"No." Sam and Kathleen replied as one. "Thank you."

Neither embellished. Didn't have to. They'd be as unable to speak as James would be, and for the same emotional reasons. Nor did any of them say, because it didn't need to be said, that Ian wouldn't care.

Ian had said enough final farewells to friends and colleagues that he would've known the healing power of such a coming together. But he would've encouraged speeches only from those to whom such speaking mattered, and who felt comfortable doing so. He would've felt the same way regarding flowers, music, a video tribute, a photographic display.

All of which, as it happened, were in the works and for the right reason: the busyness of such projects, having something to do, was healing for those who'd taken on the various tasks.

The menu for the reception was also in the works. And, an hour ago, it would've been another issue of no consequence.

But that was an hour ago.

"Scones," Kathleen said. "With apple butter from Sarah's Orchard."

"He loved Sarah's Orchard apple butter." James drew the kind of breath he would've needed to draw, often, during a eulogy for Ian. "He kept a supply for everyone to enjoy in the coffee room at the office. I'm not sure how much he had in reserve. A case or two, maybe, but definitely not enough. I'd better track down the Apple Butter Ladies and give them a call."

"I'll do that, James."

Hearing the same precariousness of emotion in Sam's voice as he'd felt in his own, James accepted the offer without questioning it. "All right, Sam. Good. Thank you."

That was all they really needed to discuss.

But James had made an interesting discovery. "I took

a look at Ian's will. Since you're both here, I might as well tell you what it says. You were half right, Kathleen. Sam's a principal beneficiary—"

"What?" Sam whispered.

"And so," James said to Kathleen, "are you. Ian left his estate equally to both of you."

"That can't be. Ian told me he'd last revised his will ten years ago."

"That's when he added you."

Both beneficiaries were stunned. And reluctant. And saddened. They wanted Ian, not his fortune. It would take a while for Sam and Kathleen to process the revelation, much less think of the numerous issues that would logically arise.

"Next week, or the week after, we can begin to discuss the inheritance in greater detail." James paused, letting that sink in, before posing a question to Sam. "Have you been in touch with your mother?"

"Not for twenty years."

"Then you don't know. She left a message for a Realtor friend of ours." James's glance toward Kathleen made it clear she was included in the "ours." "She's interested in this property—for her son."

Sam's smile was wry. His eyes were cold. "Her other son. My half-brother, Tyler."

Sam hadn't been in touch with Tyler, either, for twenty years . . . in touch with Tyler—ever. Vanessa and Mason had made good on their vows to keep the boys apart. And believing there was something terribly wrong with him, Sam had been an accomplice to their mission. He'd made a point of staying away from Tyler Nathaniel Hargrove, even though he'd longed to be close.

There wasn't anything wrong with Sam Collier, after all—except that he had a brother he didn't know. But would know.

"Did your friend talk to her?" he asked.

"No. Her message was that she'd be coming for the memorial and wanted to see the property then."

"She won't be coming for the memorial." The tone of Sam's voice, the sudden sense of danger, made his sleeping puppy stir. He stroked her gently, banished the sound of his fury. "Or stepping foot on the property. Ever. That's another call I'll make. Right after the call to Sarah's Orchard. In fact, maybe I should make those calls now—unless there's something else?"

"No. That's all."

"Okay." Sam transferred a limp Holly from his shoulder to Kathleen's. "I'll phone from upstairs. I don't plan to raise my voice, but my tone may not be a happy one for either of you to overhear."

"Holly and I will walk James to his car," Kathleen said. "And thank him over and over for all he's done."

Sam's first call was to Clara MacKenzie, placed from the cream and lavender bedroom where he and Kathleen had made love.

Clara was delighted to hear from him again, and so soon, and before Sam could explain the reason for his call, she updated him on events since New Year's Eve.

Ryan's Susie was possibly the loveliest young woman she'd ever met, and the newlyweds were definitely moving to Sarah's Orchard in June, and Ryan was very much hoping to work for Sam. He'd been trying to reach Sam, to talk about that, plus schedule a time when he, Susie and Clara could meet Sam's puppy.

When they finally got around to Sam's reason for calling, Clara expressed immediate sadness about Ian Collier. She knew he'd died. She'd read about it in the paper. What she hadn't known, and with the revelation her voice grew sadder, was that Sam was Ian's son.

Sam told her about the memorial and the apple butter they wanted to serve. And serve it they would, she replied. She'd start defrosting the autumn harvest this instant and whip up as large a batch as Sam could possibly need. Ryan and Susie would drive the cases of apple butter to Seattle and—

"They can spend the night at the Wind Chimes," Sam suggested. "My treat."

"That's not necessary, Sam."

"But I'd like to, Clara."

"Well," she said, "I know they'd love it."

Sam's second call was answered by the man who'd wanted to return him to Ian three decades ago.

"It's Sam, Mason. Is my mother there?"

"Yes, Sam. She is."

Sam heard as hisses the whispers from three thousand miles away. Then the familiar voice of the mother whose own happiness had nothing to do with the happiness—or unhappiness—of her firstborn child.

"Sam! You can't imagine how often I've prayed for this day."

"Save it, Mother, and listen. I'm in Seattle, in Ian's home. You're never going to own this property, and you'd be well advised to steer clear of Seattle, and of me."

"I'm not going to listen to this!"

"Yes. You are. I know about your lies, you see. I'm prepared to share everything I know with Mason and Tyler. I think they'd be interested, since you lied to them, too. You had to punish Ian, didn't you, for loving me and not you? You wanted me to hate him as much as you did. Well, guess what, it didn't work."

"You have no idea what kind of man he was!"

Her voice, shrill and wary, gave ample proof that Sam had hit the mark. Ian Collier had loved Sam but not Vanessa—and Ian's spurned lover made both son and father pay. "Why don't you put Mason on the other line? He and I can compare notes."

"No!"

Sam heard fear in her voice, as if Mason would be more displeased about her lies than she could easily handle. It seemed her adoring husband wasn't as tightly wrapped around her little finger as he'd once been.

"No? All right. Actually it's Tyler I'd like to talk to."

"You *can't.*"

Sam hadn't expected his thirty-year-old brother to be at the family home, and he knew full well that his mother's vehement *cannot* was really a *may* not. But he asked, as if he didn't know, "He's not there?"

"What? No. But you can't get in touch with him. I won't—"

"Allow it? You really don't have that kind of control. Not anymore. We both know I can find him on my own. And will find him. But I'm also willing to make a deal with you. I'd like you to tell Tyler that you were mistaken about my father, that he wasn't a monster and neither am I, and that you believe—as I do—that it's time for the two of us to have a chance to be the brothers you and Mason wouldn't permit us to be."

"I *don't* believe that."

"Then lie. We know you can, and I assure you it's worth your while. In exchange for making it possible for Tyler to get in touch with me—without prejudice—neither he nor Mason will be told the truth about Ian and me."

"Do you promise?"

It was a plea, not a demand, and it was as surprising to Sam as Vanessa's fear. And as real. "I'm not the liar in the family. The more relevant question is, do you promise?"

"Yes."

"Good. You know where I am. The number's listed in Ian's name. I'll look forward to hearing from Tyler. Soon."

"I'm hanging up now, Sam." The familiar haughtiness had returned. She was the aggrieved mother who'd devoted her life to an ungrateful son. "Please don't ever phone here again."

"I wouldn't consider it," Sam whispered into the already disconnected line.

He listened to the emptiness before hanging up. It was a while before he left Kathleen's room.

And it was without thought, but no hesitation, that he went to Ian's bedroom before joining Kathleen and Holly downstairs.

No embroidered Welcome Home, Sam pillow adorned Ian's never-slept-in king-size bed. Ian's bedroom, Sam's bedroom, was hardly an embroidered pillow kind of place.

But its decor—white, blue, steel, teak—was a very male blend of snow and sea.

Of father and son.

Of welcome home, Sam, welcome *home.*

Sam crossed sea-blue carpet to a windowed wall. Ian's bedroom wasn't the largest, Kathleen had told him, nor did it have what most home buyers would regard as the mansion's most fabulous view.

But it was the room Ian had wanted, precisely because of its view of apple orchard, Seattle skyline and, on a clear day, Mount Rainier.

Today wasn't clear. But it was silvery. And fingers of winter sunlight caressed the dormant volcano's freshly fallen cloak of snow.

Sam had seen such an image once before, on the cover of the Rain Mountain prospectus he'd requested a week before he turned sixteen.

Once before? The query came from deep within. How about an infinity of times? An eternity of memories so treasured they could be misplaced, perhaps, but never die . . .

All the happy memories would be recalled and reunited with the emotions that had been orphaned for so long, and they'd be as bright and joyful as the one that came to him now in the silvery light. . . .

"Daddy! Daddy! Daddy!" the boy in the orchard squealed as he pointed. "Look!"

Ian looked, of course. And because it was also part of their happy game, he said, "Well, what do you know, Sam, it's Mount Rainier."

And Sam, laughing, gazed from snowy mountain to loving eyes. "No, Daddy!"

The father's eyes grew wide. "No, Sam? What's your name for it then?"

"Rain Mountain, Daddy! Rain Mountain."

21

Atrium, Wind Chimes Hotel
Monday, January 6, Epiphany, 3:15 p.m.

The official memorial for Ian Collier wouldn't begin until four o'clock.

But the impromptu memorial had been going on since two. It consisted of the very people who had loved Ian most—and couldn't possibly have delivered eulogies without uncontrollable tears.

They'd arrived early to check that floral deliveries had been made, and that an ample supply of easels had been provided for the many pictures of Ian to be displayed, and to worry about seating—the Grand Ballroom suddenly seemed far too small—and myriad other details the hotel staff had entirely under control.

There wasn't much, really, for the volunteers to do. And even less that the staff wanted them to do. With a little encouragement, and a bounty of Sarah's Orchard apple butter and freshly baked scones, they turned their full attention to reminiscing about Ian. Some sat at pink-clothed tables. Others strolled beneath the emerald-glass wind chime made by Giselle Trouveau.

All were glad to be here, among friends, sharing memories.

The killer had known that his quarry would arrive early. James Gannon had legitimate pre-ceremony things to do. And it was quite wonderful, in the psychopath's opinion, that Ian Collier had been so popular that *he* could walk, unobserved, through the milling crowd.

The murderer needed to avoid being seen by either Natalie or James. It wasn't hard to do. The auburn-haired real estate agent and the Rain Mountain attorney only had eyes for each other. The discovery of a relationship between Natalie and James made the killer's plans even more delectable—and gave him something to do between now and four, when he'd make the call he was so restless to make.

He'd have waited until four, despite his restlessness and even if the delectable twist hadn't presented itself. *Her*self. He felt very strongly that Ian Collier's memorial should proceed as scheduled.

He hoped it would be quite wonderful, too, and looked forward to watching its televised portions later, on tape.

The killer felt a fondness for Ian Collier and wished they'd met. During the past few weeks, ever since learning the name of the woman Ian Collier intended to marry, he'd made a study of both bride and groom. In the beginning, his Internet investigation had focused on the bride alone. It had been a specific search, in pursuit of straightforward answers—yes or no.

The questions were similarly straightforward. Was Kathleen Cahill the daughter of Mary Alice? And, if so, was there a physical resemblance between the two?

The answer to the first was easily found. And, because the answer was yes, he moved—with some urgency—to address the next. But locating an online photograph of the good doctor proved problematic. He broadened his search to include Ian, in the hope that he'd uncover an engagement photo in a Seattle newspaper. There was none.

Eventually, he'd come upon a just-posted addition to the Queen Anne Medical Center Web site, a black-and-white headshot of the newest member of the hospital staff. He had his answer—another and emphatic yes. By then, however, he'd become intrigued with Ian Collier. And since he had nothing better to do while he waited for Boston Homicide to tumble to the obvious, he passed away the restless hours reading every Ian Collier article he could find.

Hour upon hour. Article upon article. Viva l'Internet, he'd mused. And long and healthy lives to the bleeding hearts who'd decided that, among other luxuries, prisoners should be entitled to unmonitored access to the World Wide Web.

He and Ian had much in common. Born with nothing, they'd both fought tooth and nail for even the most basic necessities. And both had achieved far more than anyone would have imagined men from their impoverished beginnings ever could.

Then there was the greatest bond of all: both had murder flowing in their veins.

Admittedly, Ian was merely descended from a killer, whereas he, the kindred spirit Ian had never met, was the real McCoy. But in his magnificently timely death, Ian Collier had helped him immeasurably.

Had Ian not died exactly when he did, thus creating a distraction for James Gannon when the killer needed it most, all the clever planning leading up to today's murders might well have been for naught.

Today's murders. How he loved those words. And he had three killings to look forward to now, three to savor when the time came—not just two. He had Ian to thank for that as well.

If Rain Mountain's CEO hadn't wanted to buy a new home, no telling how long it would've taken for James and Natalie to become the lovers they so clearly were.

The killer owed Ian Collier an unblemished memorial.

And Ian would have it.

"Where's Holly?" James asked when he rejoined the others at the table. He'd been called away—there'd been an issue regarding where, in the ballroom, the speakers would sit—just moments after introducing Natalie to Sam.

"At home," Sam answered. Home. Where, in less than three weeks, he and Kathleen would be welcoming his brother. Tyler wanted the chance to be brothers. He'd longed for it, too.

"Ryan and Susie are puppy-sitting," Kathleen explained. "We'd been planning to leave Holly alone, thinking she'd be more comfortable by herself, but there was so much tail-wagging when Ryan and Susie arrived with the apple butter we were happy to accept their offer to stay with her this afternoon."

"I can't wait to meet little Holly," Natalie said.

"You will," Kathleen replied. "We should have had you two over this weekend." But we were learning about each other, she thought. Being with each other, saying hello to our love even as we were saying good-bye to the man we loved . . . the man who in his death, by his death, brought us together.

"No, you shouldn't have!"

Kathleen smiled. "Well. We *will* have you over. To meet Holly and see the house. Ian made everything so beautiful. . . ." Her gaze fell to her hands, folded on that pink tablecloth. As she stared down, adrift in sadness, Sam's left hand lightly covered both of hers.

"Ms. Davis?"

Natalie followed the sound of her name to a uniformed bellman. "Yes?"

"I'm sorry to intrude, but someone from your office is in the lobby. He says it won't take long, but he really needs to speak with you."

"Oh! Okay." Shrugging, she explained to the others. "There are no true real estate emergencies. But there are plenty of issues that are perceived to be. I'll be back soon."

Very soon, she vowed, glancing at her watch as she made her way across the atrium floor.

It was three twenty-five. And even though she and James, like Kathleen and Sam, were planning to sit toward the back of the ballroom, it seemed prudent to begin finding those seats by quarter to four.

Three twenty-five. Quarter to four. Already this January 6 was almost two-thirds gone. It had been a lovely day, the anniversary of her first baby girl's death, a day during which there'd been uninterrupted stretches of time, calm between storms, when James had been able to stop long enough to say the things about Ian that his heart had been needing to say.

James had said those things—his love, his grief, his fury at the unfairness—to her.

The remainder of the day would be lovely, too. A gentle, cherishing farewell.

And tonight, after midnight, once Epiphany had come and gone, Natalie would tell the man she loved about his baby.

Natalie was smiling as she neared the lobby. Smiling and floating and not seeing her assailant, even when he stepped from the shadows, until his hand gripped her arm.

"*Grant,*" she gasped. "What are you—let me go!"

"Sorry, Natalie. No can do. And your only hope of keeping your boyfriend alive is to come with me quietly. Got that?"

"What are you talking about?"

"Nice try. But too little, too late," Grant informed her during their short journey to the elevator reserved solely for guests of the hotel's Olympic Suite. The gleaming brass doors opened promptly when Grant inserted his keycard, and closed just as efficiently after he'd guided Natalie inside. Once alone, he continued where he'd left off. "You know everything, don't you? Don't bother to lie. It was all over your face when you realized it was me. For fun, let's review the bidding. James thinks I killed Paris. That's a given. I made sure that's what he'd think. In case you're wondering, I did kill her. What I'm curious about is what else James thinks—or knows—or thinks he knows."

"You killed Paris?"

"Don't pretend to be shocked. I've been watching you and James. You're lovers. Obviously. Which means that unless you never talk, he's told you something about me. And you do talk, don't you? James isn't a meaningless sex kind of guy—even with someone like you. You're looking shocked again, Natalie. Yes, you heard me, someone like you. We're not in his class, you and I. We're beneath—figuratively and, in your case, literally—the great James Gannon. Speaking of the upper classes," he said as the elevator's bell signaled that its penthouse destination had been reached, "I wonder if Christine's tiring of being bound and gagged. . . ."

"Let's go find her, James."

James nodded at Sam. "I'm not sure why I'm so worried. But I admit I am."

Sam Collier knew all about emotions that didn't make sense. How very real they were—and how they had to be obeyed.

"It's probably just the first true emergency in real estate history," Kathleen said as she, too, rose from the table in the now-empty atrium.

The memorial would be starting in five minutes. And because it was being televised and regular programming had already been preempted, the ceremony would begin at exactly four.

Kathleen's worry, for despite her hopeful remark she *was* worried, had nothing to do with missing even a minute of the memorial. Had Ian been here, he'd have joined the search for Natalie, too. Ian *was* with them, in their beginning-to-race hearts, when they reached the lobby and Natalie was nowhere to be found.

It was 3:59 p.m. when the concierge beckoned to James.

"You have a phone call, sir."

Even before taking the receiver, James knew.

"You're a free man," he said.

"Hello, James. And yes, thank you, I am. The man I framed to *appear* to have framed me took my place in jail late yesterday afternoon. There wasn't much fanfare. My friends at the police department honored my request to alert the media only after Christine and I'd caught the red-eye to Seattle. And here we are, twenty-eight floors up, in the Olympic Suite. It's really quite sumptuous. As you've undoubtedly figured out, Natalie's with us. I'd have her come to the phone—or perhaps you'd prefer to speak with Christine?—but I'm afraid they're both a little tied up. . . ."

When Grant spoke again, his voice was ice. "This is what you'll do, James. I've already informed the concierge he's to give you access to the suite's private elevator. You need to come now. I kid you not. Any delay will be extremely bloody for either Natalie or Christine. I'll have to decide which of your lovers you'd miss the most. Are we clear?"

"I'm on my way."

James replaced the receiver and looked at Sam and Kathleen. Neither knew what was going on, but the man who'd done sea rescues and the woman who'd spent over a decade responding to code-blue emergencies deduced it was a matter of life and death.

"What is it, James?"

James answered as, with the concierge, they strode swiftly toward the elevator.

"Grant Monroe is a murderer. He's threatening to kill Natalie and Christine. He wants me up there right now."

"You can't—"

"I have to, Kathleen. It's me Grant really wants."

That James knew. And he felt certain Grant had a plan. Making sense of Grant's plan was something else. Murder-suicide seemed unlikely. Psychopaths didn't have that kind of remorse. And they had to win.

Grant had already proved he could commit the perfect murder, and in a daring way: by making it appear he'd been the killer, but claiming he'd been framed, all the while framing an innocent man. Was that Grant's plan now? To make it appear that James, driven to madness by the loss of Christine, had gone on a rampage? If so, there'd be three dead bodies when all was said and done. Grant, the sole survivor, would say he'd eventually subdued James, killed him, but not before James had murdered both Natalie and Christine.

The hell of it was, had James been searching in the lobby alone, Grant might've gotten away with it.

He still might.

Taking his cell phone from his suit-coat pocket, James talked as he dialed, "I'll try to get an open line to

911. With luck, I'll be able to communicate something of value to the police." He frowned as the emergency number rang and rang. "Assuming the 911 operator picks up in time."

"I'm coming with you, James. We can overpower him."

James didn't reply at once. He considered Sam's offer. As the opening elevator doors signaled that his scant seconds of thinking time were up, he declined.

"It's too risky for Natalie and Christine. It's me Grant wants. And," he said, "Grant will want to play. The best hope is for me to play along until he drops his guard— or the police come up with a viable plan."

"I don't like this, James."

James stepped onto the elevator and said, as the doors closed, "Neither do I."

Despite her own terror, Natalie had reacted powerfully to the sight of Christine. Her once-shining eyes were dull, her skin was gray, her soul was . . . gone? Not quite.

"I'm sorry, Natalie," she said when Grant, having reminded them both that screaming was useless since no one would hear them, removed the gag he'd forced on his wife on the off chance that in his absence she'd managed to hobble to the phone. "So *sorry.*"

"It's not your fault, Christine."

"That's not entirely true," Grant countered after strapping Natalie to a chair and binding her hands behind her back. "If Christine hadn't somehow gotten James to fall in love with her, none of us would be here today. And if Christine had been even slightly creative in bed, it might've been another year or two before I decided the time had come to rid the world of James Gannon. By then, Natalie, James would've long since let you go. As sexually creative as I'm sure you are, as wanton and as trashy, he would've moved on to more blue-blooded pastures."

"You're wrong about James!"

"No, Natalie, I'm right. As soon as he gets here, you'll see. Assuming you're still alive. Which you may not be if James doesn't arrive within the minute. Or maybe it's Christine I'll choose. In the meantime, where was I? Oh, yes. James was going to marry Christine, remember? What more proof do you need that pedigree trumps passion?"

"The things I did with you, Grant." Christine's bewilderment was a mockery of the joyful confidence that had once been hers. "*For* you."

The penthouse doorbell sounded—and the butcher knife was revealed.

Pressing it against Natalie's throat, its razor edge drawing tiny tears of blood, Grant raised his voice ever so slightly, and ever so pleasantly called out, "Do come in."

22

Wind Chimes Hotel
SWAT Team Command Center
Monday, January 6, 4:25 p.m.

James Gannon's cell phone was broadcasting with chilling fidelity the scenario that was unfolding in the Olympic Suite.

So far, all there'd been was talk. But it was deadly talk. Grant was planning to kill the women and James, and blame the carnage on a good man—James—who'd supposedly gone insane with envy.

And as a boasting, goading Grant Monroe insisted, he'd be believed. He'd set the stage carefully. Even when he was a prisoner himself, he'd shared his worries about James with his attorneys and with the Boston police.

Grant would feel guilty, of course, in the aftermath of the slayings. He was an expert on the criminal mind. It wasn't his expertise that had failed him, though. He'd known how unstable James had become. He'd merely been in denial. James was his friend. And even in his wildest imaginings, Grant hadn't foreseen the bloodshed in the Wind Chimes Hotel's Olympic Suite.

He was a profiler, after all—not a psychic.

A boasting, goading Grant Monroe did promise to give James Gannon a tearful eulogy.

The police experts, in the business-office-turned-command-center, knew that, for the moment, Grant was enjoying detailing to his victims their inevitable fate. He loved their helplessness, savored their fear.

And when he grew tired of playing with them?

He'd begin to kill. And no matter how swiftly the already positioned SWAT team rushed into the suite, Grant would be able to commit one murder—at least. His fury would be deadly, his madness fueled by rage when he realized the man he loathed to the point of murder had tricked him . . . had won.

The inevitability of one murder—at least—came from

information provided by James. In carefully chosen words, designed to convey as much as possible to the police without raising Grant's suspicion, the former prosecutor had engaged Grant in a dialogue that painted a clear picture of the scene.

The women, bound, were seated beside each other, facing James. He stood a distance away, at the point where Grant had instructed him to stop. Grant, also standing, had positioned himself directly behind the women, his knife at the ready to slice a vulnerable throat.

Natalie and Christine were human shields. Any assault, by either James or the police, would cost one or more lives. James and the police would attack only if they had to—if, tired of the game, Grant started to kill.

Unaware of his law-enforcement audience and believing the ultimate victory was his, Grant showed no signs of tiring yet. He was enjoying the taunting far too much.

And he wanted James to know, before he died, just how smart he was. How evil.

The hope, in the business-office-turned-command-post, was that one of the sharpshooters would find a perch with a clear line of sight.

Until then, everyone in the command post, a group that included Sam and Kathleen, listened to Grant Monroe's arrogant recounting of his crimes.

The murder of Paris Eugenia Bally—and the framing of the hapless assistant professor with an office located close, but not too close, to Grant's—had been "a breeze." Although, Grant acknowledged, a lesser man wouldn't have come close to pulling off such a perfect crime.

Grant was the best of the best when it came to murder. He knew the competition, had studied them intimately. No one else was anywhere near his league.

There'd been some interesting aspects to the Paris killing, challenges that elevated it from the entirely mundane. The forgery, for example. A stroke of genius if he did say so himself.

He'd created a journal, in what had been presumed to be Paris's handwriting. In it, her stalking had been meticulously chronicled. Over time and with great reluctance, she'd concluded the stalker was none other than Grant.

The final entry, dated the morning of her murder, described her decision to confront Grant that evening. She'd have her cell phone in one pocket and her sewing scissors in the other, ready to defend herself until the 911 responders arrived.

"She did call me that night," Grant explained. "I'd told her I was desperate to have interesting sex, unlike what was available to me at home. All she had to do was call at our prearranged time and start raving about a man outside her window. I'd come running to her rescue, and we'd spend a few incredible hours in bed. You should have seen her when I arrived. She was so ready for those hours. I must say I was tempted. But I stuck to my plan. I strangled her first. I needed her dead but not bloody when I put her prints in the journal—and placed the journal beside her bed—then started the tape and dialed 911. I had to do all of that quickly, of course. There had to be still-liquid blood in her heart when I stabbed her."

"The tape?" James asked.

"Of what the police would presume to be Paris's struggle with her assailant. Remember *Dial M for Murder?*"

"Sure," James acknowledged, as if he'd seen the Hitchcock classic many times, instead of merely having heard about it from Natalie. *Natalie.* He was so aware of the knife at her throat—so aware of her—although his gaze remained fixed on Grant. He had to keep Grant talking, and talking. . . . "I also remember the Gwyneth Paltrow and Michael Douglas remake *A Perfect Murder.*"

"I considered modeling Paris's murder after the remake. The title was so apt. But when it came to choosing the murder weapon, I just couldn't resist using her own scissors to kill her. My little homage to Hitchcock, I suppose. You'll note I'm going with the butcher knife this evening."

"And the tape?"

"Even there, I *dialed* Hitchcock in. I used bits and pieces of the stabbing scenes from both films—minus the soundtrack, of course—to provide the 911 operator with the requisite sound effects."

"What happened to the tape?"

"I tossed it in with all her others. It's probably still there. Paris's tape collection was one of the reasons I chose her. The primary reason, however, was her aversion to writing anything by hand."

"She'd never have kept a handwritten journal."

"Never. She was born left-handed. Her parents forced her to use only her right. It made for an abysmal childhood and a loathing of her parents—and of writing—that never went away."

"A loathing that wasn't common knowledge."

"Her close friends knew."

"But the assistant professor you framed didn't."

"That's right. And his feelings toward me were sufficiently negative to make it plausible that he'd want to frame me for her murder. Once the journal was revealed as a forgery, however, I'd left a trail of blood, prints, phone calls that led right to him."

"How was the forgery revealed?"

"By me, but more clumsily than I'd originally intended. Shortly before Christmas I arranged a meeting with one of the investigators. I told him I remembered Paris telling me about a support group she'd been in, one for children with residual anger toward their parents. I made it sound as if I thought one of the crazies in her group might have killed her—but, of course, I also mentioned the reason for her own hatred."

"You were going to wait until the preliminary hearing."

"Yes. I was. But that was before Christine mentioned the name of the woman Ian Collier was planning to marry."

Silence fell in the suite, and in the command post twenty-eight floors below. And, in that silence, Sam curled his own hand over the ice-cold hand of the woman who was supposed to have been his father's bride.

"You didn't open the package, did you, James?" Grant asked conversationally, ending the silence but not the suspense.

"No."

"You were going to, though, weren't you? You were skeptical of my FBI profiler story and had begun wondering if I'd killed Paris—but you also wondered if I was just playing with you. Right?"

"You know me well, Grant."

"I'm just a whole lot smarter than you are, James. You've always known I was smarter, haven't you? Since day one of our freshman year. You knew, and it drove you crazy. The kid with nothing who came from nowhere being smarter than the golden boy from Menlo Park wasn't the way the world was supposed to be. Not *your* world, anyway. But you felt guilty about your envy—especially since it was envy of someone as inconsequential as me. You were supposed to be above such a base emotion. The paragon of noblesse oblige. That's why you pretended to be my friend. Deigned to be."

"I was your friend, Grant."

"I don't think so, James. You were a pretty good fake. I'll give you that. Others were fooled. Maybe you even fooled yourself. But I wasn't fooled. You tolerated me because you had to. What you really felt, all you really felt, was contempt. I was smarter than you, but you were still better. I was scum, who by some quirk of nature happened to be brilliant, but all that made me was brilliant scum. Brilliant scum," Grant repeated, "who had no difficulty in seducing your fiancée."

"James," the seduced and damaged woman whispered. "I didn't know! I truly believed he—"

"Loved you?" Grant scoffed. "I kept you guessing, didn't I, *darling?* Even today, when I told you I needed you to let me tie you up—needed that proof of your love—you were so hopeful as you acquiesced. So pathetic. I have to tell you, James, I've been very unimpressed, and incredibly bored. Was Christine really the best you could do?"

"Let's leave Christine out of this."

"Your contempt is showing, James. But fine. We'll both be gentlemen. Although, and here I think you'll agree, honor has its downside. That's the reason you didn't immediately open the packet, isn't it? You had to agonize a while. But not forever, right? If you'd known about my impending freedom, and if Ian Collier hadn't so conveniently died, you'd have taken a peek inside. I owe a lot to Ian Collier—so much so that I've been seriously reconsidering my decision to murder Kathleen."

"Murder Kathleen. Why?"

"Why do you think?"

"I have no idea."

"Meaning I haven't convinced you that I'm slaughtering women you know in revenge for your despicable treatment of me?"

"You'll never convince me of that, Grant."

"Damn." Grant laughed. "You're a little smart, after all. I guess it's out of the question to hope you'll go to your death feeling responsible for any of the other murders I've committed, either."

"I'm afraid so."

"Well. It was worth a try. For the record, though, I'd never killed anyone before meeting you. And since then, James, I haven't stopped."

"You hadn't thought about killing before we met?"

"Smarter and smarter, counselor. Or maybe you've just read my books. I thought about it, dreamed about it, for as long as I can remember. To the extent that you inspired me to act out my fantasies, you have my undying gratitude. And you did inspire me. You were just a little too good. Being around you was like being force-fed sugar. I needed meat. Craved it. The more raw and bloody the—"

"I get the picture."

"—better. I only wish I'd met you sooner, had begun killing sooner. No other high comes close. That's why I'm not sure I can change my mind about murdering Kathleen. And maybe Ian wouldn't want me to. It's possible, if Ian Collier believed in an afterlife in which lovers were reunited, that I'd be doing him a favor by sending him his beloved Kathleen. Do you know what he believed?"

"No."

"Some friend you are. Just kidding. We've already established that you wouldn't help me if your life depended on it. Which it doesn't, by the way. You're already dead. If I find out Ian would've preferred to let Kathleen die of old age, I'll factor that into my decision-making. How's that for honorable? I must admit, scum though I am, I doubt I'll have enough honor to let her live. There's something quite thrilling about murdering both a mother and her daughter."

"You murdered Kathleen's mother," James repeated, as he'd repeated other horrific revelations Grant had made, in the hope that even if his cell phone wasn't capturing Grant's words, it was transmitting his.

"I did. During our so-called ski trip to Seattle. I went out that night, remember? Every night. I'd had it with sitting in the fraternity house watching the rain and listening to you rhapsodize about what a great place Seattle would be to live. Mary Alice Cahill was my first kill. She wasn't happy about it. Not that any of my thirty-three victims—and counting—have been happy about dying. But Mary Alice was particularly adamant. She didn't care about herself, she said. As if somehow that would sway me. But she worried about the effect her death would have on her daughter, Kathleen."

"There's something in the packet concerning Mary Alice Cahill's murder."

"You're sounding so lawyerly, James. Like you're trying to make points for the jury. There's no jury, friend. This is a bench trial, and I'm the judge. And guess what? The verdict's in. You die. And your lovers die."

"You don't want to tell me."

"What's in the packet? Sure I do. I'm a little surprised you haven't guessed."

"Photos and souvenirs from murders you've committed."

"Bingo." He grinned. "You must remember my Polaroids, James. The dirty pictures of girls I'd known. You made such a point of not looking at them. The first few pictures in the packet are dirty pictures of Christine. Very dirty. Too bad you'll never get a chance to see them. Christine's quite photogenic—in a pornographic way. There's also an extremely nice picture of Mary Alice Cahill, among others, taken just moments after her death. It's better than the original Polaroid I took. It's an eight-by-ten now and digitally enhanced. The pose is also different than the way I left her for the police. I didn't know if you'd seen the crime-scene photos. But I was afraid that when you saw the photograph of Mary Alice, who's a dead—" Grant smiled "—ringer for Kathleen, you'd make a point of looking at them."

"And I'd realize the photograph of Mary Alice Cahill could only have been taken by her killer. You."

"You're doing it again, James. Speaking to a nonexistent jury. But desperate times call for desperate measures, don't they? There's even more incriminating evidence your invisible jury might like to consider. A locket, worn by Mary Alice, and kept as a memento by her killer. She showed it to me before she had a clue I was going to kill her. She wanted me to see the photograph of her dead husband. Daniel Cahill was your kind of guy, James. Noble. A soldier who gave his life for his country."

"Mary Alice was proud of him."

"And of her daughter. She went on and on about her heroic Daniel and her brilliant Kathleen. It was a relief, as well as a pleasure, to shut her up. To shut all of them up—all thirty-three and counting."

"You're the killer whose murders have spanned states and years."

"That's me. I'm a little embarrassed by those random killings of strangers. Too easy. That's why I've moved on to the more intriguing challenge of committing perfect murders of people I know."

"Why did you want me to have the crime-scene photos and souvenirs?"

"You tell me, James. I've given you enough hints. Or maybe not. I keep forgetting you're not very bright. Would you like one more hint?"

"Please," James replied. He knew, of course, why Grant had given him the incriminating evidence. He'd long since figured it out.

Long since . . . meaning sometime during this dialogue with a killer. James had to keep the conversation alive, in the hope of keeping the women alive, until a marksman with a high-powered rifle had Grant in his sights. Such a shot was possible. In his arrogance, Grant had made a crucial mistake. He was fully visible through the windowed walls, and the penthouse wasn't alone in its perch in the sky. Not far away, and one floor up, the corporate headquarters of Rain Mountain Enterprises were housed.

The offices were lightless and empty. Ian's memorial was underway. But James believed he'd seen, prayed he'd seen, a glint of something—a gun barrel?—in his own darkened office. That had been a while ago. And maybe it hadn't been real.

Or maybe the sharpshooter had realized his killshot would be more certain if he made it from the office next to James's, the death-black place that until recently had belonged to the man to whom Grant proclaimed he owed a debt of gratitude—and about whom Grant had spoken as if he and Ian had been friends.

Ian Collier would have hated Grant Monroe with every fiber of his being. The psychopath had stolen so much from the woman Ian loved. He'd have welcomed the sharpshooter into his office, and, if the shot was as clean and clear as James believed it might be, Ian would gladly have pulled the trigger himself.

The gunman was in Ian's office. He had to be. And Ian's spirit was right beside him. All James had to do was buy a little more time.

"One more hint," he said to Grant.

"The only fingerprints on the packet are yours."

"And had I opened it, the prints on the photos and souvenirs inside would also have been only mine. You were planning to frame me for the killings."

"I *have* framed you, James. Admittedly, I'd intended to hammer many more nails in your coffin between now and August. But that was before I learned that Ian's fiancée was none other than Mary Alice's look-alike daughter. I was pretty sure you'd open the packet once Ian was in the ground. So instead of a scenario similar to this playing out in eight months' time, it had to play out today. It wasn't a change I was happy to make. But I'm feeling better now. The pleasure of murdering Natalie as well as Christine has improved my mood considerably. You're not looking very happy, James. But don't worry. You'll still get credit for the killings. Your prints on the outside will be incriminating enough—once I begin filling in the blanks. I'll tell the cops about the pornographic pictures you took of your college girlfriends, and how strangely you behaved during our ski trip to Seattle in freshman year, and you'll become quite famous, notorious, in your death. I'll write a book about you, and there'll undoubtedly be a movie. Any casting suggestions you'd like to make before you die?"

As Grant laughed at his own wit, James merely felt

grateful that he was talking. Every second, every minute, made a difference.

Grant went on, feigning a look of thoughtfulness. "You know, as I think about it, I may just have to give Kathleen Cahill a stay of execution—for a while. She'll turn up dead eventually, the victim of a copycat killer who idolized *you*. But she won't die until after the book comes out. I'll want her to write the foreword. Who better than your first victim's daughter *and* the fiancée of the man who trusted you as if you were the son he never had. I'll want a picture of her, too. The copycat killer has to know who she is. What would be ideal—yes, *perfect*—would be a photograph of Kathleen wearing her dead mother's treasured locket. Care to tell me where the packet is?"

"Sure. As soon as you let the women go."

"This isn't a hostage situation, James. Nobody walks out of here but me. On that point, though, since you brought it up, you need to begin deciding who I should kill first. It's entirely your choice. I have no preference. It will be a revealing choice, won't it? Your true colors finally exposed. My guess is they'll be as blue as your blood." Grant smiled. "You know what? The suspense is killing me. I'm ready to know—right now—which of your lovers is most disposable. So tell me, James, whose throat do I slice? Trashy Natalie's or frigid Chris—"

Grant heard more than felt the bullet to his brain. And, if realization ever dawned, he was dead before the news traveled to his smile.

So that was how he fell, how he died, smiling his pure evil smile.

James rushed toward Grant's body. He wanted to be sure Grant was dead.

Three SWAT team members were right beside him, and two others untied Natalie and Christine. Each woman, suddenly freed, made a decisive movement of her own.

Christine went straight to James. It was a short journey, and a wobbling one. She hadn't slept, hadn't eaten, in days. James held her when she reached him, and she clung to him as she spoke.

"I love you, James. I never stopped. I was just so . . . confused. He wanted to confuse me, didn't he? To make me believe I was loved one moment and despised the next. And if I questioned his love for me, he'd make me feel ashamed—and so guilty I'd do anything, *anything,* to have him love me again. But it wasn't real. None of it was real."

"Grant tricked you," James whispered to the bewildered creature in his arms. "He tricked us both. But it's over, Chris. He's gone. And everything's going to be all right."

Natalie saw their embrace. Heard their words. But it wasn't the reunion of lovers that compelled her to flee.

Liquid heat gushed, it felt like it was gushing, from the place where this baby girl hadn't been any safer on the Feast of Epiphany than her sister had been.

Natalie had no destination beyond leaving the suite. That accomplished, she caught the suite's private— empty—elevator and leaned, bleeding, against its mirrored wall.

• • •

The Olympic Suite elevator had been summoned to the lobby once the command center received word that Grant was dead. Kathleen had been given permission to go up, along with paramedics and police. It was an unusual authorization.

But, the SWAT team captain acknowledged, everything about what had transpired in the past ninety minutes was unusual. Kathleen Cahill had been only halfway through making her case—the physician argument, not the crime-victim one—when he'd acceded to her request.

"Are you sure you want to do this?" Sam asked as blinking lights signaled the elevator's nonstop descent.

"I'm positive. I have to see him." Before Sam could suggest less grim ways of seeing an image of the man who'd murdered her mother, Kathleen added, "In the flesh."

"So you can kill him again?"

Sam's question, posed softly, focused her chaotic emotions. She hadn't known what she wanted—beyond seeing Grant's dead body—or why she wanted even that.

But Sam knew.

"Yes," she whispered. "And again and again. What does that make me?"

"The woman I love. Who needs," he said, "to vent a little of her entirely understandable rage before she can spend time with more important—and more difficult—emotions. She loved you, Kathleen. She died loving you, caring about you, being so proud of you."

"I know. And you'd think I could just forget about my

anger and concentrate on that. But you're right. I need to look at him. . . ."

"So that's what we'll do."

"You're coming with me?"

"There's nothing and no one that could stop me."

But there was, in the person of the dazed and ashen woman who appeared before them when the elevator doors opened.

"Natalie."

"I'm bleeding, Kathleen. I'm losing the baby!"

Plans changed without a second thought. And, just as quickly, Kathleen's fury was no more. Mary Alice's beloved daughter had better things to do than rant at a dead man. And there was room, in the heart emptied of its anger, for Mary Alice to come along.

Dr. Cahill's voice offered reassuring calm.

"We don't know that, Natalie. I'd like to examine you, though, and run some tests, and see where we are. Okay?"

"Yes."

"I'll get the car," Sam said. Calmly. He'd already scanned the lobby and identified the nearest street-side exit. "I'll pull up over there."

23

Queen Anne Medical Center
Eight South
January 6, 8 p.m.

"James." Natalie's greeting was more despair than welcome. Why was he here? She didn't want him here. A little anger, just enough, gave her the energy to sit up in her bed. Anger and disbelief. "Kathleen told you I was here."

James didn't understand the anger, but he heard it. He moved as close to Natalie's hospital bed as she seemed to want him to be.

Not very close.

"She had no choice, Natalie. I was determined to find you." *But you didn't want to be found, did you? Not by me.* "You left so quickly."

"I had to get out of there."

"I know." James would have left quickly, too, had it been possible for him to do so. But the police had questions, and James had answers, and the former prosecutor was mindful of the falsely imprisoned man in a Boston jail cell, and of the families of Grant's victims. He'd personally contacted the family of one of Grant's living victims—Christine—and now, at last, he was with the other. "I'm so sorry, Natalie."

Don't feel sorry for me, James. Please. Just go away. "I'm fine!"

"No, you're not. You've been through a terrible ordeal.

I hate what Grant put you through—and even more what *I* put you through because of him."

"You didn't put me through anything, James." *Just falling in love . . . and losing love.* "And as for Grant, he really defined psychopath, didn't he?"

Her faint teasing gave James hope. "He really did." James moved closer. She didn't move away. "I wish I'd followed up on the movie connection you made."

"It wouldn't have mattered. Grant's 911 tape would have pointed away from him and toward the man he framed."

"But it was an important clue, and you identified it months ago."

"Only because I've spent so much time lying in bed watching movies."

"Lying in bed and watching movies sounds awfully good to me." James could see, even in the night shadows of the lightless room, the sadness on her lovely face. "Talk to me, Natalie. Please?"

"Kathleen told you why I was here, didn't she?"

"Yes." Kathleen was a silhouette in the doorway. "I explained that not surprisingly you were in a mild state of shock. I also predicted that with a good night's sleep, you'd be ready for discharge first thing tomorrow morning."

"First thing?" *First* thing meant no post-miscarriage D & C—and no miscarriage?

"I think so. Like the exam I did, your blood tests are fine."

Kathleen had told her, following the exam, that she believed her pregnancy was still viable. Now the blood tests had confirmed it. And Natalie's bleeding had stopped. Although it had felt like an exsanguinating gush, it hadn't been.

"I'll be in my office for a while," Kathleen said. "And I'll look in on you before I leave."

Natalie smiled at the physician she trusted with her baby's life—and her own. Kathleen hadn't betrayed either trust. James didn't know, would never know, about his baby girl *who was alive.* "Thank you, Kathleen."

Kathleen waved away her thanks, and was on the verge of leaving, when James, too, expressed his gratitude.

"I heard what you and Sam said to me, Kathleen. About my responsibility, or rather lack of it, regarding Grant. I appreciate what you said, and at a rational level I may even know it's true. I'm just not feeling very rational at the moment."

"How could you be?" The rhetorical question floated briefly. "*So.* I'm leaving you two alone."

Then they were. Alone.

And so lonely.

"Marry me," James whispered. His loneliness worsened when he saw her response. "What is it, Natalie?"

"She *did* tell you, didn't she?"

"Who?"

"Kathleen."

"Tell me what?" When her only reply was a slight shake of her head, James continued, "I don't know what you're talking about, Natalie. But I want to know. Please."

"What about Christine?"

"What *about* Christine? Do I want to marry her? Is that what you're asking?"

"She's in love with you, James. And what happened between her and Grant—he was determined to take her from you. To steal her from you. And even that wasn't enough. He had to batter her, bewilder her with the psychological games he loved to play. The fact that he succeeded with his emotional abuse shows how clever he was. I'd have thought Christine, of all people, would be immune to such manipulation. She was so confident, so centered. She can be that Christine again. *Your* Christine. It may take a while. But she'll make it. And she's so—"

"I agree, Natalie. Christine's all the superlatives you were going to list. And she has many friends, myself—and you—included, who'll make sure she gets all the help and support she needs. She might become *my* Christine again, if by that you mean the woman she was when she and I met. I hope she will. But," he said softly, "I'll never again be *her* James."

"You won't?"

"Never. I'd like to be your James, though—if you'll have me."

"Oh, James."

"You're frowning."

"You really don't know?"

"I know I love you."

"James . . ."

"Is it so bad?" he asked, kissing her tears and her trembling smile.

"No," she whispered against his lips. "Not so bad. Not bad at all."

He sensed the "but" and pulled away just enough to see her shimmering eyes. He'd been falling, as he pulled away, fearing—but now he was saved. "But?"

"We may not be able to make love for a while."

"Did Grant hurt you?"

"No! *No.* What time is it?"

"What *time?*" James squinted at his wristwatch. "Eight-seventeen."

"Before all of this happened with Grant, I'd planned to wait until midnight to tell you. I now know that was a mistake. She needs both of us, you see. Our baby girl needs both her mommy and her daddy to get her safely through this day—through every day."

"Our . . . baby girl?"

"It's because of her—until we're certain she's secure inside me—that we can't make love."

His eyes shimmered now, his love shimmered, a perfect blue. "I can live with that, Natalie, if I can spend my life living with you—and her—and loving you both."

Natalie was sleeping when Kathleen looked in on her, as promised, at ten.

Let her sleep. That was, of course, the logical thing to do. Not that awakening her would cause harm. But if it was rest Dr. Cahill's patient needed, then rest she should have—particularly when it was filled with happy dreams, as Kathleen imagined Natalie's were.

James had stopped by her office after his visit with Natalie. He was elated about the baby and wanted to know what he could do to make the pregnancy safe for Natalie, easy for Natalie. He wanted to do something.

Anything. He was already doing it, Kathleen had told him. He was already loving the mother-to-be.

Natalie was dreaming happy dreams, and Kathleen had her own dream, too.

That dream, Sam, had gone to the mansion while she reviewed Natalie's medical records. He'd thanked the lovebird puppy-sitters and sent them on their way—but only after discussing with them something he'd been planning to propose. There was an apple orchard he knew of, and a farmhouse, too, and it was theirs if they wanted it. Who better to keep the Apple Butter Ladies supplied with their favorite apples than the favorite grandson and his lovely bride?

Kathleen had called Sam once her chart review was finished and she was about to check on Natalie a final time. He'd meet her in her office, he said. He was probably almost there, and she'd been away from him far too long, and there were compelling reasons to let Natalie sleep.

So why did Kathleen enter the room? And touch, very gently, her pregnant patient's shoulder? And whisper her name?

Kathleen didn't know.

She knew only that this dictate was one she had to obey.

"Kathleen?"

"Hi."

Natalie sat up. "Is there a problem?"

"No, Natalie. No problem at all. I've just been reviewing your records from New Jersey."

"They're already here?"

323

"They arrived late today. And there's information in them I thought it was important for you to know tonight."

"Information?"

"Positive information." Kathleen smiled. "An epiphany, actually. Your baby didn't die because you stepped in front of an oncoming bus."

"She didn't?"

"No. Your first pregnancy was ectopic. In your fallopian tube. It could never have been carried to term—or even till the end of that day. I think it's very likely that the rupture of your tubal pregnancy caused you to stagger into traffic. I remember your telling me that everything hurt, even the feel of snow on your face. I wonder if what hurt most was your right lower abdomen."

"I don't remember."

"You don't need to. And it's possible there wasn't any pain. You could have been staggering from blood loss. You *were* staggering, according to witnesses. And as was discovered during your emergency surgery, the internal bleeding from the rupture was significant. It's the reason your right ovary had to be removed."

"So I didn't cause her death?" Natalie asked, repeating, reaffirming.

"No," Kathleen repeated, reaffirmed. "And this pregnancy, the baby you're carrying now, is where it—she—needs to be, in your uterus, not your fallopian tube."

Kathleen's words settled, like a comforter, soft and warm. It was from that billowy cocoon that Natalie spoke.

"You were right, Kathleen. I did need to know. Tonight. Thank you so much for sensing that. . . ."

24

Once upon a time, not so long ago, Dr. Kathleen Cahill would have attributed her decision to awaken Natalie to her intuition as a physician, a practitioner of both the science—and the art—of her chosen career.

But Kathleen had known, before awakening Natalie, that something other than the art of medicine had been guiding her. A different kind of instinct.

A womanly instinct, she thought as she made the short trip back to her office. A woman's intuition.

She'd believed, not so long ago, that she lacked an essential womanliness. She'd never experienced the sexual desires women were supposed to have, much less fallen in love. But now . . . her heartbeat quickened in anticipation of her imminent reunion with the man she loved and desired, and who loved and desired her.

She was womanly, after all, when it came to passion.

And when it came to the bonds of sisterhood? Maybe. *Yes.* There'd been a closeness with Natalie from the start. So it must have been that bond, the sisterly one, that had compelled her decision.

And yet . . . there was that other womanly instinct, the one Kathleen had revered from afar in her patients and had feared—her greatest fear—didn't exist within her. She'd learned more about that instinct just today, how it could make a mother plead for her life, not for herself but for her daughter.

The memory had traveled with Kathleen, as Mary Alice had. And now, as Kathleen laid a protective hand on her lower abdomen and sensed, before it was possible to know, the new life deep within, she felt Mary Alice with her, touching, sensing, knowing—and smiling, as her daughter was, a womanly, motherly smile.

"Sam?"

"Hi." He greeted her with love, with welcome. He didn't see, until he reached her, the new glow in her smiling eyes. "What is it, Kathleen?"

"I think I might be pregnant. No. That's wrong. I'm sure I might be pregnant." That still wasn't glorious enough, or accurate enough. "I *am* pregnant."

"Pregnant? But . . ."

"It's too soon to confirm it. Scientifically." But who cared about science when you had art? The art, ancient and true, of motherhood. "But I am. Is that okay?"

Kathleen already had his answer. But he spoke it anyway.

"So much more than okay."

"I even have a feeling—no, I'm positive—that he's a baby boy. A son. How magical is that?"

"Just the usual magic I've come to expect since falling in love with you." The teasing became wonder. "*Kathleen?* We're having a baby."

"Yes, we are."

"And you're fine."

"Deliriously fine. And I'll continue to be fine, no matter what kind of hormonal chaos this little one might provoke. He's too young to cause symptoms—yet. Symptoms, that is, other than pure joy."

"Pure joy is a pretty impressive symptom for a five-day-old. Or four-day-old. Or . . . what are you thinking?" he asked softly when her lovely glow faded ever so slightly. "Tell me."

"Or a seven-day-old."

"Seven?"

"He could be Ian's, Sam. I was ovulating the night of the accident. While Ian was at Crystal, I inseminated myself."

"The baby is his, then. If that's when you were ovulating."

"The window's not that narrow. I could have conceived on that—" *seventh time's a charm* "—night. Or on any of several nights after. I wanted to conceive on that night. For Ian. And me. Until he died, I believed I had."

"Ian's baby." Sam drew a breath, looked toward the night's darkness.

"*Our* baby, Sam. The little boy you and I will love and cherish . . . won't we?"

Sam's gaze remained on the world beyond the window. From where he and Kathleen stood, the only view was sky. The city lights below did little to illuminate the blackness.

From where they stood . . . like his joy, that had changed. As her "won't we?" went unanswered, she'd backed away . . . into darkness, too.

"We will love him," Sam said at last. He spoke to her, despite her shadowed retreat. "And cherish him. *I* will, Kathleen. I promise. I'm sorry I hesitated, that my reaction disappointed you. It did disappoint you, didn't it? I disappointed you."

"You didn't disappoint me, Sam. You never could. Your reaction surprised me, I guess. And it shouldn't have. *Of course* your immediate response would be to feel let down that he might be Ian's, not yours. I suppose I'd already moved on to the symmetry of that possibility. The magic of it."

"Symmetry?" *Magic?* "I don't understand."

"Your loving Ian's son as you would your own—and as Ian loved you."

"I will love this baby, Kathleen. Whether he's Ian's or mine. You know I will. But I really don't see the symmetry of the situation." Nor did he feel the magic. Ian's baby would be Sam's brother. Maybe that was something he and Kathleen would decide they'd never need to know. And it was certainly something they'd never share with the boy who'd be raised as a son. But . . . "Explain it to me."

"Loving another man's son as much as you'd love your own."

"But I wasn't another man's son."

Sam heard her gasp. And he saw, as she stepped out of the shadows, the sheen of tears.

"It never even *occurred* to me that she would've lied to you about that. But she did, didn't she? She told you that you were Ian's son."

I *am* Ian's son. The emotional protest was silent. And defiant, despite a contradictory message from his brain. His mother might lie to him. Kathleen would not.

Kathleen saw his torment. It was hushed, but not invisible—not to her. And she sensed he needed to hear it all, every truth she knew, even as he was reeling from the devastating lie.

"Ian made the discovery just hours after you were born. His type AB blood made it impossible for him to father a type O baby. He could've run away from the responsibility of caring for a child who wasn't his. But Ian didn't run away from you. You were his little boy, Sam. From the moment he first held you, you were his son."

And he *was* my father. The protest wasn't quite loud enough to mute her words. Nor was Sam deaf to the relentless chorus pounding in his brain. Not your father. Not your father. No matter how much you want him to be.

And no matter the joy he'd felt, the soaring hope, knowing that Ian's blood, Ian's goodness, flowed in his veins.

"Ian didn't care about the biology," Kathleen said, as if reading Sam's soul. "He couldn't have loved you any more than he did. But when your mother took you away and her attorney informed him that Vanessa knew the truth and he had no legal standing . . ."

"How long had my mother known?"

"She knew she was pregnant before she and Ian met. But she wanted Ian. For herself, not for you. And Ian wanted you. And," she said, "you don't want this to be true."

Sam smiled, a little, for her. "I want to be Ian Collier's son."

"You are, in the only way that counts." Kathleen touched the corners of his mouth, a soft landing for his falling smile. Then, as he'd said to her when her own emotions had been in turmoil, she whispered, "You also happen to be the man I love."

"And I love you, Kathleen." He touched her, too, a gentle caress beneath her loving—and tired—eyes. "It's been an eventful day. It's time, I think, for me to take you home."

And for me to take *you* home. Kathleen didn't speak the thought. It wasn't time, not for him. Oh, he was trying—for the pregnant, tired woman he loved—to pretend the emotional tempest had passed. It was a valiant effort. He'd come close to hiding every shred of pain.

But not close enough.

There was more talking to do, and some raging perhaps, and maybe even a symbolic killing or two.

"I just don't get it," she said.

"Get what?"

"Why your mother maintained that lie. A random act of unkindness, maybe?"

"Not her style. I'm not defending her as a human being, much less as a mother, but random she's not. There had to be a reason."

"To lie to a little boy when everyone else knew the truth?"

"No one else knew."

"Mason must have, and your maternal grandparents, and the psychiatrist."

"No. My mother knew. And Ian knew. And, as you've just told me, her attorney knew. But as far as everyone else in her life was concerned, I was Ian Collier's biological son."

"I'm really not getting why that was important to her."

"There must have been something worse, from her standpoint, than my being the son of the monster she portrayed Ian to be. Something worse about the man whose son I really was."

"But she didn't know who that man was. She'd had a number of one-night stands."

"So she said. We know what her word is worth." Sam looked beyond her to the night sky, searching for truth in the darkness, and speaking to blackness when the truth was found. "It's Mason. He's the mystery man. That's why she was so afraid I'd tell him what I knew."

"Until their ten-year class reunion, five months before she took you away, she hadn't seen Mason since high school."

"Not true. The two families were close. She and Mason saw each other all the time. Whenever my grandparents, the Worthings and the Hargroves, got together, they'd bemoan the fact that my mother and Mason had broken up—again—just weeks before she and Ian met. She knew she was carrying Mason's baby. But she wasn't ready to follow the matrimonial path her parents wanted her to follow. After four years with Ian, playing a distant second fiddle to her son, Mason and his adoration must have looked pretty good to her."

"She didn't dare tell him you were his son."

"I imagine he'd asked her when he learned she was pregnant. She'd lied, of course, preferring life with Ian to life with him. My guess is that she was planning to tell him after they'd been married for a while and he and I had bonded. It wouldn't be a confession. But she'd begin wondering if she'd been mistaken, especially when she saw Mason and me together. They'd do the tests and the Hargroves would live happily ever after. I foiled her plan, though, by becoming so distraught when I was taken away from Ian. Mason and I didn't bond. Quite the opposite. My first memory of him is overhearing him tell her he wanted to send me back to Ian. To get rid of me."

"I wonder how hard he tried."

"To get rid of me?"

"No. To love another man's son."

"I don't know, Kathleen. We'll never know."

It happened to Sam, then, as it had happened to Kathleen hours before. The chaotic emotions simply disappeared—and for the same reason. There were better things to do. More important issues to discuss.

"I will love our baby," he said. "I already do."

Epilogue

The Collier Home (the old Worthing estate)
December 6, Eleven months later, 4:45 p.m.

Christmas decorations went up early at the mansion on Queen Anne Hill. And as Sam and Kathleen Collier had promised each other, they always would. Or maybe they'd keep them up year-round, to make up for all the Christmases lost. Either way, decorations or not, every day would be Christmas in their home.

This evening would be their first dinner party of the season. It would be a small gathering, just the seven of them, the usual group. Their guests, James, Natalie and five-month-old Emily Anne would be arriving soon.

Evenings began and ended early these happy days. Sometimes it was three-month-old Ian Daniel Collier—Danny—who got cranky first. And sometimes it was Emily Anne. More often it was one of the moms who, although not cranky, began to yawn. Or a yawning dad.

Of the seven, only Holly had never once been the reason the two young families called it a night.

They saw each other all the time. All seven of them.

James and Sam worked side by side at Rain Mountain, keeping Ian's dream alive. Keeping Ian alive.

And they sailed. Sam taught James. And they skied. James taught Sam. Like brothers.

And when Sam's biological brother came to town, as Navy pilot Tyler Hargrove did whenever he could, there were three brothers, not two, and the third brother taught them both to fly.

And like sisters, Kathleen and Natalie, accompanied by babies and dog, went wherever weather, play or errands happened to beckon. And, on almost every outing, they dropped by to visit their men.

Sam and Kathleen were ready for their guests to arrive. Dinner was in the oven. And dessert, Susie MacKenzie's deep-dish apple pie, would be served warm and à la mode—in the festive living room, perhaps, in front of the chattering fire and near the fragrant tree.

They could sit on the plush carpet, if they liked, as Sam's family was doing now.

His family, he thought as he returned to the living room after answering the phone. His own circle of love.

"That was Marge," he said, joining them, making the circle complete. "She loved the photographs you sent her of Danny and Holly. She's pretty impressed with what a people-puppy Holly's turned out to be. Haven't you, Holly?"

Holly, who was busy ravaging a candy-cane-shaped chewy, acknowledged her name with a wagging tail.

"That's because you made her feel safe." Kathleen had intended to look at Sam as she spoke, but tiny hands had a sudden urge to pat her cheeks and nose. "Isn't that right, Danny? So safe."

Danny smiled at the sound of his mother's voice. But, like Holly, he was busy, in pursuit of the shiny locket always worn around Kathleen's neck. James had returned it to her; because of James, jewelry from Grant's other victims had also been returned to their families. It had taken a while, but all the victims had been identified, and the families found. James had been instrumental in the process, working tirelessly to help law-enforcement bring a little peace to the surviving loved ones.

Mary Alice's locket brought great peace to Kathleen. It surprised her how much. And inside, and undamaged, was the photograph of her soldier father—how young he'd been—and the Daniel for whom Danny had been named.

"We're so lucky."

"Yes," Sam said softly. "We are."

He extended a hand to his baby boy. He couldn't help it. He had to touch. Danny did, too. The locket forgotten, he grabbed his father's finger and held on tight.

"He loves his daddy so much."

"I'm the luckiest man in the world, Kathleen. The

luckiest, and the happiest."

"And he's the luckiest little boy."

They didn't know if Danny was Ian's. He *could* be. His blood-type—A—was the same as Kathleen's. Either type-AB Ian or type-O Sam could have been Danny's father. Without DNA-testing they'd never know.

And never wanted to know.

And, Kathleen thought, they didn't really know which truth—Sam's baby or Ian's baby—they would have preferred.

She wondered if Sam shared that truth with Ian during one of his many visits to the cemetery where Ian's ashes lay. If, perhaps, Sam even confided that he hoped this firstborn Collier baby, his precious Danny, was Ian's— that he'd be so proud to be the father of Ian's son, and would love Ian's boy as Ian had loved him.

The place Ian had chosen for his ashes, but truly for his loved ones, was the perfect spot to make such private confessions. Only Ian's mountains were watching, and only Ian was listening. Yes, Ian was with Sam, with both of them, always. But it was there that both Kathleen and Sam spoke to him aloud.

They visited him together, and alone. And both hoped, as they both told him, that he didn't mind their replacing the gravestone he'd chosen for himself—his name, the relevant dates, in dove-gray granite—with "Loving Friend, Loving Father, Beloved Man" engraved in marble the color of snow.

Kathleen didn't know, would never know, which man had fathered her baby. But what that baby would know was love. Danny would remember being held in Sam's arms as they stood at the window in the room that had been Ian's but now was his, talking about the view. They'd marvel at the apple orchard—how bountiful, with *their* nurturing, the trees had become.

Ian Daniel Collier would remember, too, that on a clear day, or a silvery one, they'd see the mountain. And as he listened patiently, even as he was preparing his excited reply, his father would point to its snow-capped majesty and say, "Look, Danny, there's Mount Rainier. Isn't that what I see?"

"No!" the little boy would reply.

"No?" Sam would echo. "What is it then? Tell me."

"Rain Mountain, Daddy! Rain Mountain."

Daddy.

Center Point Publishing
600 Brooks Road • PO Box 1
Thorndike ME 04986-0001 USA

(207) 568-3717

US & Canada:
1 800 929-9108

12-06